A Capital Union

Victoria Hendry

Victoria Hendry

Saraband

Published by Saraband
Suite 202, 98 Woodlands Road
Glasgow, G3 6HB, Scotland
www.saraband.net

ISBN: 9781908643346
ebook: 9781908643353

Printed in the EU on sustainably sourced paper.

1   3   5   7   9   10   8   6   4   2

VICTORIA HENDRY has worked in the London Museum of Jewish Life and Kirkcaldy Museum and Art Gallery, both of which stimulated her appetite for the stories behind the collections. She has an MSc in Creative Writing from Edinburgh University and was shortlisted for the Society of Women Writers and Journalists International Life Writing Prize in 2012. Victoria lives in Edinburgh, and this is her first book.

1

My mother said I was like jam in a bad year, sweet but with too many pips, and when I asked her what she meant, she said that some of the things I said got stuck in people's teeth and worried them. I didn't think that was a kind thing to say, so when Jeff asked me to marry him I said yes. Once I was a fine Edinburgh lady I wouldn't need to think about the things Mother said, or chickens and sheep and muck. After the wedding, when she saw the size of our braw flat in Morningside, she said there was no limit to the doors a bonny face would open. I didn't expect to miss her when she left for the farm, but I did. I was seventeen and it was 1942.

Jeff was good-looking, and my aunties said he was a catch, tall like my brothers but a bit of a skinny-malinkie, and he had a sort of dreamy look in his eyes that made them dark when really they were blue. It made me feel funny inside when he looked straight at me, and when he carried me over the threshold after the wedding, he said he was the happiest man alive. I was happy, too, despite the war. Germany seemed very far away and I thought Hitler wouldn't be interested in a wee place like Scotland. Jeff used to have a German neighbour called Professor Schramml but he moved out just before the fighting started and went to Geneva or somewhere. They used to walk to the university together in the morning and have a blether.

It was lonely Monday to Friday when Jeff went to give his lectures, or write his book, or whatever it was he did at work. He said he was saving the Scots language for future generations. He had come to Ayrshire to collect words but collected me instead, saying it saved him searching all over the country when all the old words could be found right on the tip of my tongue.

I tried to keep the house spick and span. There were no beasts needing feeding, or coos to milk, so I hoovered the flat every day, although I was afraid the dust bag would explode, the fabric swelled up so tight. I did one other big chore, too: beat the rugs, or cleaned the bathroom, and that kept it all nice. Once a week we took it in turns to clean the common stair. It was a gloomy place in our tenement with spiral steps and black railings. The sun never reached all the way down from the skylight and I missed the fresh air blowing across the fields. Once I walked up to the top but there was nothing there, just another two landings the same as ours. I asked my neighbour Mrs MacDougall why we couldn't pay someone to clean it, and she looked at me in yon thrawn way she has and said perhaps I hadn't noticed that there was a war on, and not everyone had a husband bringing in a good wage. She said we all had to pull our weight. Then she flicked a glance at my stomach to see if I was expecting, and kind of sniffed as if to say, 'I didn't think so'. What she said was it would be nice to have some bairns about the stair again. That was when I started leaving the stour under her mat, just to annoy her.

I was cooking herring with orange sauce from my *War-Time Cookery* book when Jeff got back from work. He crept up behind me and put his arms round my waist. I screamed because I hadn't heard him come in, but his Bay Rum aftershave smelt so good that I leant against him, feeling how strong and cosy he was. 'How is my girl?' he asked. 'Pip, Pip?'

His pet name always took the sting out of what Mother had said, and made me laugh.

He was tired after his day at the university, and put his feet up on the range while I finished cooking. For once, he didn't complain about the smell. I never really paid much mind to the things he read out of *The Scotsman*, but when he shouted, 'Hell's teeth, Hitler has invaded Egypt,' it was so unexpected it made me jump half out of my skin. I told him I didn't really care. I was getting tired of the war and ration cards. I didn't like seeing the Anderson shelter in the back garden and I told him I wasn't gaun in any hole with Mrs MacDougall, even if the Luftwaffe were right overhead. He said I should care because the Germans were in Norway, too, and that was just across the North Sea.

'You can coorie up wi' her, then,' I said, 'and I will stay here and finish your best malt so it doesn't fall into the hands of the Germans.'

He said I wouldn't dare, and I told him it was for the war effort, so he had better get used to the idea of real sacrifice.

As a treat that night, we went to the Dominion Cinema on Newbattle Terrace to see a Betty Grable film. He put his arm round me as we walked. It was five minutes away; a grand, white building with wide steps and a balcony on the front. I was enjoying myself until the programme started, when the newsreel showed Hitler's armies marching through the streets of Berlin. They were all pressed together in tight rows like the letters in Jeff's paper. Jeff took my hand but I couldn't concentrate on the film because I felt scared and couldn't help thinking that if a bomb fell on the cinema, we wouldn't be able to get out over all the seats. There was an injured soldier sitting a few rows in front of us with a bandaged head, but it kept lolling on his shoulder and his wife propped a jumper round his neck so he could keep upright. She was no older than me.

On the way home I asked Jeff if he had thought about signing up to fight, but he said he had more important work to do and I wasn't to ask him that again. I told him I only brought it up because I had seen the men enlisting at the Assembly Rooms in George Street, but he dropped my hand and told me to haud my wheesht. He walked ahead of me all the way home and I had to run to keep up with him because I didn't like the auld trees in the park at night. The sound of my heels tapping on the pavement echoed on the walls of the blacked-out flats, but he never looked round once and said he didn't want any cocoa when we got in. The cauld air got in between us under the quilt when he came to bed, but I didn't say anything.

2

I woke up before him in the morning. I was always an early bird, and I liked to look at him when he was dreaming. I would pull back the curls of his brown hair, which was almost black, and lean as close as I could to the hollow in his neck to smell the sweetness of him without waking him. He was brown from playing golf, my sleeping man. He kissed me when I opened the blinds to let the sun in, and the light seemed to cheer him up. I think, looking back, that perhaps it was the last time things were right between us.

I took extra care getting dressed, just to please him, and I picked out my navy blue, polka-dot dress. He smacked my bottom on his way past to the bathroom to shave, and said, 'How about it, Dotty?' but I said a real academic would have his mind on higher things, and picked up my basket to go to the butcher's.

It was bright outside and the milkman let me pat his horse as he went past on his round. He swore the wee soul went mair slowly up our street looking for me. Flash reminded me of my dad's horses and I gave him a sugar lump, although I did keep most of the ration for Jeff, who hadn't noticed I had stopped taking sugar in my tea. I liked the feel of Flash's soft lips on my hand. There was pink blossom flying in the air as I doddled along Canaan Lane for my messages. The old houses stood behind stone walls with crumbly mortar, twisted shrubs hanging over them, full of flowers. I picked a piece of honeysuckle for my hair and the smell reminded me of our honeymoon. At the end of the lane, Morningside Road was like a canyon with sandstone tenements on either side. We were registered halfway up the hill, at Black's the Butchers, for beef dripping and meat. His sign read, 'Purveyors of Finest Quality', but he didn't have much in his window. There was a new, handwritten notice pinned to his door saying to remember to send something nice to our brave boys.

'Good morning, Mr Black,' I said when I went in, but he didn't reply, which was not like him. One of the women in the queue whispered that Mr Black's son had been injured at the Front and was in hospital in England. 'They're not sure if he'll walk again,' she added. Mr Black looked up when he heard that and said it was time for all the men to get a hand to the wheel and get us out of this mess. He was staring straight at me. I think he knew Jeff hadn't signed up, so I said, 'I agree with you, Mr Black.' Everyone's head swivelled round to look at me and they stopped talking. Then the woman from the hairdresser's said, 'Perhaps you could give that husband of yours a nudge, eh, Mrs McCaffrey?'

I said my man was doing very important work at the university, collecting words for a Scottish dictionary, but Mr Black said, 'Well, it will be a German dictionary if he doesn't get his finger out.'

They all laughed and I felt my cheeks go beetroot. I could have shrivelled up and died, but it was my turn to be served. He gave me an older bit of bacon than the rest of the ladies and it seemed a bit less than the usual ration, as if he had kept his finger on the scale when he was weighing it. Just thinking about it made me cry on the way home, although I tried not to show it in case someone I knew passed me and told Jeff they had seen me greetin' in the street like a bairn.

The door to the stair felt heavier than usual. It banged shut with such a thump that Mrs MacDougall opened her door as I passed and asked in her snippy, wee voice if I could please keep the noise down. Our hall was no brighter than the stair. Wool rugs that Jeff's dad had bought in Persia were laid on the black, painted floors to cheer them up, but I could hardly make out the birds and flowers in the patterns he claimed were so rare.

As I took off my hat, I noticed there was a letter on the mat. It was in a brown envelope with a black crown printed on it and I put it on the silver tray on the dresser, just the way Jeff liked. He shouted, 'Where's my Pip?' when he got in that night and I ran into the hall to tell him about my trip to the butcher's. It had been going round in my head all day, like a dog chasing its tail, but before I could hug him, Jeff picked up the letter and took it into his study. I heard him open it and the sound of the paper tearing under the knife seemed very loud. Through the open door I could see him rubbing his eyes, and when I asked if everything was all right, he said it was fine and could I please put the kettle on.

He looked a bit wabbit when he came into the kitchen and he pushed away his new copy of the *Scots Independent*, which I had put out beside his tea, thinking it would cheer him up. Although I never dared say, I thought the subscription was too much. He got out his bottle of Talisker and poured himself a dram, saying, 'Time for a little of the strong stuff.' He poured me a glass, too. 'Agnes,' he said, and I knew it was serious because he usually called me Pip, 'Douglas Grant is coming tomorrow. We will have some important matters to discuss.'

And that was the first time I heard his name. It didn't mean anything to me then. I asked Jeff if he would be staying for tea because I wasn't sure what I could feed him. I had dug over part of the back garden, and put in some early cropping tatties, but they weren't ready just yet. Jeff said a scone would do, and then he took his whisky into his study and shut the door. He called it his 'sanctuary' and insisted he would clean it, but he never did. I put on the wireless in the drawing room, but it was all about the war and some German plane which had come down in the Pentlands, so I put it off and darned some of Jeff's socks instead. I didn't want to think about men falling from the sky.

3

Mr Grant arrived at exactly two o'clock, just as Jeff had said he would, and when I took tea through to the drawing room, Mr Grant stood up to be introduced. Jeff said, 'May I introduce my wife, Agnes Thorne? As sweet a martyrdom as any man could wish.' I couldn't hit him as I usually did when he said that, so I just smiled at our visitor. Jeff liked his jokes. Mr Grant's head was as high as the top of the press, nearly at the picture rail, and I said to him, 'I hope you can't see any stour up there, Mr Grant?'

'I can assure you it is spotless, Mrs McCaffrey,' he replied, shaking my hand. His grip felt like a bear's. He had black hair, which he had to keep pushing out of his eyes, and a muckle great beard. He said Jeff was doing a good job helping him with his current trouble and I asked, 'What trouble would that be, Mr Grant?' and passed him a scone. Jeff gave him a look and sort of shook his head. It made me feel cross but I didn't want to be rude to a visitor, so I just poured the tea and sat down with my sewing. I remember Mr Grant said my jam was delicious, and I was able to tell him that the Roslyn Glen was a great place to pick rasps and brambles, even in a war. I cycled out there with Jeff last summer and that was when he asked me to marry him.

Mr Grant put down his cup with his great bear paw and said, 'Perhaps you can advise me, Mrs McCaffrey? I am trying to grow some soya beans and Jeff told me you are a farmer's daughter.'

I had never heard of them. Dad grew neeps and barley, but Mr Grant seemed very excited about what he called the high protein-value of beans and how well they cropped. He was trying to grow some. 'I think you might be better to raise hens, Mr Grant,' I said, 'although feed is in short supply. I am planning to get some for the back green. I thought I might start with four.'

'Mrs MacDougall will love that,' laughed Jeff, but Mr Grant looked at me kindly and said that anything was better than powdered egg. He expected that even the wrath of the legendary Mrs MacDougall would be worth tholing for fresh eggs.

'Now tell me,' he said, 'how do you get your scones so light in these difficult times of rationing?' And I told him the secret was buttermilk, but perhaps his mother had already told him that?

'Unfortunately my mother is sorely disappointed in me at the moment and only communicates with me by letter,' he replied. 'The temperature at home in Fife is currently ten degrees colder than in Glasgow, so I am obliged to spend much of my time at the Scottish Home Rule Association, just to keep warm.'

'How so, Douglas?' asked Jeff, and Mr Grant said that his mother's minister had put ideas into her head that he should buckle on the armour like a good Scotsman for the sake of puir, old Scotland.

'That old dunderhead can't see it is Scotland's interests I am fighting for,' he added. 'Independence of body and soul, Agnes. That's what matters.'

I wasn't sure what he meant, and then he said to Jeff that MacCaig's exam hadn't gone well in Glasgow. I asked what he was studying. Mr Grant laughed and said the triumph of hope over experience, and Jeff joined in. I was tired of people having a laugh at my expense, so I got up to go and put more water on to refresh the tea. Jeff never even noticed I was upset although

I banged the teapot down on the tray as I went out. He said they would be in the study if I wouldn't mind just leaving the tea at the door when I came back. Mr Grant smiled apologetically at me and shrugged.

I was watching the kettle boil on the range when I decided to go out. It got on my wick that Jeff made me feel like a skivvy in front of our visitor, so I put on my wellies to walk up the Blackford Hill. It was just a stone's throw from our flat and I felt a lot better in the fresh air. Being inside so much confused my mind. As I walked past the pond and up the path to the Observatory, I calmed down. Perhaps I had been a bit daft to leave the men without their tea?

From the ridge, I could see the whole city lying round Arthur's Seat, and the castle looked like a toy on its black rock above the Forth. The Pentland Hills lay just behind me in a long, blue line to the south and I could see almost as far as Stirling in the west. It was too windy to sit on the bench at the top and, although it wasn't the most sheltered, I decided to go home down the steep side. I had hidden a snare in the gorse and, sure enough, there was a rabbit in it, stone dead. I wondered if Mr Black would buy some from me if I could catch more, but I didn't think he liked me now. Anyway, Jeff wouldn't have thought it was ladylike to make snares out of old garden wire from the foot of the stair. The rabbit felt soft and heavy when I put it in my bag and I hoped it wouldn't bleed all over the steps, because Mrs MacDougall would no doubt have got right back on her high horse about that, too.

The men were still talking when I came in. I stood very quietly in the hall. I didn't even breathe and I could hear Mr Grant saying something about the Act of Union being no better than the Anschluss. Jeff said that seemed a bit strong.

'*Komm der Tag*,' replied Mr Grant. I think it was German, and then the door opened and Jeff said, 'Oh, there you are, Agnes. I thought it had gone very quiet. Why didn't you tell me you were going out?' His eye fell on my hand. 'What on earth have you got there?'

Mr Grant laughed when I held up the rabbit by its back feet. 'I think this will taste better than your magic beans, Mr Grant.'

He looked less fierce, then. 'You have married a warrior woman, Jeff, not just an Ayrshire lass.'

Mr Grant helped me to skin my catch at the kitchen table. Jeff looked a bit haunless and disappeared behind his paper. It was when Mr Grant was standing there with his hands all bloody that he said I should call him Douglas, and I jokingly suggested Red Douglas instead. But he replied he was too true-blue a private school boy to be red. Jeff didn't join in the banter but read us bits from his paper, adding, 'Your appeal is mentioned in here, Douglas. The ninth of July.'

'Aye,' he said, wiping his hands, 'the shades of Barlinnie prison are not yet to close about me, as far as I can gather, but no doubt I shall end up in the Bastille sooner or later.' He looked at me. 'Don't worry, Agnes. I have got Jeff and others to rescue me.'

Jeff gave him a sharp look and I think he looked a wee bit afeart. At the time I thought it was for his friend.

'You do the onions, Agnes,' said Douglas, 'and I'll joint the rabbit for you.'

I looked away when he pulled the eyes out. That bit always made me want to boak but Douglas didn't seem to mind. He said to Jeff he was sure he would be able to expand on the skeleton case he had flung together before the last trial. 'There is no way that the Act of Union gave a Scottish court the right to enforce English conscription up here.'

Jeff wasn't so sure. I remembered the letter that had come for him with the black crown on it.

Douglas added the meat to the onion I was stirring, while Jeff wrote a list on the back of an old envelope. 'You could try citing the Dumfries Proclamation against the Union,' he suggested. 'Not many know there was an English man o' war in the dock at Leith when the Three Estates signed away the country in Parliament Square. I wish I had been there to kick the door in with the rest of them.'

For some reason I wished that Jeff wouldn't talk so much and do so little.

Douglas wasn't sure it mattered now. 'I'll fight at the head of a Scottish army,' he said, and he sounded so old-fashioned that I couldn't help laughing, and I asked him where he would find a horse big enough to carry him into battle if the milkman wouldn't part with Flash. Jeff banged his pen down on the table.

'It is serious, Agnes,' he muttered, and I wondered if he might be the same as Douglas and have to go to court, too.

'I don't want you in the jail,' I said.

'Yes, what would Mrs MacDougall say?' asked Douglas.

'Plenty, that's for sure,' Jeff replied.

He was right as it turned out, and I only thought later that Douglas' joke had got in the way, and that Jeff hadn't answered me.

After we had eaten, Douglas gave us a tune on the piano. Jeff sang in his bonny baritone, and gave us a Gaelic air or two, which Douglas joined in with on the chorus. Jeff's dad was a Highlander and used to take him up north in the summer on a grand tour of aunties and uncles on Skye.

'You'll need to give me a hand with translating Sorley's poems, Jeff,' said Douglas. 'I had forgotten you were all but a native speaker. I am hoping to get his *An Cuilithionn* published in Lallans. I think the poor sod is fighting in Africa at the moment. He was a bit quick to sign up, having missed the Spanish Civil War.'

'Scope there then for an Arabic edition, too,' said Jeff, 'if the Germans ease off.'

'*Tapadh leat*,' said Douglas, 'I'll be sure and suggest it to him in my next letter.'

Douglas left at nine o'clock for a train to Aberdeen. He was a lecturer in Ancient Greek at the university, although I don't know what use that was to anyone. On my way out to the back green to get the washing, I passed Mrs MacDougall on the stair. She said she noticed we'd had a visitor, as if it had a capital letter or something, and I said yes we had. It was Mr Douglas Grant, and she said, not that rotten nationalist chap? I replied that he was very nice and she just sort of snorted and said well, he needn't think he could climb on Graham's Dyke and hold the Romans back a second time, because everything was different now, and Hitler wasn't going to stop at Scotland just because men like Mr Grant thought they were too fancy to fight. I didn't like the sharp way she said it and I told her he was busy with very important things, and Jeff was helping him. Mrs MacDougall said I was a bonny fool, and I don't think she meant it kindly. Maybe she had noticed the stour I'd left under her mat, and was cross with me.

I ran down the rest of the steps. The air smelt sweet and I unpegged my washing and held it to my face. I loved the smell of soap and grass. I was full from the rabbit stew and I thought everything would be fine again soon. Perhaps the war would end before I lifted the tatties in the autumn and Jeff could stay safe at the university.

Upstairs, although I was tired, I set the iron to heat on the range and it sizzled when I spat on it to test if it was hot. Jeff said it was unladylike but I told him real ladies didn't need to iron so he better get used to it if he wanted his skivvy to put creases in his shirt sleeves. He said he was glad to know he would look his best at the SNP annual conference, but I was cross because he hadn't told me he would be out at the weekend, too. I hardly saw him, and now people like Douglas were being taken to court, I felt worried. It was only because I started to greet that he said I could come with him if I was so upset, and that Douglas would be speaking. He patted his knee and I went to him and cooried in like a bairn.

'We'll find a way through this, Pip,' he said. 'The war can't last much longer.'

4

That Saturday was very hot for the time of year, so we decided to walk down to the conference on Shandwick Place rather than wait for a tram. It was always so smoky and everyone smelt so bad, squeezed together like sardines. I put on my new dress, which I had run up from a bolt of blue cloth my mother had in the attic. The utility stuff was too thin. I sewed small, puffed sleeves and put pearl buttons down the front. The skirt wasn't as full as I would have liked, but I didn't want to look as if I was using more than my fair share of the cloth ration, so I kept some back for a blouse. Jeff thought I looked bonny when I gave him a twirl, and after I pinned on my straw hat with the red ribbon we were ready to go. I took his arm on the way out just to show Mrs MacDougall, if she was keeking out her curtains, that I didn't agree with the bad things she'd said about Jeff and Douglas. It was good to be out together, and if it hadn't been for all the brown tape stuck to the windows in criss-cross patterns, I could have believed there wasn't a war on. I took a deep breath and pretended it was all over, and this was how it would be, me and Jeff walking in the sun, arm in arm.

Women were sitting on the benches on Bruntsfield Links with their wee ones propped up in great big prams, shoogling the ones that were crying. One of the bairns looked like a flower with a halo of woolly loops on her wee, pink bonnet. The warm air and the sound of the women talking made it feel as if their men were nearby, and not far away overseas in danger. They looked up with thin faces as Jeff passed, wondering why he was there and not in uniform, but he looked straight ahead and I had to walk a bit faster to keep up with him. He only slowed down when the path opened out onto the Meadows with its view of Arthur's Seat. Boys were playing pitch and putt and an old man with an unlit pipe between his teeth stood in a booth taking money and handing out clubs.

We turned past Barclay Church and down onto Lothian Road with all its shops and bars, but we didn't see a crowd of folk until we got to the Shandwick Galleries at the West End. It was a very smart sandstone building, about four storeys high, with big, glass windows, which were boarded up on the first floor. A printed banner outside read, 'SNP Annual Conference', and a Saltire flag drooped beside it. Jeff passed me his copy of the agenda so that I could fan my face. He began to wave and nod to various people as we went in, and led us proudly up to the front where Douglas had reserved him a seat. He hoped we could both squeeze in and, sure enough, a kind, old man gave up his seat for me and moved to the second row.

'Best seats in the house,' said Jeff, smiling, but I was worried that if I got bored, I wouldn't be able to leave without being rude. The agenda was very long with the typing close together to save paper.

'I think you'll find this very informative, Pip,' Jeff whispered.

I didn't think so, but I was just glad to be there and hoped to meet some of his friends. People didn't drop by the house in Edinburgh the way they did on the farm.

Jeff pointed out who was sitting on the platform, naming all the men in their smart suits. They looked a bit het up. John MacGilvray, who Jeff said had started the Party, kept looking over at Douglas as if he was cross, and saying something to an older man called William Strang, who nodded and adjusted his tie as if it was too tight.

'Douglas is standing for Chairman against William Strang,' said Jeff.

Douglas was the only one smiling, and even sitting down he was almost eye-to-eye with the men standing beside him at the end of the table. He looked over but didn't seem to see me. Then he waved at Jeff and gave me a smile as he realised who I was. Perhaps he hadn't recognised me in my hat. The noise of people talking and chairs scraping got louder and louder, and Mr MacGilvray had to bang his gavel on the table several times before the room settled down.

'Ladies and gentlemen, welcome to the SNP annual conference of 1942, and although the sun has seen fit to shine on us, I particularly thank you for coming in such challenging circumstances. As you know, there has been considerable debate in the press, and in our own ranks, with regard to our position vis-à-vis the interests of Scotland in this time of war. A particular debate has been opened by the conviction served on Douglas Grant by the tribunal in Glasgow's Sheriff Court with regard to the issue of conscription in Scotland. I can confirm that whatever stand might be taken by individual members, the SNP is the enemy of fascism and the friend of freedom.'

There were shouts from the floor of 'Hear, hear,' and Jeff shouted, 'Free Douglas.'

Mr MacGilvray raised a hand for silence like a schoolteacher, and continued speaking. 'With regard to the election of office bearers, we will take a moment of calm reflection to consider who might best represent us as Chairman in the coming term. Let us bear in mind that large numbers of the Party are already serving courageously in the armed forces. Now, before we consider such weighty matters, the first item on the agenda is the report by Dr John Ranald in his capacity as editor of the *Scots Independent*.'

There was a jeer at the back of the room and then someone booed.

'Order,' shouted MacGilvray.

'Why are they booing?' I asked Jeff.

'Because he published an article some felt was a bit critical of Douglas' stand.'

'Order,' shouted MacGilvray, and he banged the table with his gavel again. The noise hurt my ears. It felt like this could go on all day. I took a pencil from my handbag and doodled a plan for my chicken coop on the back of an old envelope. Jeff sighed but I ignored him. The hands on the clock behind the platform moved on a whole hour before they stopped bickering and passed Dr Ranald's report. After a cup of tea, and a quick trip to the powder room, which had very fantoosh mirrors, I had to take my seat again. Jeff whispered, 'This will be exciting now. You are about to witness a revolution.'

I decided to write my shopping list later. There was just enough room for it beside my drawing.

In a very grand voice, the Vice-Chairman, Mr Macleod, invited William Strang and Douglas to leave the room, and their proposers and seconders to speak. Douglas winked as he passed us, and it was like being noticed by a fairy-tale giant. I could see the people seated across the aisle through his legs. The angry man called MacGilvray stood up to speak for old Mr Strang. MacGilvray had nice, wavy, brown hair. Several people booed him, but it didn't put him off. I wouldn't have known what to do.

'I regret to see that so many people, who have done so little for the Party, are so vociferous against Mr Strang, one of its most established members and committed stalwarts,' he said.

There was more booing.

Mr Macleod shouted, 'Silence, all members have a right to speak.' But it was lost in the racket. Mr MacGilvray took a sip of water and said both he and Mr Strang believed it was important to work for Scottish home rule. There was a cheer this time, and he added, 'We must work with friendly elements in other parties. I have already spoken to Tom Johnston, Churchill's Secretary of State for Scotland, and he might consider adding it to their agenda.'

The jeering started again. Someone shouted, 'Away and boil yer heid.'

I stood up to leave, but Jeff put his hand on my arm and pushed me back down into my chair. It was the feeling I had of being trapped in the cinema, but he didn't understand.

'Why can't I go?' I asked.

'Because this is important; Douglas' proposer is next.'

'I don't care,' I said. 'I want to go home.' But the next man had begun to speak and it would have been embarrassing to stand up. He went on about Douglas' court appeal, while I kept my eyes fixed on the door at the back of the stage and wished I could run through it. 'Douglas will never allow the red tape of the Union to strangle our rights as a sovereign nation. We say "no" to conscription,' he shouted.

There was cheering and booing. Everyone looked round to see who was doing what, and a wee man wi' a ba' heid jumped up and tried to shoosh them. The proposer raised his voice. 'Douglas may not fight abroad, but he will fight at home to ensure that our returning servicemen do not suffer the unemployment they endured at the end of the last war. He will see that we do not lose our industries to the South. He will champion full employment and independence.'

I was thinking of the farm, and the green hills where I grew up, trying to cut out the noise, but Jeff poked me in the ribs to borrow my pencil and marked his ballot paper. When the votes had been counted there was only a difference of two in Douglas' favour.

'We will have a recount, ladies and gentlemen,' said Mr Macleod, but he was shouted down.

'Don't bother,' said Mr MacGilvray, 'I wouldn't insult Mr Strang by asking him to lead such a rabble.'

'Well then,' said Mr Macleod, 'I duly elect Mr Douglas Grant as Chairman of the SNP.'

Jeff jumped to his feet punching the air, but Mr MacGilvray had a face like a soor ploom. I couldn't believe it when, instead of congratulating Douglas, he said he was resigning as National Secretary, and added, 'If anyone wants me, I will be in the Rutland Bar.' Half the room trooped out with him like bairns.

Poor Douglas looked shocked. Then Mr Strang stood up and said it looked like he had been defeated on a point of principle, and no offence, but he was resigning, too. Douglas shouted something after them in Russian, I think. The men in the room sounded like animals, hooting and jeering, but Jeff was smiling at Douglas, clapping like a wild man. I told him I was going home, and this time he didn't try to stop me. He was shouting, 'Tell MacGilvray's caucus to go hang themselves.'

The street outside was quiet by comparison. People were looking from the conference door to the Rutland Bar, and back again, at the stream of angry people, and someone had marched off with the flag. It was all so confusing. Jeff and Douglas had seemed so calm and clever at home, and Jeff was so anti-war in his slippers, but here they were hopping mad that MacGilvray had stormed off. It didn't seem worth it for two votes. Jeff said it was just that MacGilvray didn't want a political, conscientious objector as leader.

I began to breathe again as I walked over to Princes Street Gardens and sat by the gold fountain at the foot of the castle rock. Sculptures of naked women, piled three high, poured water into the pond. The most beautiful woman rose up out of the middle and it seemed strange because they used to drown witches here when it was the Norloch. It was like they had come back and were reaching up to heaven, dripping wet. Thinking about them gave me the willies, and I had no one to cheer me up. The pigeons walked up to me, dipping their heads, but I didn't have any bread for them, so I left by the railway bridge and walked home. The mothers had gone from the Links. There were just rows of empty benches, and the back streets were deserted apart from a few bairns running between the gardens with guns made of sticks.

I wondered when Jeff would get back but I could imagine he would be late. He would be drinking with Douglas somewhere, banging on about democracy. I think the ceilidh they'd planned for later was cancelled. No one would have dared to walk out of the conference if Mrs MacDougall had been standing there with the gavel in her hand.

5

The house was very quiet when I got back. It was just as I had left it, and I missed the stir of the farm with my brothers tramping in and out, leaving clothes and newspapers strewn everywhere, and filling the house with their laughter. I remembered Mother's cheery fire in the kitchen and the cooking smells, and it just felt like the flat had no life. I was looking after a museum full of Jeff's late mother's things. Her china knick-knacks were still in a glass case in the drawing room and her clothes were in our double wardrobe. They still smelt of her perfume. I put my hand on the door handle to Jeff's study, gripping the cold metal. I wanted to look for the letter with the black crown on it but he trusted me not to go in, so I made a cup of tea in the kitchen instead.

The trees out the back were thick with leaves. A fat wood pigeon was waddling along one of the branches, but when the window upstairs opened, he flew off with a crack of his wings. I put my teacup down in the saucer and heard footsteps crossing the kitchen floor above, and then water running. Maybe Mrs MacDougall was also lonely if she was cleaning Professor Schramml's empty flat again. I thought maybe I should try to be more neighbourly and invite her in for a cup of tea. I ran up the spiral stairs and chapped on the door, which had a brass knocker in the shape of a thistle. There was no reply, so I tried again, and then Mrs MacDougall's voice said, 'Who is it?'

'It's me, Agnes,' I replied.

'What do you want?'

I was surprised because she was normally so quick to open a door. 'Nothing. I wanted to ask you something.'

'Just a minute.'

I heard her footsteps moving away and then some keys being lifted and Mrs MacDougall came out into the stairwell with her pinny folded in her hand. I glimpsed a dresser covered with a white dust-sheet in the hall. Mrs MacDougall's eyes were very blue, which I hadn't noticed before.

'Couldn't you wait until I am home to speak to me?'

'I'm sorry, Mrs MacDougall. I heard you cleaning and since it is just you and me, I thought you might like a cup of tea.'

'You heard me cleaning? Have you nothing better to do than to sit listening to folk going about their business? If you have so much time on your hands, this stair needs a bit of attention, but I expect your man will be back soon and he will be looking for his tea. You should be too busy for a fly cup at this time of the day, Agnes.'

'Well, he is going to be late tonight. We were at an SNP conference.'

'Don't talk to me about that gang,' she said, pushing past me and running her finger along the banister. 'It is time this war ended so that we can get sensible men like Professor Schramml back. He always took his turn on the stair and went that wee bit extra with the duster.' She looked at me. 'He is sadly missed.'

She was just one of those wrong-headed folk. She clumped down the stairs and banged the door of her flat shut. I sat down on the landing and it grew very quiet. I knew the family opposite the Professor had gone to their cottage in Fife, and the two bachelors on the top floor were away fighting. I grew cold sitting there looking up at the skylight and I leant over the railing to see how far it was to the bikes chained at the bottom. I counted twenty-one steps down to my front door.

In my bedroom, I took off my dress and lay down under the quilt, and even though it was only six o'clock, I tried to sleep. At the farm, the coos would be coming in to be milked and for some reason the thought of them walking together, with their heads nodding, made me want to greet.

Jeff and Douglas didn't get in until two in the morning, laughing as they stumbled through the hall to the kitchen. I heard Jeff saying, 'It will all be different when you are Gauleiter of Scotland, Douglas.'

'Let's hope it won't come to that,' Douglas replied.

There was the clink of whisky glasses being put on a tray. I thought about going through to tell them there was soup in the pan, but Jeff put his head round the door before I could get up, and slurred, 'How is my sleeping beauty?' He didn't wait for an answer.

6

Douglas slept on the divan in Jeff's study but was gone before breakfast, and Jeff left after a cup of tea and a couple of aspirin. Later that day, I could see from my kitchen window it was one of those sudden, heavy rainstorms that all farmers dread. The trees at the back of the house began to shake as the ball of wind jumped from one to another, pushing the soft, summer leaves down. Sunlight struck Arthur's Seat in the distance, turning it gold against a charcoal sky and it grew darker and darker until, just for a second, the wind dropped and the first splashes of rain fell. It was soon driving against the glass at the front of the flat and the stair door banged. After running round to push up all the windows with my pole, as Jeff still hadn't replaced the ropes, I looked over at the empty mansion behind us. The windows were dark and bare of curtains, and it made me feel mair lonely. Jeff was at another evening talk at the university so he would be late. As I stared at the black trunks of the trees they seemed to twist themselves into figures, standing with their arms raised up to the sky or pointing fingers at their neighbours. Some of their faces looked like they were greetin'; others kept a calm sough.

There was a small movement at the foot of the largest wych elm and it gave me a shock when a figure detached itself from the trunk and sat down with its head resting on its knees, a coat pulled over its head. The rain was so heavy that it bounced off the fabric, and was falling in such grey gusts that I could barely make out the figure any more. It stopped moving altogether and I was less sure it was human and not some trick of the gloomy half-light. I put my hand under the dishes I was washing to look for the last piece of green soap, and when I looked back, a person was nearing the tree, their arm stretched out as if they were approaching a stray that might bite. For a moment I thought it was Mrs MacDougall in her green mackintosh, but she was sure to have her feet up in front of her fire, knitting socks for servicemen and listening to the latest list of casualties on the wireless. I could imagine the thick, white wool slipping round the knobbly joints of her hands. Then Jeff burst into the kitchen, much earlier than I expected, shaking his coat and hanging it near the range. He kissed me, sat down and opened his paper. 'Fancy the latest?' he asked, smoothing out the creases. 'Here's one for you: "Plan for Action. Wars are won by planning. This is as true whether you are fighting Germans – or germs. Each harmless, tiny drop of Milton – as it slips into the water – carries within it a scientific plan for action that would be the envy of any general."'

I was concentrating on the figures walking towards the gate and didn't answer him. When I looked round he was bent over the pages, peering at the print, with the towel from the range over his shoulders.

'There are two people out there, Jeff. They're drookit.'

'Nonsense,' he replied, 'no one would be out there on a night like this. I got a lift and that was bad enough.'

'Come and see for yourself.'

He stood beside me, his reading glasses sliding down his nose. It was raining even harder than before.

'I can't see a thing. Your window is all steamed up. Mother always kept hers crystal clear. I expect it was an ARP warden, if anyone.'

'Well, if it was, there were two, and one of them was sitting down.'

'That's unlikely,' he said. 'Perhaps you have been peering at too much sewing?'

'Why don't you believe me?' I banged the plate onto the draining board.

'Mind you don't break that,' he said. 'It's china. None of your old crocks here.'

'My mother has china, too.'

'Must you be so shrill?' he asked, and, folding his paper under his arm, he walked towards the door. 'Call me when you're finished. I'd like to read you a bit of my address for tomorrow night at the university, see if it resonates with a true native speaker.'

I stuck my tongue out when he left the room. I hadn't done that since I was ten but his high-falutin' ways made me cross. I took longer than I needed to dry the dishes, remembering how much he seemed to value me when we first met at the farm. I had been so shy of him when he set up his recording machine on the kitchen table, a real university man, and I hid my hands as the nails were broken. Mother had agreed to let him record me speaking as part of his research. He said it was important to capture Scots words now as they were disappearing like sna' aff a dyke and I laughed at the way he said it, all posh as if he wasn't really Scottish. He was a man of two voices, his town voice and his country voice. I only had one then, and it disappeared into the desert of my throat as the wheels began to wind the tape from one reel to the other with a slow, grinding sound. He pressed pause and told me to talk about a typical day on the farm. 'What did you do this morning?' he asked, and pushed the microphone closer to me. It was easier to speak now he'd told me what to say, and he scribbled in his notebook, saying, 'Marvellous, marvellous, it is pure Burns, poetry.' I blushed, and he leant forward and said, 'I'm so grateful to you, Agnes. Ayrshire lives in you. You are the living receptacle of an ancient tongue.'

I had never been called a receptacle before, but he looked as if he wanted to lean forward and suck the words right out of me, so instead of laughing, I stood up and asked him if he wanted more tea. He made three more visits after that, always hungry for words, but when Mother suggested she might be able to help him, too, he said he really only needed one subject typical of each area and that I was doing nicely. 'I'm sure she is,' said Mother.

'We're hoping to get Scottish language and culture onto the university curriculum,' said Jeff.

'That would be a wonder,' Mother replied. 'It's the language of plain folk, even when it hides behind a bonnier face than most. We were taught to speak properly at school.'

'You underestimate your heritage,' replied Jeff. 'The speech of someone like Agnes would be the cornerstone of our research. I am a mere foot soldier in the fight against the totalitarianism of the English language and its bureaucracy.'

'You've lost me there, Jeff,' said Mother.

'Its ideology spreads like tentacles through our native consciousness, suffocating the innate philosophy enshrined in our very speech; a democratic, socialist consciousness that is itself the enemy of fascism.' He had jumped to his feet.

'Well, it is braw that you care so much about the auld tongue,' said Mother, 'but you needn't worry, I'm sure it is alive and well here, and always will be.'

'I wouldn't be so sure,' said Jeff.

'Well, you tell me, how many angels can sit on a pin?' said Mother. 'There are some questions not even the cleverest man can answer, so I find it pays not to worry.' She pulled the tea cosy down on the teapot she had just filled to signal the end of the discussion. She never liked people to get too heated. 'Tell me again, do you take milk with your tea?'

Those old days on the farm faded as I tidied my hair in the bathroom mirror, rolling it back round its foam shapers and pinning it in place. When I tilted my chin up, I looked a bit like Rita Hayworth. Then I took off my pinny and joined Jeff in the drawing room.

'Much better,' he said when I went through.

'Now sit here,' he said, pulling out a chair for me in the bay window, 'and pretend you are at my talk.'

I tried to look interested, like a good wife. The rain was still drumming down and the whole block creaked in the wind. There was a mark on my skirt. 'Agnes?' said Jeff, and leaning an elbow on the mantelpiece, he cleared his throat. He began to scan the pages without speaking.

'I'm waiting,' I said.

He took a pencil from behind his ear and altered a line before turning to me. 'Ladies and gentlemen, I am pleased to announce that I have temporarily taken over as principal researcher for the Scottish Dictionary, following the sad death of the previous incumbent, who took this mighty work to "C".'

'"C" isn't very far on,' I said.

'That is the point, Agnes. It is all still to do.'

'How can you do it when there is a war on?'

'Well, someone has to.'

'But why now? Why not after it is all over? Aren't you scared the Germans are coming? Mr Black said you will be writing a German dictionary if you don't watch out.'

'Did he? And what would a butcher know about the value of words?'

'They say his son is in hospital down south. They weren't sure he would survive.'

'And did he?'

'Well, Mrs MacDougall says he's a bit glaikit now, and he lost his leg. He is only nineteen.'

'Poor sod.' Jeff's eyes went back to the papers in his hand. 'Well, he shouldn't have signed up.'

'Jeff, everyone is signing up.'

'Exactly. That is why we are in this mess.'

'How can you say that?'

'Well, if they didn't dance to the tune of some jumped-up motorcycle courier called Adolf, or a load of English generals on this side of the Channel, there wouldn't be a war, would there?'

'I don't understand you.'

'You don't understand much, Agnes.'

'What's that supposed to mean?'

'Nothing. Now, do you want to hear this speech?' He corrected a word with his pencil.

'No, not now. I'm not in the mood.' I got up to close the blinds. I heard the scuff of his slippers on the carpet and he pulled a curl loose at the nape of my neck. 'Don't be cross, Pip,' and I felt his breath as he nuzzled into the top of my collarbone and pulled my ear lobe with his teeth. 'You are a very beautiful and brilliant girl, far too beautiful to need brains at all.'

He wound my hair round his finger and pulled my hips back against his. His hand ran down my thigh. It was dizzying, and I let him carry me through to the bedroom with the wind still beating in the trees.

I was lying with my head pillowed on Jeff's arm when I heard the floorboards creak upstairs in the Professor's flat, and a short, scraping sound like a match being struck. It was so unexpected that I stared at the ceiling and held my breath, but it didn't happen again. I began to doubt I had heard it at all when I heard the Professor's front door shut, and then the tap of feet on the stone steps. They stopped at Mrs MacDougall's flat. Her door opened and clicked shut and then it was all quiet again. Jeff opened his eyes and gazed at me. 'I love you, Pip,' he said.

We kissed. 'Why would Mrs MacDougall be in Professor Schramml's flat at this time of night?' I asked.

He leant back and looked at me. 'Don't mention Mrs MacDougall.' He dropped his voice to a baritone. 'It kills my ardour.'

When I didn't laugh and sat up instead, pushing his arms off, he suggested, 'Maybe she left a window open? She likes to keep everything ship-shape. The war will be over one day and I expect he will come back. She always had a soft spot for him, used to call him "that poor German widower" and take him bowls of soup. She was as pleased as punch when he left a key with her.'

'I thought I heard more footsteps upstairs just now. Listen.'

He walked his fingers along my arm without answering.

The last drops of the storm ran down the windowpane. The sky was dark. 'I don't like the war,' I said.

'I know, Pip. No one does.' And he held me close. He rubbed my tummy and said, 'Maybe this time we'll be lucky and you'll have a new life to think of.'

But I didn't want to bring a bairn into this war. I felt like the marching feet in the newsreel were bringing death closer, and I tried not to imagine the Nazis on Morningside Road, carrying their swastikas to the castle.

7

I was very nervous about meeting Jeff's colleagues for the first time, although he claimed they would be very nice to me as the wife of the speaker. He thought it was time I went out and made friends, instead of worrying about pernickety, old Mrs MacDougall. I spent a long time washing my hair and rinsed it with the last of Jeff's beer to make it shine. He had dug out an old dress of his mother's from the wardrobe and laid it on the bed. It was white satin, cut on the bias, and looked a bit 1930s to me. He said a corsage from the garden would bring it right up to date and I could wear his mother's Arctic fox stole. It was the most expensive kind, caught in its white winter coat. He said she had worn it with a blue ribbon when the National Party and the Scottish Party joined together in 1934. Jeff kissed me before we left and said he was proud to have me on his arm, but he must have forgotten because when we arrived, he left me by the mantelpiece with a glass of sherry, which I don't like, and went off with a colleague to fine-tune his speech.

The room was panelled with glass-fronted bookcases, each closed with a little, gold key. The books looked very old. There was cornicing like ours, which made the white walls look like a wedding cake, and the floors were covered with a deep red carpet.

'You seem to have been quite abandoned, dear,' said a middle-aged woman with wee, round glasses and a tweed suit. She held out her hand. 'Dr Gray, Classics, but you can call me Sylvia.' She removed a small whistle from round her neck and put it in her pocket. 'I have this for the bloody dogs but keep forgetting to take it off. You are?'

'Agnes,' I said, and we shook hands, like Jeff had told me to. 'What kind of dogs do you have?'

'Mad, bad and diabetic. Schnauzers – probably be rounded up for being German if this war goes on much longer. What are you reading, Agnes?' she asked.

'I'm not a student,' I said. 'I'm just Jeff's wife.'

'Jeff McCaffrey? How marvellous. What a talent he has for languages. I think he'll take that dictionary to "Z" before 1943. What do you think?'

I couldn't think of anything to say. She spoke so fast and stared at me through lenses that made her eyes very big.

'So what do you do all day?' she asked.

'I am at home looking after Jeff.'

'Quite right, dear, someone has to,' she said with a smile. 'I must say he has been looking much better since you took him in hand. More dapper and, some would say, more fragrant.' She nudged me. 'He went a bit downhill after his mother died.'

I took a sip of my sherry and Sylvia grabbed the arm of a woman just a little older than me, who was passing.

'Let me introduce you to one of our bright, young things. Millie Dow. This is Agnes McCaffrey, Jeff's wife. Agnes, Millie.'

'Lovely to meet you,' said Millie. 'I'm very much looking forward to Jeff's paper. I expect he has bored you rigid with it. Read it a hundred times in search of the perfect conclusion?'

'No,' I replied. 'He just showed it to me last night.'

'Really?' said Millie. 'I would have thought you'd be the perfect captive audience.'

'Jeff doesn't tell me much about what he does.'

'Oh,' said Millie, 'you're lucky. I can never get him to stop talking. Not that what he is saying about the genesis of Lowland Scots isn't very interesting, of course.'

I took another sip from my glass.

'What a beautiful dress,' she said. 'Where did you get it?'

'It was Jeff's mother's,' I replied, but she didn't answer. Her eye had fallen on a small moth hole I hadn't noticed on my shoulder strap. Our eyes met. I was going to say, 'make do and mend', but she had turned away, waving her empty glass and shouting across the room, 'Ewan, you simply must get me a refill. This sherry is ambrosia, darling.'

I was alone again. Jeff looked over from the dais, where he was now discussing his paper with a very old man. He waved, but was leafing through the pages before I could mouth the word 'help' at him. The sound of it was sitting on my tongue, half-swallowed, when Sylvia emerged from a sea of backs carrying a plate of wee cheese pies. 'Some genius has rustled these up,' she said. 'You must try one.'

I took a bite and the pastry crumbled down my chin.

'Good?' she asked as I wiped the crumbs from my dress and lips. 'Now don't tell me that fly-by-night, Millie, has abandoned you?' But before I could reply, she added, 'Of course, she really is leaving us. Joining the WAAF. Said all the best-looking boys are airmen. Something about a squadron of angels. I'm past all that myself. Gave up on men years ago. I can heartily recommend it.' She smiled at me. 'Ever thought of signing up? Even Jeff can't be a full-time job.'

'Well, it takes a long time to clean the flat and queue for rations. It's hard to keep everything nice when he won't let me into his study to clean.'

'He won't let you in his study?' repeated Sylvia. 'All top secret and hush-hush, eh?' She bit into another cheese pie.

'I don't really mind. I am very busy. I grow my own vegetables and I keep a snare on the Blackford Hill for rabbits.'

'Do you really?' she exclaimed.

'A veritable Diana,' said a deep voice behind me, and I

turned to see Douglas standing there. He bent and kissed my hand. Suddenly I didn't feel like my dress was second-hand any more. 'A vision,' he said, brushing the stole at my shoulder, and moved to kiss Sylvia on both cheeks.

'Our one-man Bannockburn,' she laughed. 'Any date for the appeal?'

'July the ninth,' he said.

'Any hope of a defence?'

'Watertight, of course. You know me. Jeff has been helping me research it but I am going down the line of the sheriff acting *ultra vires* in view of the statutes of 1369 and 1371. The 1707 treaty never gave him more authority than he had before that date, ergo he can't enforce edicts like conscription in a Scottish court when that edict originated in England. And the Crown is not above the law here, a principle established in the Declaration of Arbroath to keep Bruce in his place.'

'Well, I don't know where you dug up your dusty statutes but I hope they serve you well. The war isn't looking too good what with this Northern Front in Norway. The Free Norwegians are cobbling together boats here.'

'I salute their Viking spirit,' said Douglas, 'but the fight against Nazism can come when we have home rule, or at least a Scottish army under our control.'

'Well, let's hope there is time,' replied Sylvia, and as she spoke I imagined the Nazis stamping down the hill to Tollcross, even nearer the castle. 'We need people like you, Douglas. I don't want to see you locked away in some dungeon for treason,' she added.

'It's all mod cons at Barlinnie, Sylvia,' he laughed.

He didn't seem to notice the tears in her eyes from his great height. Someone tapped on a glass with a spoon and everyone moved towards the seats, which were upholstered in blue velvet. Jeff was standing on the podium two rows away, but I was more aware of Douglas' warm thigh against mine. Even though I tried to hold my leg away from his without moving my foot, every time I relaxed I felt him next to me.

'Ladies and gentlemen,' began Jeff. He had insisted on wearing a dinner suit with a white tie as ladies were present, but I didn't see that it mattered. I must have been away in a dwam, or perhaps it was the sherry, because Douglas nudged me and nodded towards the podium. Jeff had started speaking.

'It is an honour and a privilege to be present tonight as a caretaker for the Scottish Dictionary while its prospective editor is exiled in Beith.'

There was a smattering of applause. 'While I don't expect the war to last long enough to get the work finished, I hope to contribute more than a little to the letter "C". In the meantime, I propose to speak to you tonight about the declension of Scots verbs in the German model, using those active words which might be said to take a common Germanic root.'

Douglas got out a small pen and paper. 'Prepared for any eventuality,' he said.

Jeff took a deep breath. 'The verb "to go",' he said. 'Past tense, imperfect, as we have it from Burns, and the Scottish vernacular, "ging". Perfect, from the German perfect tense as we know it today, "*ich bin gegangen*". We drop the auxiliary verb "*bin*" and the prefix "*ge-*", and the suffix "*-en*", and arrive at "gang". "I gang", meaning, "I went".'

I was looking at the clasp of river pearls in Millie's hair in front of me when I realised that Jeff was adding, 'As any native speaker might say intuitively, without a full understanding of the origins of their speech – a speaker such as my lovely wife, Agnes.'

'Aye,' I said, standing up, and then the room laughed. I sat down.

'Very good,' applauded Douglas, but I wasn't being funny. Millie turned round and whispered, 'Spoken like a true native,' and her red, red lips split open like a wound. I felt a tear spring to my eye. I never used to cry in Ayrshire. Mother always said I had a smile for the world.

Jeff talked for a long time and Douglas made occasional notes – '*Ich meine*: I mind: loosely, I remember' – shaking his pen over the floor to get the ink flowing. Then, with a sigh, he took a pencil out of his pocket. 'Sometimes the simplest solutions are the best,' he said.

Jeff continued with his long list. 'Common misunderstandings of Scots words by our English neighbours, who believe them to be a corruption of their own tongue rather than coming from a different root: "man" meaning husband, from the German word "*Mann*" as in, "*Mann und Frau*", man and wife; "coo" from the German "*Kuh*", k–u–h, not a mispronunciation of the word "cow".'

Jeff was getting very heated and paused to take a drink. I heard Millie whisper, 'Rather obvious,' to her neighbour. Then Jeff leafed through his papers to find what he called his interesting aside. I turned to Douglas, whose eyes fell on the moth hole on my shoulder strap.

'May I?' he smiled and reached towards the corsage over my left breast. He unpinned it with his bear's paw and delicately pinned it over the hole. His fingers felt huge against my skin as he pulled the satin up to fasten the pin. 'Make do or mend. That is the real choice. Mend – never make do.'

'Thank you, Mr Grant,' I said. Millie's head turned a fraction. The pearl drop in her ear swung like a tiny pendulum on its silver chain. She reminded me of Mrs MacDougall listening through the wall, as if there could be no secrets in the world. 'Please excuse me,' I said.

I stood up as quietly as I could, but the room that had seemed so large suddenly seemed very small, and I had to squeeze past three other people to get out. Jeff stopped talking for a moment, which made everyone turn to look at me. I mimed drinking a glass of water and he started talking again. There were too many words in the room, coming so fast they all fell over each other and lost their sense. Jeff should have slowed down and given them space so that I could try to understand what he was talking about, but they came at breakneck speed as if he was challenging his colleagues to keep up. I pulled the heavy, wooden door shut behind me, only releasing the handle at the last minute so it wouldn't make a noise. The hall was cool and I wanted to lean my hot forehead against the windowpane, but the blackout blind was down. I didn't dare lift it in case some light escaped, so I stood there waiting for Jeff to finish. I longed to walk back across the Meadows by myself, to see the stars and smell the cool, night air, but for the first time in my life, the big, open spaces seemed dangerous, as if a German plane might drift over from the Forth on owl wings, and the silver necklace at my throat felt like the rabbit snare I had left on the hill.

Douglas stayed with us again that night, but apart from asking if the moths had been issued with the appropriate ration cards before hanging his jacket in the cupboard, we never spoke. I fell asleep to the sound of his laughter in the kitchen and the low murmur of my husband answering him.

8

Jeff was happy all week after his talk and insisted I come to the next Party meeting and see the Bannockburn rally, although it was out of town. Stirling was much smaller than Edinburgh and there weren't so many signs of the war. Only the station was sandbagged. We paused by a newspaper stand while a man checked our tickets. It read, '1,000 bombers leave Bremen blazing'. The headline wriggled under the criss-crossed wire in the breeze, trying to escape. I wondered where Bremen was.

As we walked up the hill below the castle, I could see the Ochils in a long line and Jeff pointed out the Witches' Craig at the foot of Dumyat. The hills were soft and round, and the Wallace Monument stood out against them with its craggy hat on. 'It is God's own country,' he said.

Smartly dressed old men, and a few women were also walking up to the Miners' Welfare Institute at the Craigs, and some carried rolled-up flags and banners. There was a sign outside which read, 'SNP Special Conference'. We had to queue to get in. At the far end of the hall there was a platform with a long table, draped with the Saltire.

All the blethering in the room tailed off when the Convenor stood up to welcome everyone. When they stopped rummaging in bags for sweeties, and turning round to say hello to people, he begged leave to remind them that, on this occasion, Stirling

Council had not seen fit to allow them to march through the town with a pipe band in honour of Bannockburn. Someone shouted, 'Shame.'

'I regret to inform you, ladies and gentlemen,' he continued, 'that a certain councillor and the baillies of this small but once glorious place are of the mind that a pacifist organisation, as they choose to call us – heavily influenced by the press, I might add – cannot claim to represent the fighting spirit of Robert the Bruce. The recent election of Douglas as Chairman has persuaded some misguided people to share this view.'

There was a gasp from the audience. Jeff jumped up and shouted, 'No one can stop us flying the flag for Scotland.'

The Convenor rose to his feet and patted down the uproar. 'There will be an opportunity to unfurl all the banners you want at the Bannockburn rally itself in the King's Park tonight at 7pm. We must accept their assertion that we have been rebuffed on the grounds of traffic control and, in the meantime, I am obliged to ask you to respect the wishes of the local community, or at least their representatives. Let us demonstrate the good discipline of our Party for the greater good.'

'Down with the baillies!' shouted a lone voice.

'Freedom from tyranny!' shouted another.

'Order, please, gentlemen. I give you our new Chairman.'

Douglas bowed. He looked tired. 'My dear friends, despite the recent reports of a split in our Party, we know that we remain true to Scotland's interests. We are fighting for her rights and freedom, just as England fights for hers against the Nazis, but we have another yoke to lay off; the yoke of English oppression – oppression of our industry, our trade, and our young women, who are transported as mobile labour to war factories down south.' He lowered his voice. 'Let us not forget the sad case of Jessie, who was forced under threat of imprisonment to leave her dependent and disabled mother and travel to England to work.' His voice rose. 'We need to bring the defence of Scotland home. If the British government can transfer the defence of Ireland and Iceland,' he paused to look round the room, 'to the United States, then why can't they transfer the defence of Scotland to a Scottish government?'

There was applause and a rumble of feet stamping on the floor.

I wasn't really in the mood for all this tub-thumping again, so I squeezed out to help the women in the kitchen. They were cutting sandwiches and preparing tea in great, big metal pots. A baby was drinking tea from a bottle held in place by a nappy tied round his chin. Someone pulled a pinny round my waist to protect my blue dress and I felt happy as I cut the bread. The girl next to me said she wouldn't mind starting a revolution with that Douglas Grant and everyone laughed.

Three hours later, we were on our way to King's Park. The houses were very big with tidy lawns, and had shiny, brass knockers on the doors that Mrs McDougall would have waxed lyrical about. She always made out she was born to better things than keeping a dusty Edinburgh stair, but Jeff said it was all nonsense as her mother was in service. He was a bit Morningside about these things.

At the park, we stood in the crowd with the Trossachs lying across the horizon behind us. Jeff pointed out the blue tip of Ben Lomond away in the west. Sheep were grazing on the golf course to keep the grass short while the men were away fighting. I wondered if we could go to one of the tents for another cup of tea before the speakers got on stage, but Jeff wanted to be near the front. The first speaker sounded very tinny, as if the microphone was chewing up his words, so I gazed at the castle on its rock above the knot garden where Jeff said Queen Mary used to play when she was a bairn.

Applause started as Douglas appeared on the stage with a man dressed as Robert the Bruce, carrying a great, long sword. Douglas waved at Jeff, who had stuck a wee Saltire in his hatband, although I thought it looked daft. And then Douglas nodded at a man standing near us. He was all dressed in black and he raised his hat to the stage very politely. His voice was English, just like the ones on the wireless, and the man next to him began to write the things Douglas said in a wee notebook. He wrote very fast in a kind of squiggly writing when Douglas spoke about not sending the lassies away, or not transferring German spies to London when they were caught here in Scotland. 'Reject conscription. We will fight for a Scots army led by Scotsmen,' he roared, and the crowd shouted back, 'Long live the Bruce,' but in such a big park it all sounded no louder than the sheep bleating. The branch banners were up now, hiding the view to the hills. Douglas said he commended his February article in the *Scots Independent* to us if we wished to read more on the subject. Everyone cheered again, and Jeff nudged me, so I cheered, too. I was annoyed that he put so much money in the bucket that went round for the Scottish Mutual Aid Committee. As I passed it on, I noticed that the man in the black hat had gone.

I was anxious to ask Jeff about conscription and the letter. I knew he would be fit enough to fight as he was always up on the Braids playing golf, but I didn't know how to raise it because he got so crabbit last time. At the station, he said, 'You are very quiet, Pip,' but he didn't wait for a reply. He started blethering on about how great the meeting had been and how good Douglas was. I sat in the compartment, beside two old ladies who were knitting, and watched his jaw going up and down as he kept talking. The sun shone on the bristles on his cheek and I wondered why he never noticed that I was bored rigid and just nodded to look polite. He fell asleep outside Falkirk and the sun shone in my eyes as it got lower. Jeff became a sort of hazy shadow against the light. How could he sleep when the Nazis were spreading everywhere like ants? As we drew into Waverley, Jeff stretched and blew me a kiss. He reached for my hand as he stood up.

Waverley was very busy and men were crowding onto the platform for Southampton to go and fight. A woman was greetin' so hard that she bumped into Jeff and then she said, 'Sorry, son, are you going for this train?' and sort of held open her arm as if to guide him onto it, but Jeff shook his head. She looked a bit confused before stepping aside.

'They are no better than sheep,' he said to me, and we had to push through the crowd to get up the steps to Princes Street. I felt like we were going the wrong way and when I said so, he replied, 'This is the right way. We are going home.'

I said, 'That's not what I meant.'

A muscle in his jaw began to twitch. I tried to ignore him until the tram came, and then I looked out the window or down at my bag. A corner of the leaflet I got from the rally was trapped in the clasp, and I opened my bag to push it further down inside.

'I am not signing up, Agnes,' Jeff said in a whisper, and he got off the tram early, leaving me on my own. He said he wanted to walk home to clear his head, but I arrived well before him and had forgotten my key, so ended up sitting on the wall outside the flat. The blossom was dead now and it rustled at my feet in shrivelled heaps that smelt foostie as the wind whipped them up. When Jeff finally got home he opened the door, but didn't hold it for me.

The range was on its last puff when we got in and there wasn't much coal left. I made some pancakes and we ate the last of the broth, but my spoon sounded very loud in my bowl and Jeff went to his study instead of reading the paper to me as I washed up. I was singing Come awa' wi' me to Gallowa' when Jeff came in and asked me to be quiet. 'I am writing something important,' he said, 'and you are making a racket. Mother always had more consideration.'

I looked at the bubbles on my hands and then over at him. He was like someone I had never seen before, so pernickety and crabbit. Not cheery like Douglas.

'I wish I had never left the farm,' I said and, although I wanted to go to him, and have him hold me to make things better, it seemed too far to walk. I noticed the lino was cracked. When I looked up he was gone and I didn't feel like singing again anyway. I sat on the window seat and looked out at the deserted mansion. Jeff was still typing when I went to bed after my bath, and the snap of the letters hitting the paper was like distant gunfire, which bothered me even when I put my head under the pillow.

9

Jeff left for a meeting in Glasgow early the next day and said I could phone him at the Scottish Home Rule Association if I needed him. He left the number on the phone table and I looked at his beautiful writing for a long time after he had gone. Each letter was so carefully formed.

After some porridge, I walked out onto the Blackford Hill to check my snare because it would have been wrong to leave an animal to suffer in it, but there was nothing. The little silver 'O' was like an empty promise and could hardly be seen against the grass. I felt sad as I walked back empty-handed. My feet skited on the gravel on the way down the path and when I reached the street, the concrete seemed to smother the land.

After lunch, to try and cheer up, I was polishing the brass on my front door, to be more like the bonny houses in Stirling, when the phone rang. I wiped my hands on my pinny and said, 'Morningside 4125,' like Jeff taught me, and he said, 'Oh, for heaven's sake, Agnes. It's me.'

He sounded as if he had been running and said that something very bad was happening. I was to take the key to his desk from under the plant pot and burn all the letters in the first three pigeonholes on the left. I was to be quick because there was not a minute to lose, and he was going for the train at Queen Street now, and would be home as soon as possible.

My hands were shaking. I had only been in Jeff's study once. It smelt of old books and dust motes danced against the window. The wastepaper basket was full and I thought I could run a duster round the place once I had dealt with Jeff's letters. The bundles of envelopes rustled as I pulled them out. Some came loose and fell on the floor, so I stuffed what I could into my pinny and went through to the kitchen. The fire was almost out when I opened the range door, and the grit left in the coal scuttle seemed to smother the flames when I put it on. Smoke bit at the back of my nose and made my eyes water, but I poked the letters in and went out to the garden to find some twigs to get the blaze going. I couldn't ask Mrs MacDougall for any coal as she was on her own, and not nearly as well off as she made out. I climbed over the mansion wall to pick kindling from under the trees. The grass was long and damp, and white moths flew up from the plants as I walked through them. The wild garlic smelt bitter as it crushed under my feet, and I had to watch for the nettles. I had forgotten what good soup they make, so I picked a few of the young tips. They don't sting if you grip them just right, and then I added some dandelions. I was sitting astride the wall, trying to work out how to get down without dropping all my sticks and field greens, when a voice said, 'Mrs McCaffrey?'

I looked up to see the English man from the rally yesterday. Before I could answer, the policeman with him said to watch I didn't kiss him, in case I was a fairy in my green dress. My hair was full of leaves and bits of sticky willow, but the man in the suit didn't laugh. He didn't know he would disappear for seven years if I was one of the Gentle Folk. He was looking at my legs and just said, 'Help her down off the wall, officer.'

Mrs MacDougall's curtains twitched. I expect she heard him say that they were here on Crown business and had a warrant to search the flat. I told them Jeff wasn't in and they said they knew that as they had been upstairs already.

'I am not sure it is wise to leave your door open when you are out, Mrs McCaffrey,' the man said, so I told him I always left it open when I was out at the back green because maist folk were honest.

He held my arm very tightly on the way up the stairs, and when I said, 'Get your hauns aff me,' he laughed and said, 'You'll need to translate for me on this one, officer.'

Then I remembered I was an Edinburgh lady now. I stood up straight and said a real gentleman would introduce himself. He bowed and said he was Mr Grenville Ford, Assistant Director of Intelligence for His Majesty's Government. I told him I didn't care if he was King George himself, he had no right to enter my house uninvited and he showed me his warrant and declared I was mistaken on that point, he had every right.

There was a smell of smouldering paper as we went into the hall. I knew then that none of the letters had burnt. I wondered why Jeff wanted rid of them. Mr Ford guided me into the drawing room and asked me to take a seat. I didn't want to because I was all maukit from climbing over the wall, but he said, 'Sit down, Mrs McCaffrey,' in a very stern voice, as if I was back in school and about to get the belt.

'I haven't done anything wrong.'

'That remains to be seen. I need to ask you some questions about your husband. Can you look at me when I am speaking to you?'

I was pulling the leaves out of my hair and when I looked at him, he sighed and opened his notebook. 'Let's start at the beginning to keep the record straight. What is your full name?'

'Mrs Jeff McCaffrey,' I said.

He stopped me with his hand. 'Your first name,' he said.

'Agnes Margaret. My maiden name was Thorne and my husband sometimes calls me Pip. He makes a joke about...'

'Address?' he said, and it was then I felt like I was waking up in Jeff's world and that I had been lost in a dream before, and nothing had been real. I didn't like Mr Ford with his grey moustache and the lines on his forehead that pulled the skin onto his eyebrows, or his eyes that were as sharp and black as a craw's.

'How long have you been married, Mrs McCaffrey?' he asked. I told him it would soon be a year, and he glanced at my belly like Mrs MacDougall, and I put my hand across it. 'Children?' he asked, and I said, 'No, not yet.'

'Seems our man is neglecting more than one of his duties, eh, Mrs McCaffrey?' And he looked at me as if he expected me to laugh.

'Why are you asking me all these questions?'

'I think you know,' he answered.

I told him I had no idea and he said, 'So why are you burning letters in your kitchen and not making bread, or whatever it is that a good Edinburgh housewife usually does?'

'Because my husband asked me to.'

The wrinkled skin above his eyebrows shot up, but he just nodded and made a note in his book. The officer came into the drawing room and asked him where he wanted the papers to go. He had a box full of Jeff's things. I jumped up and shouted, 'You can't take those,' but Mr Ford told me to sit down in a sharp voice, as if I was a dog. I insisted I wouldn't unless he told me what was going on.

'There is a war going on, Mrs McCaffrey,' and he added that Jeff had declared in a letter to *The Scotsman* that he would not accept conscription. 'Your husband has set himself against the government at a time of national emergency, Mrs McCaffrey.' It put him beyond the usual niceties and what did I know about that?

'It's not my fault if people take me to rallies, or use funny German words.'

He leant forward. 'What kind of German words?' But the only one I could remember was '*der Tag*'.

'Can you remember who said that?'

'I think Douglas said, "*Komm der Tag*".'

'So was that Douglas Grant, Mrs McCaffrey?'

'Mr Grant, but you needn't think anything bad about him.'

'I am not thinking anything yet, Mrs McCaffrey, but can you remember what he meant when he said, "*der Tag*"? It means, "Come the day". You will be helping your husband if you cooperate with us. I wouldn't like to have to ask him the same question down at the station.'

I said I thought maybe they were talking about Douglas' appeal, or Hitler in Norway, or something. He nodded and wrote some more in his book, then lifted his head as if he was listening and I recognised Jeff's feet on the stair, taking them two at a time. When he rushed in, I was so glad to see him I began to greet. He looked as if he wanted to hit Mr Ford. 'How dare you come into my house and distress my wife!' he shouted.

I was proud of him. He looked so brave. Mr Ford held out his hand and said he was sorry to spring this visit on him but in the present circumstances he was sure he would understand the reason for his call. He passed him the search warrant. The wind went right out of Jeff's sails and he sat down and glared at Mr Ford, who seemed to be enjoying himself. His eyes sparkled. He was sure Jeff would understand that since a certain German had dropped in outside Glasgow so unexpectedly last year, His Majesty's Government had been understandably alarmed at the prospect that certain, and he paused before he said the word – Nationalists – might have been tempted to accord him a warm welcome.

Jeff went bright red and said no Scotsman would have anything to do with a Nazi like Hess, but Mr Ford only replied that some Scotsmen were finding it a problem having anything to do with Churchill, either.

'Scottish Nationalism is not National Socialism, Mr Ford,' Jeff said, as if he was talking to a tumshee-heid. It went very quiet. They glared at each other and I asked if I could go to the bathroom but Mr Ford snapped, 'Just a minute, Mrs McCaffrey,' and they kept staring at each other, although I was bursting.

'The day your lot added a capital letter to the word "nationalism" it became my business, Mr McCaffrey – it threatened the body politic,' said Mr Ford. 'Politics is semantics writ large.' He paused. 'Your wife tells me you are a close associate of Douglas Grant?'

Jeff looked at me and then nodded. Mr Ford straightened his cuffs. 'I believe I noticed you, and your lovely wife, at the Bannockburn rally yesterday.'

'Did you?'

'Can I assume then that you are of the same mind as Mr Grant?'

'Don't pigeonhole me, Mr Ford. I have my own opinion on these matters and I certainly don't like to be told what to do by Westminster. They aren't forcing conscription on Northern Ireland.'

'I am sorry you see it like that. It is a matter of some urgency that we garner sufficient forces to fight the Nazi menace and at the same time preclude an attack on another front. As you know, the Germans are in Norway on a northern offensive.'

'No one will let them in here.'

'Stable doors, Mr McCaffrey, stable doors. Who will hold them back if not you, or Mr Grant, or others like you?'

'The SNP are forming a new resolution to clarify the situation,' said Jeff.

'I fear the time for resolutions, however worthy, is past, Mr McCaffrey. It is the time for action.'

'If you would just let me finish? We are considering a resolution that would allow us to raise a Scots army under the umbrella of the "United Nations".'

'And how will your pigeon-post resolution find its way past von Braun's rockets? Scratch for feed in bombed-out cities? Wake up, Mr McCaffrey.'

Jeff looked like my father's dog when he had a rat in his jaws. I asked to go to the toilet again because I couldn't wait any longer. Mr Ford called the officer, who came with me along the corridor and waited outside the door. I was so embarrassed that I almost didn't need to go any more. After I pulled the chain, I took a moment in front of the mirror to tie back my hair. It was getting very long but Jeff didn't like me to cut it. I was tired of all the men's talk and worried that Mr Ford might be right about the Nazis. If Jeff didn't want to fight, maybe he could go to work on the farm with my brothers, but he seemed set on being like Douglas. For a moment I wished he was Douglas, and not just running after him. I rubbed some carmine on my lips because they looked a bit pale and wondered what it would feel like if Douglas touched them.

The policeman gave me a smile when I came out of the toilet, as if he thought I looked nice, and he whispered, 'Dinnae fash yersel', hen, it will all pass,' but I ignored him and walked straight into the drawing room.

'I'd like to go out to the garden, Mr Ford,' I said. 'My vegetables won't grow themselves and I need to water them.'

He nodded, and turned a page in his book. 'Dig for victory, Mrs McCaffrey. That's the spirit.' He looked at Jeff, who stared straight ahead. A muscle was twitching in his cheek.

I wondered if I could sneak Jeff's letters out and dig them into the earth, but the boxes had already been taken away. They were probably in Mr Ford's car. The officer winked at me as I passed, as if he guessed my plan.

The garden was in shadow, and the birds were picking insects from the earth I'd hoed over, when Jeff came down to the back green. He put his arms round my waist and I leant against him, my hand still on the hoe. 'You are a child of nature, Agnes,' he said.

When I turned to face him, he was greetin'. I wiped away his tears, and he said, 'Pip, Pip,' and gave a watery smile. We stood there a long time, leaning together. He said Mr Ford was away now and the house would be quiet if I wanted to come up, but I knew the door to his study would be standing open, his papers gone and nothing would ever be the same again.

It was midnight before he came to bed that night. His typewriter rattled and the bell on the carriage rang again and again as it reached the end of the line. I could hear sheet after sheet being torn up. I worried about where he could get more paper if he ran out. The moon had almost moved out of the top pane of glass in the bedroom when he came through. I hadn't wanted to look at the blackout blinds, so I had left them up and a cool breeze was coming in at the top of the window. He was wearing the silk pyjamas Prof Schramml had left him when he went abroad, and he wiggled his eyebrows and said, 'How do I look?' But I wasn't in the mood and turned over in bed. He said I wasn't to be a soor ploom and that everything would be fine, but I didn't see how it could be. 'Don't trouble yourself over it, Agnes. The Party will support me,' but I told him I was tired of only getting half the story and that most women didn't spend the evening sweeping up the ash from their husband's half-burned letters. 'I don't want men I don't know stamping round my house,' I said, but he replied that the police were only doing their duty.

'Well, why don't you do yours?' I shouted, although I didn't mean to.

I wished I could call the words back but I couldn't. Then I heard Mrs MacDougall's light switch go on, although it was late, and I bet she had her glass to the wall.

'You only ever give me half the story,' I said. He brought through the letter with the black crown on it. He was to go to the Conscientious Objectors' Tribunal in Glasgow next week.

'They can't make me fight,' he said, 'as long as I can prove that the Act of Union didn't give English jurisdiction precedence in Scottish courts. I have been looking into it for Douglas' appeal.'

'Not that again. I am tired of that man and the way you follow him like a dog. Why can't you think for yourself?'

He swallowed and said he was sorry I felt like that, pulled up his pillows and the quilt and went to sleep on the divan in his study. The bed felt cold without him and I wondered if this was how it would be if he went to prison. I looked at the stars of the Plough through the window and heard Mother's voice telling me that the last one always pointed north to the Pole Star, the only fixed point in the sky.

10

By morning my head ached, but I decided to go to the early Mass anyway. I knew Jeff was a half-baked Piskie when I married him, so I just let that flee stick to the wa' and went alone as usual without waking him.

The church was full of flowers and candles and it made me feel as if there wasn't a war on after all, as if I could come out the door afterwards and find my house was clean and sparkling and Jeff still had a kiss for me on his bonny lips. I prayed for the war to be over during the intercessions. So many of my neighbours' menfolk were mentioned, and some were even named in the list of those whose anniversaries we keep. As I stood in the queue to receive communion, two little boys started fighting in the line next to me. One raised his wee hands, clasped in prayer, and used them to hit his brother, and the younger one swung his praying hands back in his brother's belly like a club. They laughed and their mother stared straight ahead at Jesus hanging on his cross, and bit her lip.

'Body of Christ,' said Father Michael, holding the wafer up in front of me. I put it on my tongue and crossed myself. I prayed for Jeff and Douglas as I knelt in the pew. On the way out, I put my last sixpence in the box to buy a candle for Mrs Black's son at the Shrine of the Venerable Margaret Sinclair. The light looked very small on the sanctuary. I thought of the nun sleeping with folded hands under the stone, and the people she nursed while she lived, even though she was poorly. I prayed she might send us a miracle.

A blue wind from the south was shaking the trees as I walked home across the Meadows. My mother said each wind had a different colour, as any fisherman could tell you. I envied her not needing to lose any of the men on the farm to war, and she always prayed to Mary, Star of the Sea, when the boys took the boat out. I wished the farm had a phone so I could have heard her voice. No one around me was making any sense, but Father Michael had said The Lord is my shepherd in his homily and I felt less lost. I was humming the psalm to cheer myself up when I reached the flat and had just got my key out when Mrs Black came up to me. 'Mrs McCaffrey,' she said, 'I have something for your husband.'

I thought she meant something nice, but she snapped open her bag and took out a white feather. I put my hands behind my back so she couldn't give it to me, but she pushed it towards me, right in my face. It looked like a feather from an angel's wing, curling over at the edges and fluffy at the quill. I couldn't think where she had got it, which birds were white in the garden, and then I realised that she must have pulled it from her pillow in the night, or plucked it from a chicken at the shop. Her eyes were red-rimmed.

'I am not taking that,' I said, and pushed past her. She said we all had to face up to things, that Jeff was a coward and the worst kind, hiding behind his politics, as if Herr Hitler would give two figs for nationalism when he was sitting at Holyrood with a whisky in his hand. I took the feather from her and tried to throw it on the ground, but it was so light that it floated down between us, and blew in to the stair as I opened the door.

'Your husband is a skiving coward, scrievin' nonsense while laddies get blown to pieces.' She looked like she was going to swing her bag at me.

I ran upstairs and banged the door, but Jeff shouted, 'Don't bang the door, Agnes.'

I thought my head would explode, pop like a puffball, and all the dust inside would float away on the breeze, growing fainter and fainter until it disappeared.

'Don't you shout at me when Mrs Black is out there saying you are too feart to fight.'

Jeff went quiet. 'I'll go down and have a word.'

'You're too late. She has gone to bend the ears of her friends about you. I will never be able to go to the butcher's again.'

The feather was still at the foot of the stair the next day, although I tried not to look at it lying in the corner, and then two days later it was gone. I don't know who picked it up or brushed it away. Maybe the wind took it.

11

The week passed slowly and on the first dry day after a spell of rain I got up early and walked out onto the Blackford Hill. There were only a few days left until the tribunal and the words buzzed in my mind as I walked; 'C' for conscientious, 'O' for Objector. It was as if the pages of a dictionary were flashing before me and Jeff was pressed like a trapped insect as the book snapped shut. There was no Scots word for such a thing. He was in a foreign land. As I climbed the hill above the battleships shoaling on the Forth, I saw that the world was pressing into Edinburgh, making the familiar view unfamiliar. My legs ached as I walked along the ridge to my snare. I suppose it was lack of food. A neighbour next door had said there was fruit at McColl's, but last time I queued for oranges there was only one left by the time I got served. Mr McColl had thought he might have some more by the end of the week, but I didn't go back. There were wild strawberries and rhubarb growing over the wall.

My snare was empty, although there was a little dried blood on it. I moved it further into the gorse bushes just in case someone had discovered it and was helping themselves. It was peaceful on the hill. I could just make out the Forth Bridge although it was always blacked out of the photos in

Jeff's paper, and I wondered what the exiled King of Norway thought of the view of its red legs from his new home in South Queensferry. I supposed a Viking chief like him would like a fiord, even a Scottish one.

The smell of the grass warming in the sun made me feel sleepy, and the bees were humming in the yellow gorse, living their little bee lives, never knowing that the Germans were coming. I lay back on a flat patch of grass, just off the path, beside my silver snare, which arched against the Forth. I could have picked the ships out of my net like minnows. It might have been an hour later when I woke up. My cheek was hot from the sun, and for a moment I couldn't tell if it was morning or afternoon, or even who I was, or where. Then I remembered Mr Ford, and Jeff most likely facing prison because the dunderheid agreed with Douglas. I wished that we had never met the bear and that there was no war and that we were still happy.

From the height of the sun, I guessed it was almost midday and I hurried home past the duck pond, which was covered in scum. Some trees had tipped over in the gale but there was no one to clear them away. All the good, green places were going to sleep as if they were enchanted, and the hard streets and barracks and docks were sucking all the men away, so that soon there would be nothing left but old people and women and bairns. By the time I reached Falkland Terrace, I had decided to tell Jeff that I would volunteer to become a Land Girl. There were farms in the Pentlands I could cycle to, and then, if Jeff was taken to prison, I could bury my hands in the good earth and not be lonely.

I heard the noise of the saws at the top of the street before I saw the sparks flying from the railings as they were cut down. Mrs MacDougall was out shouting at the workmen that they had better agree to pay for new ones after the war, and one of them paused with three on his shoulder, spiky like spears, and said, 'Aye, Mrs, if you'd like to pay for the ships during it.'

'A war is no excuse to ration your manners,' she said, but he laughed and clattered the railings into the back of his truck. She sat down on the wall at the end of a row of metal dots as she spotted me. 'Agnes,' she said, 'get Jeff down here to have a word with these vandals.'

'Jeff is a wee bit busy at the moment,' I said.

'What on earth could he be busy with at a time like this?'

I didn't want to tell her in front of all these men that he might be going to prison. One of them winked at me. 'Look boys, it's Rita Hayworth,' he said.

Mrs MacDougall sighed and stood up. 'I want your husband out here to deal with this. My Struan would have protected his property and not let these ruffians take good railings to make bad boats. These hooligans are just stacking them at Leith docks. Mr McColl saw them rusting down there when he went for fruit.' She dabbed her eyes with a corner of her pinny while peeping at the men. 'Struan would never have left me to deal with all this and only a slip of a girl for support.'

I don't know why she thought I supported her. I didn't like her or the railings.

'I'm going in now, Mrs MacDougall,' I said, but I had to pull the bell as I had forgotten to take my key. There was no answer from Jeff so I tried again. Mrs MacDougall said, 'Oh, for heaven's sake, I'll get it,' but as she stepped forward, she clutched her chest. She shrugged off my arm when I asked her if she was all right.

'Don't make a fuss. It's all this commotion. If you could just get out my way so I can get in, I'll be fine. This carry-on is more than I can bear, what with the police running up and down the stair yesterday as well.' She looked at me as if I was to blame for the whole stramash.

I was happy to let her past, then. I followed the nippy sweetie up the stairs, but she took them one at a time, clutching onto the banister and always putting the same foot up first.

Jeff was towelling his hair dry at the door. 'Where have you been?'

'I'll be in in a minute,' I said, and he walked back into the hall. I could hear the wireless playing.

Mrs MacDougall had dropped her key. I opened the door for her and took her arm. 'The blind leading the blind,' she said, and tried to smile. Her flat was the mirror image of ours. I steered her into the front room and sat her down in a wing-back chair.

'I don't really use the drawing room,' she said, 'it's for visitors.'

She remained seated, although she didn't lean her head back against the starched antimacassar. I made a pot of tea and put mats out to stop the cups marking her wooden coffee table. She mouthed a thank you and her cup rattled as she put it back on her saucer. 'Not enough milk,' she whispered.

'Are you all right?' I asked, kneeling beside her.

She squeezed my hand. 'Not really. The police gave me a bit of a fright the other day.'

'Me, too,' I said.

'That sort of thing doesn't generally happen in Morningside.'

'I suppose it doesn't,' I replied.

'I am not saying you are a bad influence, dear.'

I let go of her hand and sat back in my own seat as she continued. 'But all those officious men walking round the garden as if they owned it, and piling out the door with boxes of I don't know what. Jeff's mother would have taken a turn, but, of course, she would never have let them get away with it. She was a great guide to Jeff after his father died.' She mopped her brow with her handkerchief. 'You are very young. One must make allowances. Not an established woman.'

I stood up to leave, but she reached out for my arm.

'Don't leave yet,' she whispered.

'I need to sort things out at home,' I said. 'Chap on the door if you don't feel any better. Jeff could telephone the doctor for you.'

'I don't want to be alone,' she mumbled. 'I'm scared.'

'But your colour is better now. Let's get you tucked up in bed and I am sure you will be as right as rain.'

'It's not that. The police might come back.'

'Well, they won't bother you. They said they would return Jeff's things in a few days. He hasn't done anything wrong.'

'If he is one of those objector chaps like Grant, he'll bring them back at the drop of a hat, running all over the place, willy-nilly, scaring decent folk.'

'You've nothing to worry about, Mrs MacDougall.'

'But you see, dear, I do.'

'Don't tell me you are a Party member, too?' I was trying to cheer her up, bring back her fighting spirit.

'Most certainly not. My Struan fought for the British Empire in the last war. I still have his medals. He was proud of the Union. Look what it was like before: Highlanders jumping about the heather, bashing men in red coats. Uncouth and unshaven, the lot of them, and the women left to feed hungry bairns on thin air.'

She looked a bit stronger and waved at Mr MacDougall's framed medals on the mantelpiece. The clock beside them chimed and to my surprise a cuckoo popped out. 'A gift from Schramml, that old fool. That is exactly the problem. The very nub of the matter.'

'What is the problem?' I asked.

'Ask me no questions and I'll tell you no lies. You would be the first to admit that we haven't exactly seen eye-to-eye, although one has a duty to maintain friendly relations with one's neighbours, while being careful not to live out of each other's pockets. Especially,' she added, 'in times like these.'

'With the Germans coming?' I asked.

She paused and looked towards the door. 'What if they're already here?'

'I don't think you need to worry about that. The Home Guard would be firing real bullets from their pill boxes, not crawling round the streets making eyes at housewives.'

'Oh, for heaven's sake, I need your help, Agnes. I have most unexpectedly got myself into a spot of bother, and it's a cross I can't bear alone.' She blew her nose. 'I want you to promise me that you won't betray my trust, even if you don't agree with what I am about to show you.'

I was so curious that I promised. 'Cross my heart and hope to die,' I said.

'It's not a game,' she said. 'Swear on the Bible,' and she made me take it down from her mantelpiece and place my hand on it. Small pieces of paper were sticking out from various pages. 'Swear,' she said. 'May you be struck dumb if you ever betray the trust I am about to place in you.'

'I swear.'

I thought perhaps Mrs MacDougall was losing her marbles, but her eyes were very earnest. She looked afraid, like the sheep at market. 'Don't keep me in suspense any longer, Mrs MacDougall. I'm on tenterhooks.'

She took my arm and we went upstairs to Professor Schramml's flat, pausing to listen for anyone approaching before opening the door. 'Can't be too careful,' she said.

There was a sweet, sickly smell in the hall, which was in darkness. All the doors were closed. A little light from the stained glass above the front door fell in fragments of colour on the polished lino. She put her fingers to her lips and picked up a broom, which was propped against the wall. 'Take your shoes off,' she whispered. 'Jeff might hear us.'

'Why would that matter?' I asked, but she pressed her fingers to her lips. 'Don't talk.'

She opened the door slowly, holding the broom like a weapon and keeked in. Then she opened the door fully and beckoned me to follow her. The smell was stronger here, a smell of unwashed bodies and illness. There was a man with a bandaged head lying in the large double bed. The curtains were drawn. A vase of dried hydrangeas stood on the dressing table. 'I'm having problems keeping him clean,' said Mrs MacDougall. Dirty sheets were piled in a corner.

I walked forward. 'Don't go too close, dear. He might be a bit unpredictable.'

The man's eyes were glazed and his face was flushed with a fever. He was young, helpless in a nightshirt two sizes too small for him. He tried to sit up as I approached, but slumped forward at an angle and I guided him back onto the pillow. '*Wer sind Sie?*' he whispered. His eyes rolled towards the window where the sound of the men cutting down the railings had grown fainter as they moved down the street.

'You see the difficulty,' said Mrs MacDougall, beckoning me. 'Come through to the kitchen.'

I followed her through the hall past photos of Professor Schramml's family on the beach or posed for weddings and christenings, all smiling, never knowing they were now in limbo in Edinburgh in a war, with no loving eyes to look at them. A few frames were missing, just lighter patches on the wallpaper to show where they had been.

'He's German, isn't he?' I said.

'Evidently. But remember you promised to keep my secret.'

'Mrs MacDougall, it's not about secrets now. He looks like he needs a hospital. He might be dangerous when he gets better.'

'Nonsense, he couldn't hurt a fly, the state he is in. He has had a wee bump to the head. Anyway, I have my broom. I'll just give him a good whack if I have to.'

'You're not making any sense. He needs help. He could be that airman who came down, or a POW.'

'This isn't about him now. It is about me. If the police are prepared to lock up your Jeff for holding daft views, what might they do to me when they find I have a pet German? I was only doing my Christian duty. I thought he was ill, or maybe drunk, when I found him outside. He was on his knees in the rain. He held the cross round his neck out to me and I saw an opportunity to be a Good Samaritan. A call to serve. I thought he was one of ours.'

'He speaks German.'

'Well, he knew enough to keep schtum when I found him. I thought he might be from the hospital, wandered off. I used to be a nurse, you know. I haven't always been the old body on the stair. I was going to take him back in the morning when the rain stopped, and then I thought maybe I could do a good job for him here, save the hospital some money, put a little back in the war purse. But then the police came thundering up the stairs.'

'It's not too late. I could walk round to the hospital. See what they say. It might not be so bad.'

'The authorities might not be very sympathetic towards me. Question my motives like they are doing with Jeff. And what would Mr and Mrs Black say if it gets out, and their poor laddie with his leg blown off.'

'Well, I don't think Mr Black would take his cleaver to you. You're one of his best customers.'

She frowned. 'I'll attribute your insouciance to youth. I could never show my face on Morningside Road again. I would be cast out into the wilderness. Our Lord has left me in the storm without guidance. I am like Job in torment.'

'Don't upset yourself. You have lived here a long time. No one will blame you.'

'But they will, don't you see? They will doubt me and I will lose my good name forever.'

She looked at me. 'You are young. Perhaps you could look after him? He is bound to run off the minute he is well. Isn't that what they all do? Pledge themselves to escape. Then he'll simply vanish and we can get on with our lives. He'll never make it to the coast.'

I sat down at the table, which was covered with a white crochet cloth. The pattern of flower motifs was perfect, regular. I wondered if Professor Schramml's wife had made it. The thought of her death made me feel sad. I was tired of people dying, of fighting, of being alone.

'I'll do it,' I said. 'No one need know, and then we won't have the police back. When the German is well, he can tell us what he wants to do. Maybe he doesn't want to fight any more? And if he gets out of hand, I can take the broom to him, like you say.'

'What about Jeff?'

'I won't tell him.'

'There should be no secrets between a man and his wife. A woman has a duty to her husband.'

'Believe me, Mrs MacDougall, I've come to realise that Jeff has more than a few secrets of his own. Perhaps I should be allowed one, too?'

'You're as big a fool as I thought,' she said, 'but I am grateful to you. I always had a soft spot for Schramml. A very good man for a German.' She passed me the key to the flat. 'I don't know what you'll do when he gets hungry,' she said. 'My ration would never have stretched to feeding two.'

She left me alone. It was odd knowing Jeff was moving around beneath my feet. I tiptoed to the airing cupboard and switched on the water heater, but there was no electricity. The sheets would have to wait. I got the heebie-jeebies without Mrs MacDougall around, but I filled a basin with cold water and went into the room. He was sleeping, or unconscious. I could feel a faint pulse in his neck, but he didn't stir.

12

Downstairs, Jeff came out of the bathroom dressed in his best suit. 'You were a long time with Mrs MacDougall. Don't tell me you have sued for peace?'

'Where are you going?' I asked, as he kissed my cheek.

'Douglas' appeal at the High Court. I told you.'

'No, you didn't.'

'Well, don't make a fuss now. I have enough on my plate. We'll talk later. Perhaps you could give the place a good clean after last week's unpleasantness?' He put on his hat and walked out the door, banging it shut.

He was gone all day and came back in the evening. I was glad he was late. I had got the sheets done and had given the German a couple of aspirin and a little gravy from a fresh rabbit stew. The vegetables from the garden had made a nourishing stock.

Jeff looked scunnered when he came in. Douglas had been sentenced to twelve months in Saughton prison on the spot.

'It could be me next, Pip. Thank God, Mother isn't here to see this. He had a thirty-page defence and they took five minutes to sentence him. Douglas never had a chance. The judges all served in the last war. They weren't going to humour a CO with nationalist tendencies; said this was no time for a loose cannon as he was led down to the cells.'

'I suppose not,' I said.

'You suppose not? What do you even know? What do you do all day, anyway?'

'I look after you,' I said. It wasn't a lie.

'You look after me? All you do is wander round the flat twirling a feather duster.'

'Perhaps you'd like to try it, then, if it's so easy? You try getting food from a butcher that doesn't like you, and keep the peace with Mrs MacDougall. See how long you last before you'd be begging me to take you away from this flat. It is like a museum, Jeff. A museum to your mother.'

'Leave my mother out of this.'

'Her clothes are still hanging in the wardrobe in our bedroom. It's still her room. It is even her bed.'

'Well, you don't need to sleep in it.'

'And where would I go? I am your wife.'

'Try the Anderson shelter. What kind of country woman can't even keep a decent fire going in the hearth? You're making things difficult for me with the police.'

'How am I making things difficult for you? You're the one who had letters to burn, not me.'

'Yes, to save Douglas. There were jokes in German in there that the authorities might have misconstrued.'

'Well, why are you joking in German in a war?'

'We are linguists, Pip. It is what we do. It's a game.'

'Well, I'm not having any fun.'

'I thought I could rely on you for support.'

'You could.'

'Could or can?'

'You can.'

'Do you still love me?' He held out his arms.

I remembered Millie saying how much he talked to her, and his easy laughter with Douglas. He rationed everything with me. I had the scraps from his life.

'I love you, Pip,' he said. 'I need you. I think they are going to send me to jail, too. I'll be a nationalist martyr like Douglas.'

'Why bother, Jeff? Douglas has already made the point about Westminster. You're a nobody, like me. Why not work for an office somewhere? Drive an ambulance, anything.'

'Strength in numbers? Unfinished business?'

'It's not the time. Hitler is coming. I don't want you shouting it wisnae me, and tearing up a copy of the Treaty of Union in front of him when he marches up Falkland Terrace. You need to fight this fight. It's not 1707 now.'

'But I don't want to shoot anyone. I can't imagine taking up a gun. I am a paper warrior.' He wiped his eyes with his handkerchief. I felt annoyed with him. His nose was streaming and his face was going red. He was greetin' like my little cousin.

'Hold me, Pip.' He nuzzled his face into my breast, but I didn't kiss his curls, which smelt of cigarette smoke and hat felt. The ceiling upstairs creaked, but he didn't notice. I tried to breathe more deeply so he would think I was relaxed, but my chest ached by the time he released me and wandered into his study.

'Perhaps you could bring me some of that stew in half an hour,' he called over his shoulder.

13

A week later I saw Saughton prison for the first time. It stood in the middle of long grass behind high walls near the Water of Leith. There were bars at the windows. The flats nearby looked much poorer than ours, with drying greens at the front. The Pentlands stretched between the prison and the south. I parked my bike at the gate. Jeff had been feeling sick and asked me to go alone. He claimed it was my cooking. Cracked, white tiles lined the walls of the waiting room and two old men sat on the benches in the centre. The warder didn't smile as he took my pass and showed me into the narrow visiting room. He lifted up a bar that ran the room's length, and dropped it into place before me. Douglas was leaning on an identical metal rail opposite. The warder stood at one end between us, filling the doorway.

'Good of you to come, Agnes,' said Douglas. He looked tired. 'Is Jeff all right?'

I nodded. 'Just an upset stomach. He heard you got to play the harmonium on Sunday, so he thought you might like some Bach and Mendelssohn.' I held the music out towards him, but the warder took it from my hand and leafed through the pages, looking for writing, before passing it to Douglas.

'This will be perfect,' he said, and smiled. My eyes must have been shining with pleasure because he added, 'You look particularly lovely today, a ministering angel.'

I blushed and smoothed down my polka-dot dress. 'So, how are they treating you?' I asked, to hide my embarrassment.

'Admirably,' he replied with a glance at the warder, who stared straight ahead as if he had cloth ears. 'I attend a garden party in the mornings and spend my evenings very profitably translating Theognis.'

'Who's he?' I asked.

'Oh, a cynical Greek reprobate like myself, although considerably older. "All's gone to the crows and ruined, we've none to blame…" I might ask Jeff about a couple of points. I believe he read Greek at Edinburgh? I am allowed to send a number of letters out but, as you know, my visits are strictly rationed.'

'Well, this might help keep your strength up,' I said, reaching over a bar of chocolate from my pocket. The warder stepped forward and pushed my hand back.

'No supplementary food rations for the prisoners,' he said.

'But it's just a sweetie,' I replied.

'No supplementary food rations,' he repeated.

Douglas patted his stomach. 'Better for the figure now that I am subject to hours of enforced inactivity. I wonder if you might send a telegram to my parents telling them that King George's establishment is treating their guest tolerably well.'

I nodded and put the chocolate back in my bag.

The warder tapped his watch.

'Before you go, Agnes, could you tell Jeff that the Party is getting up a petition? Perhaps he could check that stays on course?'

'I am sure he'll try, but he is up before the tribunal any day now. He might be your cellmate before you know it.'

'Let's hope it won't come to that,' he said.

The warder steered me back to the waiting room with a hand on my back. I tried not to greet as I walked past the old men. In the corner, a woman was nursing her baby.

I was peched out cycling home up the hill from Balgreen to Morningside. On Canaan Lane, nurses in their blue and white uniforms were wheeling injured servicemen back to Astley Ainslie Hospital after some fresh air. I remembered the German upstairs, not much older than me. I didn't know his name.

Jeff met me at the door, waving a newspaper article about Douglas' conviction. 'They are calling the SNP a party which looks both ways – pro-war but anti-conscription. They are calling Douglas a Janus.'

I walked past him. Why was it only at home that I found so many words I didn't understand?

'Where are you going?' Jeff asked.

'The kitchen. I'm tired. Do you want some tea?'

He followed me through. 'How was Douglas? Did you get the music to him?'

'Yes.'

'And?'

'He was fine.'

'Did he give you a message for me?'

'Something about a petition.'

'It's in hand.' He stood at the window.

'I could help,' I said.

'Really?' He pulled a dead leaf off one of the geraniums on the sill. 'You are neglecting these.'

'Must you have so little faith in me?'

'Stick to what you know, Agnes. How many people can you call on in positions of power and influence?'

I poured the dregs of the tea leaves from the pot into my compost bin and looked up. 'Mrs MacDougall?'

He didn't laugh. 'Our Chairman is jailed and you are making jokes.'

'I mind the day you would have laughed at that.'

'It's no laughing matter. I am writing to all our major literary figures and Tom Johnston, the Secretary of State for Scotland.'

I laid out the cups and saucers.

'Do we have to use the good set?' he asked. 'Why not use the everyday ones?'

'You didn't complain when Douglas was here.'

He walked over to me. 'You like him, don't you?'

'Of course, he is your friend.'

He smacked me on the bottom with his rolled up newspaper. 'That is not what I meant.'

'What did you mean, Jeff?'

'You were gone a long time. What did you talk about on your visit?'

'Nothing.'

'You see our Chairman and you talked about nothing?'

'He mentioned a Greek poet.'

'A Greek poet? To you?'

'I am not daft. He wants to ask you about him.'

'So what was he called?'

I couldn't remember. His name had gone. 'The kettle has boiled,' I said, reaching out for it. Jeff laid his hand over mine.

'Did you comfort him?' He lifted my hand, and sucked my finger.

'What are you talking about?' I tried to pull away. 'The visiting room has rails, if you must know.'

Jeff dropped my hand and sat down. 'I don't know if I can do it,' he said. 'Live in a cage.'

'It's not too late. You could sign up.'

'I have told you,' he shouted. 'I will not fight for Westminster.'

'It's not for Westminster, Jeff. It is for us.'

'Not this again,' he said, jumping up. 'I am going out.'

'What about your tea?'

'Give it to your plants.'

14

At two o'clock he still wasn't back, so I ate a couple of boiled eggs, and poked a hole in the bottom of the empty shells, like Mother did, to stop witches sailing to sea and sinking boats. I wished I hadn't eaten both of them, as I could have taken one upstairs to the German, but I decided he could have my bread and butter. Jeff would never notice. The university was probably giving him lunch; motherly women who polished his fork on their aprons to make it shine, and called him 'Sir'. I tidied my hair and went upstairs.

Professor Schramml's flat was very quiet when I crept in. For a moment I wondered if I should pick up the broom in case the German was dangerous, as Mrs MacDougall said he might be, but he was lying on his side, gazing towards the door as I entered. I wanted to throw up the blinds and windows to let in the air, but I was afraid someone might see us from the flats opposite. I showed him the bread wrapped in a cloth and went to find a plate in the kitchen, filled a glass with water and brought it through to him on a tray.

He looked hungry but was still too weak to hold the plate, so I tore off small pieces of bread, dipped them in the water and fed him. His brown eyes watched me the whole time. The bandage round his head smelt bad, sticky with blood and pus. When I had dressed the wound with iodine and one of Mrs

MacDougall's bandages, I washed his face and hands with a cloth, and propped him up on his pillows. He touched his chest. 'Hannes,' he said. 'Sie?'

'Agnes,' I replied.

'Agnes,' he repeated.

I gave him two aspirin tablets. Then he pointed to the clock on the mantelpiece that had stopped, and I wound it up for him. He closed his eyes after that. I left him to sleep, and emptied the chanty before going downstairs.

I had just climbed into the bath to try and get rid of the smell of illness that clung to my clothes, when the phone rang. It was Jeff.

'Pip, it's me. What took you so long?' he said.

'I was in the bath.'

'It's all right for some. Listen, I have decided to go to Glasgow to the Home Rule Association. We are trying to get a Douglas Grant Defence Committee together. I don't have much time before the tribunal. They are processing people more quickly now.'

'When will you be back?'

'Sometime tomorrow.'

'Tomorrow?'

'It is only one night. I'll have a better chance with the authorities if they see we have teeth. Douglas' article about the quislings in Scotland has really set the cat among the pigeons.'

I didn't ask what a quisling was.

'I love you Pip… You have gone very quiet.'

'I don't want to lose you.'

'No chance of that. I have to go now. I'll ask Sylvia to pop round and take you out in her motor. Keep you out of mischief. She took quite a shine to you at my do in the department.'

15

The next day, although I was feeling a bit wabbit, Sylvia insisted on taking me to the zoo to cheer me up. She said all men were a worry to their wives, and sensible women sought their fun elsewhere. 'Political animals are the worst,' she said. 'I should know, my father was one.'

She was a fast driver and was pleased with her car-share petrol allowance for driving for the Women's Voluntary Service. By the time we climbed the stairs to the zoo entrance, I was feeling more excited. I wondered if the animals would look like they did in the films. I had seen Safari and was worried about meeting a lion. 'It is supposed to be fun, Agnes,' Sylvia said, taking my arm. 'You're shaking like a leaf.'

'Are they all in cages?' I asked.

'Every last one,' she replied.

There were a lot of children standing in rows as we passed through the pavilion and there was bunting everywhere as if it was a festival. The ticket lady at the turnstile told us it was a 'Holiday at Home' rally to raise morale. All the children were in their school uniforms with their little gas masks on straps over their shoulders.

'Glad I tied the dogs up outside,' whispered Sylvia, 'they would have been far too excited by all these playmates to remember their manners. Let's march up to the top of the hill and then we can negotiate the crowds on the way down. It is pretty steep.' She took my arm. 'Lead on, Macduff.'

A sea lion broke the surface of the pond as we passed, blowing air out through his whiskers and making me jump. 'I thought it was for ducks,' I said.

She laughed. 'What are we going to do with you?'

The flamingos were like pink chickens with long legs but she marched me on until we reached the parrots. Three tatty gentlemen sat on a dead branch in green coats arguing about whose perch it was. Their feathers were bedraggled and they looked towards us as if we could decide the matter. 'You'll have to sort it out yourselves, boys,' said Sylvia, glancing down the hill at the first of the bairns to round the corner, and taking my arm.

As we walked on up the steep path, the sound of the wee ones grew fainter and she told me the Latin names of all the animals we passed. 'Darwin's Rhea,' she said, looking into the grass of a cage that seemed empty. 'A most unusual bird. The male sits on the nest. Old Darwin toddled round South America looking for it for six months, and was halfway through one at dinner before he realised it wasn't chicken.'

I laughed and it felt good, but when I saw the gorilla in his cage I stopped. He was pulling at the hairs on his bald belly looking for fleas. I tried to pass him the chocolate that was still in my coat pocket, but Sylvia put a hand on my arm. 'You'll rot his teeth,' she said. 'He is more of a banana kind of a chap, although they seem to be in short supply in this blessed war. You'd think some seaman might have the nous to pick up a few as he sailed past Mombasa. Ships all over the world and we are eating from the hedgerows.'

I thought of the wild strawberries and my snare. 'It's not so bad,' I said.

She sighed. 'To tell you the truth, I'm having problems feeding myself and the dogs. They are hungry hunters, you know, and I can't quite bring myself to squabble over bones at the butcher's for them.'

'I could get you a rabbit,' I said.

'From a magic hat?' she asked, with a quizzical smile.

'From the Blackford Hill. If you walk your dogs up there, I could give you one.'

'Better get one for poor Douglas, too, then.' We could see the prison below us in the distance.

'I've just been to visit him.'

'One of the privileged few. I hear it is hard to get a pass. How was he?'

'Says he enjoys the garden party.'

She laughed. 'Well, they left him his sense of humour. That helps.'

'He's translating Theognis in the evening.'

'"Not heeding poverty that eats the heart, nor foes who slander me." How very apt,' she replied. 'Strong personal parallels with Douglas' situation. The past won't save him, although it might do something for his sanity in the short term. You can't keep a good academic down.' She tapped her head. 'It is the mind, you see, dear. Free ranging. Soars like a bird, although I haven't done much soaring myself recently.' She looked round at the animals and sighed again. The first of the children on the rally reached us.

'You need a "Holiday at Home",' I said, pointing at one of the zoo's banners.

'I prefer Italy,' she replied, 'but at least the wee mites are enjoying it.' One of the children was shouting, 'Wake up!' at a leopard. 'They don't know half the mess we are in, of course. Their mothers protect them from the worst of it. The mixed blessing of white lies.'

We found a bench and sat down. The city spread out below us.

'But how are you?' Sylvia asked, turning to me. 'You look pale.'

I wondered if she could see right through me; see the word 'traitor' emerging on my forehead?

I wished I could tell her about the German. Sylvia misread my face. 'The war will pass one day, my dear,' she said. 'All these foolish tensions will be forgotten and we will be able to get on with our lives. We just have to hope Douglas will stop stoking old fires when this is over. Not sure independence is all that relevant now. Everyone wants to chum up with America. I believe Churchill has given Roosevelt a ninety-year lease to stick his planes here. Bit like an awkward lodger: pays well, but wants a say in the running of the house.'

She seemed to have forgotten Jeff was in the Party. I didn't care about the Yanks.

'Douglas wants Jeff to oversee a petition for his release,' I said.

'Does he indeed? I rather suspect he has had his go with the authorities.'

'Jeff might be going to prison, too.'

'That is the worst of it, all you young love birds being separated.'

'I feel I have let him down.' I wiped my eyes.

'Nonsense, dear,' Sylvia put her arm round me. 'You are a good wife to Jeff and I am sure he loves you very much. You are very young. Wait until you see life through the far end of the telescope. These youthful days seem very small, like a silent movie.' She laughed. 'How would we write the captions if we could do it all again?'

I leant against her. Her tweed jacket smelt of dog but I didn't mind. She gave me a squeeze. 'Better trot on,' she said.

Near a sign reading, 'No species is an island', we came to a standstill. There was a sea of children. 'There must be thousands,' Sylvia exclaimed.

A woman was making a speech from a platform draped with Union Jacks, and at her signal to the band, the bairns began to sing God Save the King. Their voices were light and rose up into the air. Sylvia got out her whistle.

16

For days after the trip to Glasgow, Jeff was filled with a desperate energy to save Douglas, and he helped a man called Dr MacIntyre organise a Sunday march to Saughton prison. 'We'll serenade Douglas and cock a snook at the authorities. Two birds with one stone,' he said, pulling an old kilted skirt of his mother's from the wardrobe. He insisted I wear its garish tartan even though I had to secure it at the waist with safety pins. 'She was proud of being a McGregor,' he said. 'Now you are one by marriage.'

I looked like a tattieboggle pinned together in her old clothes, but I wanted to keep him happy. My secret upstairs would be safer if I did.

A small crowd had gathered on Longstone Road, which ran past the back of the prison. Jeff pointed out the poet Hugh McDiarmid to me. At a signal from a drum major, a piper stepped forward in full regalia and we marched as a ragtag army of old men, women with bare legs, and bairns up to the gate. The notes of Scots Wha Hae floated over the prison wall, and at one of the windows a handkerchief fluttered. 'He has heard us,' Jeff yelled, but I couldn't make out which window it was. Men I recognised from the conference cheered and shouted, 'Yours aye for Scotland, Douglas.'

A member of the committee began to speak. 'Friends, we are gathered here today to serenade our Chairman, and while away the heavy hours of his imprisonment in communion with him and his heartfelt nationalism. His stand tells the world that a sovereign nation will never bow to the will of Westminster, that a treaty, however old, cannot be thrown to the wind, and that a true Scot will never surrender to oppression, be it English or German.'

I had heard it all before. I felt my skirt slip on my hips and pulled it up. 'Stop wriggling, Agnes,' said Jeff.

I moved behind a woman with a pram to be out of sight. I'd wanted to wear my best dress in case Douglas was looking out, but I still couldn't spot which window he was at. 'Come here,' said Jeff, the way Sylvia spoke to her dogs. I shook my head. He frowned and his eyes went hot under his hat. I didn't want him to be angry when we got home, with Hannes just upstairs, so when the piper struck up A Man's a Man for a' That, I took his arm and sang at the top of my voice to please him. The notes soared above his baritone.

'Same time next Sunday, folks,' said the committee man. 'Thank you for coming and showing your support for our dear Douglas.'

We waited a long time for a tram. Jeff stood up to get off at the West End and said he would walk over to the university. It was becoming a habit. 'Maybe that outfit wasn't the best choice,' he said as he left, 'although Mother always carried it off.'

I thought he had been leaning over to kiss me. It wasn't just the things I said that got stuck in people's teeth.

'It was your idea,' I said, but he moved off down the tram holding onto the rails.

At home, Mrs MacDougall's door flew open as I went up the stairs. 'I was hoping to catch you alone,' she said. 'What on earth are you wearing?'

'A piece of ancient history,' I replied.

'Well, never mind that. How is our… new neighbour?' She rolled her eyes to the landing above. 'Still alive?'

I nodded.

'Walking about?'

'Not yet.'

'Good,' she said. 'Don't give him too much to eat. He might get too strong.'

'Don't worry, Mrs MacDougall. I grew up on a farm with five brothers.'

'Aye, but they weren't...' and she sketched a *Sieg Heil* in the air and mouthed the word 'Nazis'. 'They are fanatics, dear. They say Hitler is designing a rocket that could reach Scotland. The end is coming, Agnes.'

I opened my mouth to speak.

'Oh, but I don't mean you should feel guilty about what you are doing.' She emphasised the word 'you'. 'God will forgive you for lifting the burden from his servant's shoulders.' Footsteps approached the stair and she slammed her door shut.

It was a boy with a telegram for Jeff. Strips of paper were pasted onto a cream sheet. The letters were typed in large print, confirming his hearing: 'CO Tribunal Glasgow, Monday, at 11am.' The last telegrams I had seen were at our wedding; loving greetings from Jeff's family up north, and our family in Ireland. The war had stopped most of them travelling to be with us on that day, when I had been so happy. Jeff had wiggled the dark eyebrows he claimed he got from Angus Og, a distant ancestor, and said, 'How do I look?' And I replied, 'A little Og.' When he laughed I thought he was the handsomest man alive. It was my grannie who'd whispered, 'The gilt will soon be off that gingerbread,' to my aunt. I wondered what she had seen in us that I hadn't.

I couldn't thole being inside waiting for Jeff to get back, so I went and sat in the garden with my plants. A slater made his way along the bricks edging the vegetable patch, feeling the air with his antenna. The black and white cat from next door came and sat beside me to watch it. He had been wild for most of the summer, hunting mice and drinking from an old clay bowl I had put out to catch the rainwater. He licked his already white paws. A movement at the window caught my eye. Hannes was looking down at me with an expression of sympathy. We were both a long way from home. I pulled some carrots and small new potatoes from the good earth and took them into the kitchen. When they were boiled, I mashed them with a little butter and took them upstairs. The front bedroom was empty and I almost dropped the bowl when Hannes came through the hall. He was wearing an old shirt and trousers of Professor Schramml's, and looked as if he had washed. He was taller than Jeff. I stopped stock-still.

'*Grüss Gott*,' he said, and bowed. '*Wollen wir uns duzen? Ein Deutschsprecher wohnte hier, nicht wahr?*' I didn't know what he meant. He pointed to a picture of the Professor and then to himself. 'German, here?'

I nodded, and held the food out to him. He took it into the kitchen, sat down at the table and chewed each mouthful slowly. I pretended to clean: wiping the surfaces with a soapy cloth, too shy to sit with him. He looked amused, but I was wondering if all Professor Schramml's kitchen knives were still in their drawer. When he had finished eating, he beckoned me to follow him through to the front room. I was afraid he might lock me in, so I stood by the door. There was a German dictionary in a glass-fronted bookcase and he pulled it out and carried it over to the table, opening it as if it were a book of spells. He poured over the pages, leafing backwards and for-wards, and writing the words he found in a list. 'From Vienna,' he said. 'Austrian. Farmer. Go home. Not fight.' He pulled a photo of a child out of his pocket. 'Liesl. *Hast Du Kinder?*' She was wearing a dress with wee, white puffed sleeves, a black bodice and an apron over the top, just like a picture of Snow White. 'Children?' he asked.

I shook my head.

'*Vielleicht gibt's noch Zeit dafür, wenn alles vorbei ist?*' he said, and smiled, but I didn't understand.

'Perhaps, one day. *Wo ist Dein Mann?*' He pointed to his ring finger and then to me.

'My man?' I asked.

He nodded.

'At the university.'

'*Universität von* Edinburgh? Professor?'

'Lecturer.' I must have looked sad thinking of Jeff. The telegram was folded in my pocket.

'*Er will Soldat werden?*' He mimed holding a gun across his chest and waved a hand at the window.

'Not a soldier, no.'

He leafed through the dictionary.

'You love your man?'

His eyes were warm. I nodded.

'*Krieg macht Angst.* War – anxiety.'

I didn't like all these German words and stood up to go. He could have stopped me but didn't move.

'*Komm bald wieder*,' he said.

'I'll come back soon.'

He stood as I left the table, bowed from his shoulders and clicked his heels together. It was so military that I wanted to run downstairs and phone the police, but by the time I opened the door, I realised that it might make things worse for Jeff. Mr Ford would have been cock-a-hoop to kill two birds with one stone.

17

The day of the tribunal came too soon and the train to Glasgow was full of servicemen and sailors, who had docked at Leith and were travelling home. They were bearded and hollow-eyed, gazing out at the hills and the ruin of Linlithgow Palace as if they were seeing them for the first time. The carriage was full of smoke and Jeff pursed his lips, brushed at the creases in his best suit and looked through his papers balanced on his briefcase, as if he was doing something so important he couldn't look up for a moment. I brought him a cup of tea from the buffet, but he let it grow cold on the little table below the window.

'I'll drink that if you don't want it, pal,' said the soldier opposite, and Jeff nodded. 'Going far, doll?' the man asked me, as Jeff looked down again.

'Glasgow,' I said.

'A meeting,' Jeff added, with a look at me under his brows.

'Home Front?'

'You could say that,' Jeff answered.

'Glad you boys are holding the fort. I was never much good at paperwork.'

I excused myself. My stomach was churning and I only just made it to the toilet before I threw up my tea. I sat there until someone knocked on the door, and then I stood at an open window at the end of the carriage until we were almost at Queen Street.

'Where have you been?' Jeff asked, as I slid open the door to the compartment.

'You want to keep an eye on that one, pal,' said the soldier. 'A regular film star.'

Jeff sniffed as he leant towards me. 'I've been sick,' I said. He put his arms around me. 'I'm not going to jail, Pip,' he whispered. The soldiers pressed past us, down the narrow corridor.

We walked out from under the huge glass canopy of Queen Street station and through George Square to Ingram Street. The Sheriff Court was in a sandstone building with six columns that had flowery tops at the front. It stretched back a long way. I felt I was getting smaller as we walked up to it. A policeman opened the door for us.

The room where the tribunal was held was very bare. A photo of King George hung behind the heads of three men seated at a polished oak table. One stood as we entered and led me to a seat behind the door. His feet squeaked on the lino as he moved back across the room, pointing to another seat for Jeff in the centre of the floor. Jeff walked over to the coat stand in the corner. 'You won't be here long enough for that,' the man said, but Jeff hung up his coat anyway. It seemed to annoy the man who had spoken.

'Dr Jeffrey James McCaffrey of Falkland Terrace, Edinburgh?' he said. 'You know why you are in attendance at the Sheriff Court?'

'I am fully cognisant of my position,' replied Jeff.

'Do you have a valid reason not to sign up?'

'I'd like to know to whom I am addressing my remarks,' Jeff replied.

The man introduced the others at the table. One was in uniform.

'It is really quite simple,' said Jeff, 'I do not wish to fight under the auspices of conscription.'

'On what grounds?'

'On the grounds that Westminster cannot enforce the National Services (Armed Forces) Act of 1939 in Scotland under the Act of Union.'

'You are a member of the SNP?' said the uniformed man.

'Yes.'

'Then you will be aware that we have already been over this ground with your Chairman, Douglas Grant.'

Jeff opened his mouth to speak but the man held up a hand. 'Let me cut to the chase, Dr McCaffrey. All former rulings have been superseded by the Act of 1941, and as long as that remains a statute, it is the law. It doesn't matter if an individual wishes to contest it. It is law until repealed by subsequent legislation, and therefore you are bound by its jurisdiction. Do I make myself clear?'

Jeff shuffled his papers. 'I wish to invoke the League of Nations and its attendant organisations,' he said.

'Let us save ourselves the cost of another High Court appearance, Dr McCaffrey. For international purposes, Scotland and England constitute one state. Perhaps we might be more inclined to listen to your views when the guns fall silent across Europe, and your fellow countrymen return.'

'I am committed to the declared aims of the SNP to establish a self-governing Scotland,' said Jeff.

'Now be a good fellow,' the third man interrupted, 'and sign up. We can offer a man of your evident intelligence a non-combatant role with His Majesty's Government.'

'I will only fight for Scotland,' said Jeff.

The man sighed. 'Perhaps you would agree to tend the soil of your beloved Caledonia until this war is over? There are various nurseries across Scotland. I believe the work there would not be too arduous.'

'I will not surrender my principles,' said Jeff.

'Then we have no option but to recommend you for a jail term of twelve months. Do you wish to contest the ruling?'

'No,' said Jeff. 'I will be a nationalist martyr.'

'Then you are a fool, Dr McCaffrey,' said the man, 'with no thought for your wife.'

Jeff looked round at me and winked.

18

The street looked the same when we came out, but everything had changed for us. Jeff walked off under the sandstone arches opposite the court, muttering something about 'triumphal archways to my own bloody misfortune', when I stopped to look up at them. 'We haven't time for this, Agnes,' he said, and walked quickly up a hilly side street, which looked as if it led straight into the clouds. The name 'St Vincent Street' was carved into one of the tall buildings. Three-storey houses lined the pavements at the top, and on my left I could see out over the Clyde. Somewhere down there, they were building warships among the bombed-out tenements. Jeff stopped at Blythswood Square to let me catch my breath. All the houses looked out onto a beautiful garden, but it was locked behind iron gates. I would have liked to climb over the fence, sit for a while and talk. It was like a Garden of Eden, full of growing things, but he didn't want to stop. 'I don't want to discuss it,' he muttered. 'They are just misguided, self-serving plebeians afraid to shake the status quo. They won't count for anything at the end of the day.'

We walked towards Charing Cross station and I tried to put my arm through his as we reached the Scottish Home Rule Association, but he shrugged me off and took the five steps up to the door in a single bound.

Jeff left me sitting in the kitchen while he went off with a Mr Lamont to discuss whether the SNP petition should demand amnesty for himself as well as Douglas, but in the end they decided it was not a good idea. 'Douglas is a figurehead,' Mr Lamont explained as they came back through. 'Adding other names would only muddy the water. I have to ask you to suffer your jail term quietly. I secretly fear that MacGilvray might be right that conscientious objection in the membership might hinder, rather than help, the cause of nationalism.'

'MacGilvray was a fool to divide the Party,' said Jeff. 'The new Scottish Convention is just a distraction.'

'Still the same cause, Jeff.'

I dried the cup I had used and hung up the dish towel. Someone had embroidered it with thistles. 'Why can't you help my husband, Mr Lamont?' I asked. 'How will I survive in a war without him?'

'Not now, Agnes,' said Jeff. 'I can ask the Edinburgh University branch of the SNP for support. I believe they are going to campaign for Douglas for Rector, so they must be pretty active.'

'Never say never,' laughed Mr Lamont. He helped me into my coat and shook Jeff's hand. He bowed to me. 'Although I am not in complete agreement with your husband's particular stand, you should be proud of him, Mrs McCaffrey. In his way he is fighting a different kind of war on behalf of all Scots. Some wrongs need to be righted, we're just not all able to agree on when or how.'

'But we have had peace with England since 1707, Mr Lamont. My father said they lent us money. Doesn't that count for something?'

Jeff looked over at me as if I was a mental defective short of a bed, but Mr Lamont said, 'An unequal partnership does not make a happy marriage, Mrs McCaffrey.'

'That is enough, Agnes,' said Jeff, opening the front door before I could say anything else. 'We'll be late for our train. Good day to you, Mr Lamont.'

When he turned to me in the street he looked like he hated me. 'Do you think I went through that tribunal for fun? Do you think I have nothing better to do than sit in prison? My work for the Party is important.'

'I didn't mean...'

'You undermined me with your pro-Unionist comment. We were standing in the middle of the Scottish Home Rule Association in case you hadn't noticed.'

'I do support you. I am here, amn't I?' I tried to take his arm. 'But you must admit we haven't been sneaking across the border to steal each other's cows since the Union.'

'That is typical of you – take the simple view. Reduce everything to the farmyard.'

'You have a very low opinion of me.'

'I judge as I find,' said Jeff, and walked off.

'I know enough to know you are trying to plant in the wrong season,' I shouted after him, but he didn't turn round. I watched him go. The rain crept under my collar in thin, cold lines and ran down my back. I followed him as best I could to Queen Street station but I lost my way at the end of Sauchiehall Street. A woman directed me to the side entrance and I found Jeff at the barrier, urging me to hurry up.

'We'll miss the train, Agnes,' he shouted, and I ran across the concourse. He caught my arm as I slipped on the wet surface of the platform, and opened the door of the last carriage just as it began to pull out. The guard blew his whistle and waved his flag to the driver as Jeff levered me on board and jumped in after me, slamming the door. 'Let's not fight, Pip,' he said, as we found an empty compartment and took our seats. 'At the end of the day, you are my wife and it is my duty to guide you.'

He shook out his coat, folded it and put it up on the luggage rack before opening his paper. 'You don't mind, do you?' he asked, and started reading as we pulled into the tunnel out of the city.

19

During the next week, it was more difficult to get food to Hannes with Jeff around. I set another snare and made double quantities of broth and stew, which I slow-cooked in a hay box. Jeff didn't notice or at least didn't comment. When he went out for a round of golf or to the post office, I ran upstairs and left food for Hannes just inside the door.

Every day, Jeff's typewriter thundered in his study. He was also proofreading *The Free Minded Scot*, which he said was the text of Douglas' High Court appeal, as well as a leaflet and statement for the *Scots Independent*. 'This should please Professor Gilbert,' he said. 'He almost stymied the Stirling conference by saying he wanted a statement that we support the war. He never stopped banging on about it when you were blethering in the kitchen, although you'll see Douglas hasn't conceded anything on conscription.'

He made me sit down in the drawing room and read the words as if it was the Creed, but I sat there wondering why he didn't want to spend any of the time he had left with me.

'To the Scottish People
The Scottish National Party says in definite and unmistakable terms:

We stand firm for freedom…

We abhor and oppose Fascism…

In this war we see… our industries closed down, our traders crushed out, our man- and woman-power transported to alien soil and our constitutional rights strangled by the red tape of Westminster… this process can have only one end, the extinction of Scotland. There is only one way to fight it.

The Scottish people must stand as one man behind all who, on any issue, champion the cause of Scotland.

And there is only one party which can consistently and effectively do so – the Scottish Nationalist Party.'

'You see,' said Jeff. 'We don't look both ways. Our purpose is clear. Nationalism in a world without Nazism.'

'And how are you going to do that from behind bars?' I asked.

'Oh, not this again.' He sighed. 'Words can pass through bars, Pip. They won't disarm me by putting me in prison. Anyway, without the distractions of marriage, I can always work on the dictionary. There will be more than a few Scots words from all over the country in that jail. I shall be the honey bee that effortlessly sips the nectar of language.'

I turned away. He certainly hummed the loudest.

'Where are you going, Pip?' he asked.

'To clean the stair,' I said, thinking I might be able to get more food to Hannes in my pail.

'Why are you doing it again?' he asked. 'Mrs MacDougall has the card.'

'She has been a wee bit peely-wally recently,' I said.

'Well, do it later. Come and kiss me. It may be a while before I taste your sweet lips if the rails are as well policed in Saughton as you say they are.'

'Maybe later,' I said.

'No, now, Pip. It has been over a week.'

'I am not in the mood, Jeff.'

'Well, I am. Come here.' He stepped towards me.

'I said no.'

'You are my wife.' He grabbed my arm and pulled me against his chest. 'You may barely feign interest in my politics – don't think I haven't noticed – but you have a duty to your husband. Forget the stair.'

'Let me go. You never even told me you were in the SNP when we married.' I could hardly breathe and he pushed me back onto the table. The cups crashed to the ground. 'Now look what you've done,' he said as I wriggled free. 'Come on, Pip.' He was laughing. 'I have your attention now.'

'Stop it, Jeff. You're scaring me.'

I lifted the blue ironstone jug from his mother's wedding set and made as if to throw it at him.

'Put that down. It is irreplaceable.'

He stepped closer. I threw it at his head, but he ducked and it crashed onto the hearth. 'I told you not to do that,' he said.

I ran into the hall. He picked me up as I unlatched the front door and carried me to the bedroom, throwing me onto my knees on the bed and pulling my skirt up. I screamed as he ran his hand down my legs. 'I like rationing,' he said, 'there is less to take off.' He pushed my head into the quilt. 'Stop making such a fuss. Mrs MacDougall will hear you. Now be a good girl and hold still.'

The satin of the quilt was smooth against my face and the end of a tiny feather poked through it near my eye. The shout at the door startled us both. Hannes was standing there with the broom in his hand.

'*Hören Sie auf,*' he said. '*Sie hat nein gesagt.* She said no.'

Jeff jumped back, pulling at his zip. 'Who the hell are you?' he shouted. He tried to push me behind him but I scrambled over to the other side of the bed. The quilt slipped off and I fell on the floor.

'*Es macht nichts. Hände hoch!*' He gestured to Jeff to put his hands up and swept the broom at his knees, which buckled. Jeff crumpled to the floor and started crying. 'Please don't hurt me,' he said, raising a hand to protect his head.

Hannes took a step forward and put the broom on his neck, pushing his head down onto the rug.

I tried to reach him across the bed but the sheets were all in a fankle, so I shouted, 'Hannes, stop!'

He looked at me. His eyes were hard, like he wanted to kill someone.

'No, stop.' I reached out a hand, and got to the other side.

'Fucking hell. You know him?' croaked Jeff, aiming a kick at his ankles and trying to push the broom away from his neck and get up. Hannes kicked him in the stomach and his knees jerked up to his chest.

'Don't hurt him,' I screamed. Hannes stopped, with his foot pulled back for a second kick, as I fell over Jeff and tried to shield him.

'*Er ist nicht besser als ein Tier,*' Hannes said, and spat. 'He is an animal.'

Jeff was curled into a ball, crying. I knelt and cradled his head. 'Leave him alone,' I said, but Hannes didn't move. 'Leave him alone!' I shouted, and my voice came out as a screech. He backed into the hall.

'What is going on? Who the bloody hell is he?' Jeff asked me. His eyes took in Professor Schramml's clothes and he looked back at me. 'Why is he wearing Schramml's clothes?' He scrambled to his feet.

Hannes eyed him warily.

'It's a long story. I have been looking after him,' I said.

'He is German, Agnes.'

'He is a better friend to me than you.'

My nose was streaming with tears and I wiped them away with the back of my hand. 'Stay there,' I said to Hannes.

Jeff sat back onto the bed, rubbing his stomach. I walked out of the room and into the bathroom. I cried for a long time into the basin, and then I splashed my face. I unpinned my plait to brush it out, but then I picked up my scissors and cut through the rope of my hair. Jeff had wound it round his hand, pulling the hairs at the base of my neck. I put my wedding ring on the shelf. Hannes and Jeff were where I had left them, but Hannes was leaning against the wall, looking wabbit. Jeff saw his attacker weakening and became brave enough to try talking to him in halting German. *'Wer sind Sie?'* he said, but Hannes didn't reply. 'Who are you?' he repeated.

He looked at me for an answer, but I walked into the kitchen. Jeff followed me. 'I am sorry, Agnes. Please talk to me. Oh God, what the hell have you done to your hair?' he said, and he reached out to touch it. I brushed his hand away.

Hannes followed us into the kitchen and sat down at the table. I couldn't look at him. I was afraid of meeting his eyes. 'What are you going to do?' I asked Jeff.

My voice was ragged.

'I'll make it up to you.'

'I mean about him.'

'I don't know. That is an interesting question.'

He looked more focused. Hannes was rubbing his forehead. Jeff pulled his bottle of Talisker from the dresser and poured three large measures. 'To the divine insanity of war,' he said, raising his glass, but it bumped against his teeth as he put it to his lips.

Hannes sipped his whisky and put the glass back on the table. *'Wie geht's Dir?'* he asked me.

'He is asking how you are,' said Jeff, 'after being caught *in flagrante delicto…*'

'Stop using your fancy words,' I shouted. 'You are no better than a beast of the field.'

'That is a nice thing to say in front of our guest.'

Hannes pushed himself to his feet.

'Bitte, setzen Sie sich,' said Jeff, pointing to the chair. 'You still haven't told me who you are. Who is he, Agnes?'

He was feeling braver now.

'Mrs MacDougall found him, why don't you ask her?' And then I regretted letting him know she had been involved.

'Mrs MacDougall and a Nazi, for God's sake. Do you expect me to believe that?'

I stood up. 'Must you talk to me like a bairn?'

'Sit down,' said Jeff.

I could see that Hannes wasn't feeling well now. His cheeks were pale and he rested an arm on the table. Jeff pushed his chair back and looked at him. Hannes stared back. He should never have come downstairs.

'Even if you are here as a guest of my lovely wife, you are still an enemy combatant.' He began to play with a coin from the housekeeping money I kept in a jar on the table. 'But he who pays the piper calls the tune.'

He translated it into German for Hannes, who frowned.

'The question is what should I do.'

I knew he was going to start talking, tying the words together in a long, long line so they would all run together and confuse me.

'How would this cosy scene in the kitchen look to the outside world?' he went on.

'Stop talking,' I shouted. 'Please just stop talking.'

But he ignored me, sucking all the air out of the room. 'A conscientious objector sheltering an enemy soldier – a German, no less. A soon-to-be jailed member of the SNP entertaining a man whose politics the rest of the world finds... distasteful.'

He swirled the whisky round his glass. 'It might raise interesting questions of loyalty.'

'*Ich bin Österreicher*,' said Hannes.

'You might be Austrian but it didn't stop you getting into bed with Germany, did it? Or did Germany get into bed with you?' He laughed. 'I wonder who else you got into bed with.'

He pinched my cheeks together and tilted my face up. '*Meine Frau ist wunderschön, nicht wahr?* A real beauty.'

Hannes pushed himself to his feet. '*Ich bin schon verheiratet*,' he said.

'Well, you may be married, but that hasn't stopped you from taking things that weren't yours – Poland, for example.'

He poured more whisky. 'Let's drink to Poland,' he said. He took a sip. 'And Norway. What about a dram for King

Haakon? What about a dram for Agnes?'

He smashed his fist onto the table. 'A toast to Agnes.'

He raised his glass to me and drank. 'You're not drinking to my wife, Hannes. I take that as a personal insult,' and he laughed, but it ended in a gulp. He wiped his mouth with his hankie.

'Jeff, please stop. You are being ridiculous,' I said.

'Not like Douglas,' he said. 'Not like the bear. You'd like that, wouldn't you, if I were more like him?'

'*Bitte*,' said Hannes. '*Beruhigen Sie sich. Morgen wird alles anders scheinen.*'

'You shut up. I was talking to my wife. Nothing will be better tomorrow,' he shouted at him.

'Please, this isn't helping anyone,' I said. 'Why not let him go for now, Jeff? Take time to calm down.'

'Don't tell me to calm down,' he replied, his voice rising again. He looked at Hannes, ignoring me. 'I will be going away for a lot longer than twelve months if they find you here. On the other hand, I could apprehend an enemy soldier and become a national hero. You'd help me, wouldn't you, Agnes? The loyal, not-so-loyal wife.'

He turned back to Hannes. 'They assumed you died in the fire after the crash, you know. A lone pilot downed in heavy mist over the Pentlands. How clever of you to bail out. How very clever of you to find my lovely wife – a heavenly vision, an angel.'

He filled his glass again. 'To angels,' he said, 'and men who drop from the sky.'

'Das habe ich nicht verstanden,' said Hannes, looking at me. 'Please, I don't understand.'

Jeff picked up the coin and spun it on the table. 'Time to choose,' he said. It clattered as it fell flat, an edge lifting one last time before it ran out of momentum. He slapped his hand over it. 'Heads or tails?' he asked. 'I said heads or tails? *Wappen oder Zahl?* You call it, Agnes. Tails, he dies a nationalist hero. Heads, I do.'

'Stop playing games,' I shouted.

'There is no need to shout, Pip. That's not very ladylike but then I forgot: you are no lady.'

'And you are no gentleman.'

'No, maybe not. Do you think Mother would be disappointed in me? But at least I play by the rules.'

He turned to Hannes, who looked like he was trapped in a nightmare. 'Let's have a gentleman's agreement, my dear man.' He imitated the voice from the wireless. 'Keep it all civilised and above board. Heads, you get to stay. Tails, I call the authorities.'

He flipped the coin in the air. 'Call it, Agnes,' he said. 'Or I will.'

He caught it on the back of his hand. The fingers of his left hand lay across the skin. A tendon twitched. I heard the rattle of a cart's wheels on Canaan Lane.

'Heads,' I said.

He lifted his hand. The king's head stared blindly at the legend on the edge of the coin, the circumference of his world. I remembered his halting voice on the radio, the words of comfort he spoke to the nation; the German name he rubbed out of the history books. Hannes was pushing himself to his feet, but staggered and steadied himself against the table as if he might fall.

'Wouldn't you know it?' Jeff said. 'Fortune favours the brave. It's heads. Janus is alive and well and the whole world looks both ways. Herr... but I forget, we don't know your second name, do we? Herr Rank and File. Anyway, I'm off to prison tomorrow, so you can stay upstairs. *Sie können dort oben bleiben. Ab morgen bin ich weg.* Lucky for you. *Sie sind nicht der einzige Gefangener in dieser Stadt.* Both prisoners: we have that in common. Looks like we are paying the price for our beliefs. Poor saps too stupid to keep our heads down.'

I took Hannes by the arm and pulled him towards the door. 'Yes, take your rat back to his cage, dear. We are all the fools of love and war, but it looks like I am the biggest one of all, thanks to you.'

He gave Hannes a Nazi salute. 'Was it worth it?' he said. 'Do you think perhaps you should just have stayed at home? Not exported Adolf's fucking chaos?'

Hannes stumbled through the door. I listened to his feet echo on the stair as he pulled himself along the banister back to Professor Schramml's flat. I didn't know if he was safe there now, but he had nowhere else to go.

'I hate you,' I said to Jeff. It was the first honest thing I had said to him in a long time. He didn't reply. I locked myself in the bathroom and lay in the bath for hours. My body was distorted under the water and I moved my legs to see the water running over my thighs, like a tide drifting out over rocks. Some sloshed onto the floor. I turned the tap on with my toes for the third time, but there was no hot water left. I towelled myself dry, put my dressing gown over my nightdress and went into the bedroom. I didn't speak to Jeff. After folding a few clothes into a small suitcase, and picking up his book from the bedside table, he left the room without a word and slept in his study. In the morning, I heard him clean his teeth and walk towards the front door. I didn't get up. He closed the door with his key so as not to wake me, but I hadn't slept. I lay on in bed looking out the window. It was ten o'clock before I wandered through to the kitchen and found his note on top of his proof of Douglas' articles. It was weighted down with my wedding ring, which I had left in the bathroom. It was the first time I had ever taken it off.

'I apologise, my darling,' the note read, *'if I was somewhat more forceful towards you than I intended last night. Can you forgive me? Please remember I remain your loving husband and need you more than ever in my forthcoming ordeal. Thinking of you will lighten the dark days ahead.*

If you would accept some advice, I would pass your guest on to the authorities, but only telephone them if you can get him to leave the flat. He might be dangerous if cornered, although he obviously feels some loyalty to you. I am sure you can think of some pretext. It

would be safer for us all that way. Please don't take any risks.
    Yours aye for Scotland.
    Jeff/Og.

PS. Could you please post these proofs to the Editor of the Scots Independent?'

I sat staring out the window until I grew stiff. I didn't put the ring back on, but left it on the note, staring at the random letters of his empty apology trapped in its circle. The part of me that had already grown cold towards him had shattered under his assault last night, and my chest felt hollow. I used to worry about keeping everything nice. Now I wanted to destroy the cage around me. The broken jug still lay on the hearth, but instead of sweeping it up, I walked into the bedroom. I didn't recognise the girl in the mirror of the wardrobe door as it swung open. I lifted up armfuls of Jeff's mother's clothes and threw them out of the window. A coat hanger snagged on the washing line below and the dress twisted in the breeze until it broke free and fluttered into the next garden. The bonfire I made sang and crackled as I fed it, until the smell of mothballs from the clothes was replaced by the scent of the buddleia. I burnt the fox stole last. His eyes melted as fire crept over his white coat and the black hole of his nose was the last to go. Perhaps Hannes watched from the window? I didn't turn round until there was only ash and glowing embers, and I warmed myself there until it grew dark.

20

Hannes tapped softly on the door that night and, without a word, made soup in my kitchen. He watched me take the first mouthful and then left looking satisfied, but I poured the bowl back in the pan after he had gone. I found it strange to see him chopping the onion and potatoes, boiling water and lifting the kettle with a cloth, just as I did. His sleeves were rolled up and he had tied a pinny over his clothes. He seemed less like an enemy soldier and more like a parent to me. I could imagine his own mother in her kitchen, smiling at him, preparing food. It was so ordinary, so everyday. I wondered where the politics came from that swept everyone up and away from everything they knew, what it was that made them into people they had never dreamt of becoming. I thought of Jeff alone in his cell and wondered if he was sorry for what he had done to me. We had never really been able to talk. We had only played at marriage. I expected he was looking forward to being with Douglas again. Politics was his first love, I knew that now. I tried not to think of Millie.

In the morning, I tied the polka-dot bandana from my best dress round my hair to hide the rough ends, and took Jeff's letter to the post office. The woman behind the counter raised an eyebrow at the address on the envelope. 'You're Jeff McCaffrey's wife, aren't you? He was in here a lot.'

I nodded.

'I am sorry he has been sentenced,' she said. 'It was in the paper the other day. A line at the bottom of page six.'

Her sympathy made me want to cry. I didn't understand how I could have lost everything I thought was good. The only person I wanted to speak to was Douglas, but his visits were booked for weeks ahead. The people who might have campaigned for his release were getting fewer and it looked as if he would be locked up for the whole twelve months. He might even have to go back in again as I couldn't see him changing his mind any time soon. I laid the coins for the stamp on the counter and tried to smile at her. I felt like the women behind me in the queue might be staring at my shorn hair, thinking I had lost my marbles, gone mad with grief. The assistant pushed a coin back across to me. 'You've given me too much,' she said. 'Keep calm and carry on, as they say.'

I stopped outside the post office and looked up Morningside Road. I was meant to take my new ration book to the shops to re-register for groceries and give the shopkeepers the counterfoils, but I was afraid Mrs Black might have turned them against me and then I would have to walk as far as Tollcross to get food. I held the three old books in my hand in my pocket and decided it could wait. I wasn't hungry anyway.

Turning left, I walked back down Nile Grove past the terraced houses in their bonny gardens, now planted with vegetables, and tried to hold in my tears in case I met anyone I knew. Part of me almost hoped I might, so I could tell someone what had happened and ask their advice, but the street was deserted and I turned into Falkland Terrace without meeting a soul.

That afternoon, there was a knock at the door. I opened it, thinking it might be Hannes, but a policeman stood there. I heard a bolt slide shut on Mrs MacDougall's door and knew she would be standing with her ear pressed against it, listening. She must have seen the officer from her window as he approached. He was over forty, with tired, grey eyes.

'Mrs McCaffrey?' he asked, tipping his helmet.

I held on to the edge of the door.

'Yes, but I wish to be known as Agnes Thorne.'

'You are Jeff McCaffrey's wife?'

'Yes.' I straightened my back.

'Mrs McCaffrey, I wonder if you could accompany me to my motorcar?'

I looked round the hall but there was no way out. 'Do I need to bring anything?' I asked, not sure where I had put my bag. I wondered if I could leave Professor Schramml's key with Mrs MacDougall, if the officer would let me. Perhaps she would take pity on Hannes and feed him.

'No, you're alright. I have a number of your husband's papers to return for your safe keeping. Perhaps you could give me a hand?'

My heart slowed down. He hadn't noticed I was finding it difficult to breathe. I hoped Hannes wouldn't look out of the window as I went out. He might misunderstand what was happening and try to run. I could imagine the officer blowing his whistle, shouting at him to stop.

I stood beside the car in my slippers waiting for the officer to tell me to get in. I was sure that the letters were just a trick to get me out of the flat without a stramash, but he put a box in my arms.

'Too heavy for you?' he asked.

'No,' I said.

'One more? You look like a strong lassie.'

I shook my head. 'I am an Edinburgh lady, officer, not a beast of burden.'

He looked at my short hair with its uneven edges escaping from my bandana.

'I am sorry I haven't had time to set my hair,' I said.

'Well, perhaps you have had other things on your mind.' He laughed.

'What do you mean?' It sounded sharper than I intended, like a real nippy sweetie.

'With your man in Saughton.'

I blushed.

'Better out of harm's way. What would a university type do on a battlefield? Although I dare say he might have enough of a fight on in there with Jack Frost this winter. It is not the warmest place.'

I hadn't thought of the cold months stretching ahead for Jeff or me; months alone without heat or vegetables or rabbits. I wasn't sure what I would do. He saw my face fall. 'Just leave that box at the foot of the stair,' he said. 'The station can do without me for five minutes while I help a damsel in distress. Anyway, the sky isn't exactly filled with planes.' And he looked up at the blue expanse above us. 'Let's hope it is all over by Christmas.'

He stacked the boxes in the hall and came through to the kitchen for a glass of water, leaning against the sink. 'Nice place you have here,' he said, looking round. 'Plenty of room to start a family. My youngest laddie signed up last week, but they made him a munitions worker in case anything happened to his brothers at the Front and his mother was left with no sons. Must be thankful for small mercies. He's based at the old Singer factory in Clydebank. Plenty of banter to take his mind off his wounded pride.'

He looked up at the ceiling. I followed his eyes. 'Looks like you have a bit of damp starting there. You want to watch that.'

I nodded, afraid the floorboards might creak and he might ask who lived upstairs, but there wasn't a sound. He looked at his watch. 'I'll leave you to it, then,' he said, putting the glass in the washing up bowl. 'Good day to you.'

When I had closed the door, I carried the boxes into Jeff's study and sat down at his desk. The chair was upholstered in brown leather and swivelled. I span round. The three pigeon-holes on the left were empty, like three dark doorways to an empty church, but the crinkled edge of a photograph stuck out from the fourth. I pulled it out. It was a picture of Jeff and Millie raising their glasses to the camera. He had his arm round her waist and she was laughing. I wondered when it had been taken and turned it over, but there was nothing written on the back. I thought of his jealous rage, the way he had gone on at me about Douglas after just one visit – and that to a prison – and I tore it up. It lay as a jigsaw on the desk, fragments of teeth and hands, busy saying and doing things I never knew anything about. I swept the pieces into the wastepaper basket and closed the door. I walked through the empty rooms, trailing my fingers over the surfaces of the heavy mahogany furniture from Jeff's mother, and then I sat in her old wing-back chair in the sunny corner of the bay window. The room looked empty and dead, like a stage set after the play had finished. I tried to sew for a while but the picture of Jeff and Millie kept flashing over my work. I remembered the WAAF's march past Lord Provost Darling on Princes Street and I wondered if she had been there; smiling, neat and smart, at the heart of things, looking for Jeff in the crowd, and for some reason the advert for Weston biscuits popped into my mind and I began to sing, 'She really takes the biscuit. Although WAAFs may not be pilots, they fairly fly to the canteen when they hear that Weston biscuits have arrived.' I sang it in different voices, high and low, sombre like a hymn and quick like folk music. 'She really takes the biscuit.' I imagined crumbs of her caught in Jeff's teeth, and I laughed until I cried, and then I lay my head on a cushion on my lap and howled like a dog.

When my tears stopped, I didn't want to be alone so I splashed my face with cold water and took Hannes some bread and cheese. He felt like the only person I knew. He smiled at me as I went into the kitchen. He had found a wireless and was sitting with the dictionary at the table writing down words. I turned it off. 'This is not for you,' I said, feeling uneasy.

It was silent without the broadcaster's voice. He shrugged and closed the book. I put down the food, but he didn't pull the plate towards him. He stood up and moved closer to me, reaching out a hand. I flinched, turning my face away. He smoothed out the frown on my brow with his thumb and asked, '*Wie geht's?*' Then he said, 'How are you?'

He turned down the corners of his mouth and raised his eyebrows. It made me laugh. It was hard to remember he was the enemy. He gazed at me as if he was seeing me for the first time. There was a dimple in his left cheek and his neck was still brown where it disappeared into his collar. He must have seen the sun in his other life. His lips were soft as he kissed my hand, and then he turned back to the table. He pulled out a chair for me and brought me a glass of water. I took a sip but I couldn't think of a thing to say, so I took my sewing out of my apron pocket and we sat there together in the sun. After a while he brought through some cards and we played racing patience. We didn't speak. The cards piled up in number order: jack, queen, king, ace, two, three. His hands were quick and once brushed against mine. He paused, but I didn't look up and put another card on the pile. I think he let me win that time. Then I said I had to go and pointed to the clock, but time was meaningless as I had nothing to do. I don't think he was pleased when I took the wireless and carried it downstairs to be sure he wouldn't listen to it again, but he didn't try to stop me.

There were two phone calls that afternoon as I lay on my bed listening to Hannes moving about in the room upstairs. He trod more heavily now that Jeff was away. The jangling of the bell in the quiet of the flat made me jump. The first was Mr Lamont, asking if the SHRA might have the use of Jeff's typewriter until his release as theirs was broken and it was proving difficult and expensive to get spare parts sent from England. The other was from the prison, saying Jeff had forgotten his ID card and that I should bring it in on a visitor's pass next Tuesday. I could have fifteen minutes with my husband as I was a spouse, but after that, I would have to apply to see him.

'I can understand it is all very upsetting, Mrs McCaffrey,' the voice on the end of the line said, misinterpreting my silence, 'but I can assure you he is being well treated. Not quite home comforts, I am sure, but as well as can be expected.'

I was pulling a small piece of wallpaper off in a thin strip, watching as it peeled away from the plaster, leaving a trail of brown paper underneath. It tore and I scratched at the paper to start a new piece.

'Thank you for your call,' I said, the way Jeff had taught me. I hated hearing a voice and not seeing the speaker. 'I will be there next week. Yes, I will report to the main gate.'

I walked through the hall and sat for a long time at the window in the drawing room watching the neighbours come and go. The clock had just struck eight when I realised that there hadn't been any sound of movement from Hannes. The silence was unbroken. His routines had become familiar to me but although he seemed freer, I was afraid Jeff might tell someone about him. What would Douglas say if he told the bear my secret? Perhaps he could use the information to get out of jail early? I just hoped Jeff still loved me enough to keep quiet and protect me. I put on my shoes and tiptoed upstairs. The flat was gloomy and quiet. I called for Hannes in a whisper but there was no reply. He wasn't sleeping on any of the beds and I lit the paraffin lamp in the kitchen. The words '*Kino – komme gleich wieder*' were neatly written on a scrap of paper. I ran to fetch the German dictionary and flicked through the letters to 'K'. I moved my finger down the unfamiliar lines to read, 'cinema', and then, 'back soon'. A picture of Professor Schramml's jam jar of lucky sixpences in the kitchen flashed into my mind. I should have hidden it, but I never thought there was enough money there to be a danger and, to cap it all, just last week, I had told Hannes I was going to see a movie. I could have cursed myself for letting him know the cinema was so close, pressing my fingers together to show it was a short distance away and pointing round the corner. I had wanted to reassure him that I wouldn't be long, since he relied on me so much. I didn't doubt he would have found it. Taking away the radio had made him even more curious about the world outside the flat. He was looking for information. He needed to know about the war. How could I have expected to keep him caged in a drawing room for weeks – a grown man, a flyer, a fighter? Perhaps, just seeing him for a short time at a stretch, I had missed how bored he was. There was nothing for him here. It was foreign in every way.

I tied a scarf round my neck, pulled on my hat and coat and then walked as quickly as I could, without running, up to Newbattle Terrace. I bought a ticket at the kiosk, went through the turnstile and found a seat at the back. I couldn't spot him at first. All the figures were dark shapes. A soldier was kissing his sweetheart near me, so I moved forward a row and then I saw him. He was smoking. Someone must have offered him a cigarette and he was slumped down inside a coat he probably found in Professor Schramml's cupboard. The programme started with the Pathé news; pictures of German tanks crossing the North African desert came into view, throwing up the sand in clouds. Rommel was standing on a car addressing his troops, but the German was turned down and a crisp voice said the Field Marshal's assault on Egypt would founder in the desert thanks to the unstinting efforts of our brave boys. Hannes was leaning forward. And then they showed bombs falling on a German city. He turned his head to the side and wiped at his eyes with his sleeve. His shoulders heaved and he stood up to leave, with his hand held over his mouth as if he was going to be sick. I followed him out. He was standing at the door, trying to push it open. There was a sign on it saying to contact the desk to exit once the programme had started as the wind kept blowing it open. A woman was making her way over to him in a starched, blue dress with the cinema's logo as a pattern on the cloth. 'Excuse me, Sir,' she was saying, 'excuse me, Sir. Please don't force the door.'

She touched his arm and asked him to step back so that she could put the key in the lock. He stared at her.

'Are you all right?' she asked.

He didn't reply and she repeated her question. I walked up to him and said, 'There you are.'

I turned to the woman. 'He is one of my neighbour's nephews. He's a bit shell-shocked. They're hoping one of the doctors at the infirmary might be able to help.'

'Let's hope so,' she said. 'Life's hard enough without forgetting how to open a door.'

I smiled. 'Thank you,' I said. 'I hope he hasn't been a bother.'

'You're down on Falkland Terrace, aren't you?' she said. 'I see you sometimes when I'm visiting my Grannie. She's at number twenty-three.'

'I'll wave next time I pass you,' I said. 'I'd better get this one home.'

'Do you want a refund?' she asked, turning towards the box office. 'You've hardly seen anything of the programme, although the news is always good for morale.'

Hannes pushed against the door, although it said 'Pull' in large letters on a brass plate.

'Someone's keen to get home,' she said, as if he was a dog.

I nodded and took his arm. 'Don't worry about the money,' I said.

'It's nae bother,' she replied, looking through the bunch of keys in her hand, so I said I thought he might be feeling sick, and she whipped the door open after that.

I held his arm; afraid he might run or do something daft. I was so angry with him I could hardly speak and I was afraid someone might hear us, or recognise me, if I bent his ear about how stupid he had been. It was still light but we only passed one woman and she was leaning over her bairn in a pram, shaking a little knitted teddy at its tear-stained face.

In the park, I turned to him. 'Edinburgh is a village. Do you understand? Everyone knows everyone. Don't ever do that again.'

He was looking at me, more upset than I had ever seen him. I wondered if he knew people in the bombed town. A tear was running down his cheek. Somewhere a craw called and flapped in the branches above my head.

'Please come home,' I said.

He walked beside me, followed me up the stairs and I let him into Professor Schramml's flat. He never said a word and I left him there with whatever was going round in his head, unable to help him. My mother would have said he had brought it on himself, but I wasn't sure it was that simple.

21

I couldn't sleep all night, worrying that Hannes might try to escape, and I jumped at every little sound in the street. After a bath, I lay on the divan in Jeff's study at the front so I could hear if the door opened downstairs, although I didn't know what I would do if he did slip out. I would have had to let him go, but I was worried he might hurt someone if he was cornered, or they might hurt him. Then I remembered Jeff's identity card was still in the flat. I eventually found it in the drawer of the hall table. It was only six o'clock, but I ran upstairs, afraid I might lose courage before I could tell Hannes my idea. He was sitting in a chair near the back window, an empty glass beside him. He was surprised to see me so early. Using Professor Schramml's dictionary, I told him I was taking him to my family's farm near Ayr and then across to my Aunt Ina's in Ireland. I drew him a rough map on the back of an old envelope. He looked dubious, pacing up and down the kitchen, until I showed him Jeff's card and his raincoat.

'You can pretend to be my husband.' I pointed to my ring finger and then to him, and held up the coat. It looked like it would fit quite well. Jeff had always worn things a size up to make him look bigger.

He shook his head, lifting a handful of his dark blond hair, which was so different from Jeff's curls. I got the last bandages from the kitchen drawer and held them out to him. They would hide his hair, but he put two fingers to his head as if it was a gun and looked at me questioningly.

'They won't shoot you unless you try to run,' I said, but I wondered if that was true. People did strange things when they were afraid. I tried not to imagine him falling dead on the concourse at Waverley with people running about screaming. It wasn't possible, was it? 'Just surrender,' I said, putting my hands up. 'Like this. Dinnae be feart.'

He stood at the window in the half-light, looking out at the trees. He was clean-shaven and thin. There were still dark hollows under his cheekbones. He was trapped here. '*Es ist auch für Dich gefährlich wenn ich länger bleibe. Ich soll doch weggehen, abfliegen.*' He interlaced his fingers and cracked his knuckles. 'Okay, I go. Me here – is dangerous for you,' he said, and rolled his shoulders like a swimmer preparing to dive.

'Are you okay?' I asked, remembering his tears after the cinema.

He nodded and opened his mouth to speak and then closed it. He didn't have the words to express what he wanted to say, or perhaps the pain of his emotion had crawled into his throat and gagged him. I took his hand. I was standing so close that I could feel his breath on my face as he sighed. He drew his gaze away from the window. Out there far from this island someone close to him was suffering, had suffered. Perhaps it was too late for them, he had no way of knowing. His eyes were naked when they met mine and I saw the man without his bravado, his deference to me, his social grace. He looked at me and I looked back. We were both wounded and saw the other's pain, and then stepping forward he pulled me close. I leant against him, and it felt like a home-coming. His heart beat under my ear, fast at first and then slower, a steady beat, the pulse of his life.

He let me go as soon as I loosened my grip on his waist, lifting my hands from his back. They felt light and empty as if it had been right to hold him, as if I should go on holding him.

'I will miss you,' he said.

I nodded, distracted by the bow shape of his lips, which closed now waiting for me to reply. I looked down and my eye fell on his picture of Liesl tucked into the book he had been reading. He followed my gaze. 'Goethe,' he said. *'Auf dem See. "Hier auch Lieb und Leben ist."* There is… life here too.'

I stepped back and shook my head. 'There is no life here for you in this war. You need to get away.' A door banged on the stair and footsteps tapped on the steps, winding closer. There was a rattle of keys and the sound of Mrs MacDougall muttering 'Hell's teeth!' as she dropped them with a clatter. A door banged shut and then, silence.

I wasn't sure if he had understood what I'd said, then he sat down and nodded, putting his elbow on the table and tugging at his lower lip. I had his agreement, but I came down with something, and it was to be three weeks before I found the strength or courage to take him. I took to my bed, perhaps it was flu.

Fortunately, Mrs MacDougall, true to form, had knocked on the door to ask why I hadn't cleaned the stair, and when she saw my peely-wally face, she took a spare key and agreed to fetch my rations. She gathered up the main book, yellow supplement book and points book, and went to sort out the new single book. I didn't ask where she had registered me. 'Don't let a bad conscience affect your life, Agnes,' she said as she brought through some porridge. 'You are young, yet. There is a long way to go and you have a duty to our Lord to live the best life you can. "What profit is there in my blood, when I go down to the pit? Shall the dust praise thee? Shall it declare thy truth?" Psalms 30:9. You should pay more attention to them, Agnes. They might benefit you. Keep you sound of body and mind.'

I grew stronger as best I could. I wasn't sure I could take many more of Mrs MacDougall's homilies. She telephoned the prison for me to say I was poorly. They were sympathetic and said to bring in the ID card as soon as I was well.

The night before I began to get better, I was woken by a great wailing, as if the city was screaming, and the sound rose and fell across the hills, echoing on the cold water of the Forth. It forced its way inside my head, but before I could try to get up, Mrs MacDougall had rushed through and pulled me from my new bed in the spare room. My legs buckled under me, and she couldn't lift me, so she pushed me under the bed and crawled in after me. 'What about Hannes?' I said.

'He'll have to take care of himself as best he can. They are his bloody friends, after all.'

It was only the second time I had ever heard Mrs MacDougall swear. We lay there side by side, shivering until she pulled the quilt from the bed and we lay under it. There was no sound of planes passing over head, although I held my breath to listen. 'Don't worry about general engine noise,' she said, 'if it comes. You only need to worry if you hear a high-pitched, whining sound right over head. Let's hope the guns on the Forth shoot them down, although I can tell you for a fact that more than one of the laddies down there has lied about his age.'

I could see the mattress bulging through the criss-crossed wire of the bed base. I tried not to think of the people who had been crushed falling on the stairs in the Tube in London, all the bodies piled up to make a wall of dead and not a single bomb dropped. There were so many ways to die. After an hour, the all-clear sounded and Mrs MacDougall helped me crawl back into bed, and then felt her way through the hall in the darkness. She returned with my taped-up torch and two hot toddies. 'I was sorry to have to put Jeff's good single malt in them, but I couldn't find a blend,' she said, as she passed me a cup. 'Needs must, eh? Look on the bright side. At least if we drink it, it can't fuel the flames if we're hit. Not like those poor sods sitting on piles of the stuff in the distillery towns. They could go up in a fireball any day if the Jerries bomb them.'

The next morning, I huddled down in the bed, pulling the quilt and sheet up round the back of my neck. My feet were cold even in bed socks and although I was wrapped in

Mrs MacDougall's old crocheted bed jacket, the draft from the chimney crept in around me. I pressed my chin onto my chest, but had to sit up as another coughing fit took me and all the heat flew out from under the covers. As I lay back down, I heard the key turn in the lock, then footsteps and a knock at the door.

'Come in, Mrs MacDougall,' I croaked. Hannes stepped into the room. He was balancing a tray on his hip and smiled before coming in, as if asking permission. 'Sorry,' he said, waving a hand at the walls of the bedroom as if it were somehow sacred space.

I pulled the sheet up over my chest.

'Mrs MacDougall...' He lifted up the tray before laying it across my lap. '...Away.'

'Where?' I asked, wondering if she knew someone affected by the raid.

He shrugged. 'She say back tomorrow.' A frown crossed his brow. I suppose he wondered if she might return with the police, although I knew she was more afraid of them than he was. We had hidden him for so long that she must have believed she would join Jeff in prison, if Hannes was discovered. A good name was not the currency it used to be, as she was so fond of saying. I was sure Hannes would never let on when we had taken him in, but the authorities knew the day the plane had come down, and that would count against us. I imagined them picking over the wreckage on the hill, and wondering why there was no body; looking over to the city just thirty minutes' walk away, as if they might see him like an ant creeping past the flats. Perhaps they were still searching.

I looked up from the pale, yellow loops of the bed jacket, a soft chain mail of fan shapes. Hannes was watching my face. '*Noch etwas?*' he said. 'Something else?' It sounded like 'zomz-ing' and I wanted to laugh.

'Votter?' he added, and I watched the language come apart on his lips in this house of words, where every syllable had been guarded, and it wasn't funny any more.

I nodded, blowing my nose to hide my tears, and he took the empty jug from the bedside table and filled it in the kitchen. I saw him glance at the bread on my tray as he set the jug back down on its doily. He looked hungry. I held the bread out to him, but he shook his head. 'Please,' I said, worried that Mrs MacDougall hadn't been feeding him while I was laid up.

He broke half of it off and put the rest back on the plate. 'Take vegetables from the garden at night,' I said. 'No one will see you.'

He chewed without speaking, not understanding. I pointed at him and then towards the back wall with the garden beyond, mimed pulling up a carrot and nibbling on it.

He laughed and nodded. 'Okay,' he said, and rubbed the crumbs from his hands on his thighs.

'*Also...*' he said, and paused. It was very quiet. 'Goodbye.' He glanced round the room, both of us aware that it was the empty guest room and not my own. His eyes met mine. There was something more than pity in them; concern, or a last flicker of anger against Jeff, or the war, or Mrs MacDougall, who kept him hungry. But above all, there was a kind of understanding that didn't need words, a glimpse of the warmth I had seen upstairs. He took a step towards me and then stopped, looking at the bed as if he might sit on the edge. I pointed to the chair in the corner which he pulled over. It creaked as he sat down.

'This room is cold,' he said, looking round.

'Yes,' I agreed, but this time the tears came too fast to stop, and spilled down my cheeks. He passed me the napkin he had folded on the tray, and I blew my nose, then tried to smile. It was Jeff's mother's best linen. I laughed, but it came out as a burp.

'Just cry,' he said, and held my hand. The tears flowed faster and we sat in silence. The warmth of his grasp comforted me and I lay back against the pillows. He took the tray from my lap, and put it on the floor.

'Sleep now,' he said and leant forward. I flinched, I couldn't help it. The light breaking in between the curtains and shining on the quilt had brought back memories of Jeff. I pushed it off the bed, and it slithered onto the floor, a green snake-skin. Hannes picked it up and put it over the back of the chair. The room smelt of mothballs and beeswax. It seemed to stick inside my nose. I held my breath.

'Agnes,' he said. I looked at him, and he smiled, holding his arms out as he might have done to calm a frightened animal on his farm. He reached forward slowly and moved one of the pillows from behind me, tucking me up like a child as I slid down between the sheets. He lifted my head and held a glass of water to my lips.

'*Schlaf gut,*' he said, putting the glass down. 'Sleep well,' and he turned away, closing my door without a sound. I heard him pause at the front door to listen, and a minute later the pad of his feet passing down the hall upstairs. He whistled a few bars of a tune I didn't recognise and then stopped mid-phrase, as if remembering that the price of his safety was silence; that everything inside him must be silent, too, without voice. He had become his own jailer, imprisoning the man he had been, locking away his identity to preserve his future, a day that might never come.

It was on the first of the bright September mornings, after walking out early to send my mother a telegram, that I shaved and bandaged Hannes' head as if he was still injured. I whitened his face with the last of my talcum powder. His hair lay on the kitchen lino like the fur of a moulting animal. For some reason I couldn't sweep it up. He took the dustpan and brush from my hand, and knelt down. I put the last of the bread and the dictionary in a small hold-all containing my clothes. I thought it would be best to travel in the early afternoon and catch the train to Ayr from Glasgow, so that when we arrived at the farm it would be later, and fewer people would be about. My pin money and the housekeeping would be just enough to get us there if we didn't buy anything on the way. Mrs MacDougall watched from the window as we left. I waved, but she gave no sign that she knew us.

We walked down the back streets to Haymarket. Hannes walked slowly and stopped at the top of Viewforth to look at the estuary. I was afraid he was memorising the scene. It was hazy. I knew Rosyth dockyard was tucked away in the distance and tried to pull him on. He looked down at me, and his eyes held no sign of anything but warmth as he turned towards me. '*Schön*,' he said. 'Beautiful.'

I looked over my shoulder when he said the German word, but there was no one nearby, just a woman pulling her dog, which was sniffing at a wall. Large, white clouds scudded over the Forth, and we walked on down the hill past the tenements, the gates to the brewery and the canal. The swans were sailing on the water with their cygnets, nesting under the bridge as they did every year, but no one brought them bread any more.

The traffic increased as we neared the station; carts and trams rumbling across Haymarket junction. I took Hannes' arm and he leant on me, playing along and keeping his eyes lowered. There were so many men here in suits and uniforms that I was worried in case someone Jeff knew might recognise me before I spotted them, but no one did. There were four platforms, and the ticket inspector pointed to the most distant one over the bridge. 'Safe journey, folks,' he said. 'Plenty of time before the train, so don't rush.'

We stood at the far end of the platform and Hannes kept his head down, staring at the tracks. If anyone guessed his true identity, there was no escape from this station for him. We were below the level of the street and he would never be able to climb the high walls on either side, or escape into the yards, which were bustling with railway men. After ten minutes, the train roared out of the tunnel from Waverley in a cloud of black smoke, and pulled up at the platform. We sat in an empty compartment, but were joined by a real old windbag who seemed determined to have our story even if it meant she had to stop knitting. 'Going far?' she asked, as she swapped needles. Her tweed coat was folded on the seat beside her. She had eyes like river-wet pebbles. One was cloudy.

'Ayr,' I said, and then realised I should just have said Glasgow. It was more anonymous. She might have kennt people in Ayr.

'Don't know it at all,' she said. 'I'm a Balloch woman, myself. It is better up the coast and away from all this trouble. Of course, it is not the same with all the men away. Difficult to keep things on track. What happened to you, dear?' She leant forward to speak to Hannes as if he were a child. He rolled his eyes towards me.

'He can't speak,' I said.

'Bless him, the poor soul,' she replied, leaning back. 'His sacrifice won't have been in vain. We'll beat those Jerries. I said, we'll beat the Boche, dear,' she shouted at Hannes. He closed his eyes.

'Tired?' she asked me, nodding at him.

'He's only just getting better now.'

'The sea air will do him good. It's a great tonic. I swear by it.'

'I know what you mean,' I said.

'My arthritis is always worse in the city. Damp, you see. I don't like to complain now there are so many people worse off than myself.'

But she spoke about her aches and pains all the way to Linlithgow without dropping a stitch. 'Excuse me while I turn this heel,' she said, unravelling more wool from her ball.

I looked out at the ruined palace as we pulled into the station. The four towers crumbled behind the gate. Jeff had taken me there, once. High above us, traces of fireplaces hung on the wall like picture frames, with no floor beneath them. We had walked up and down the towers, edging along what was left of the corridors, while Jeff sang bright airs he claimed were from Queen Mary's court. They had echoed down into the dark hall beneath, which had grass for a carpet.

Hannes touched my sleeve and nodded towards the corridor. 'I expect he needs to stretch his legs, dear,' said the woman. 'Far too long in a hospital bed, no doubt. My mother had a sore so septic it had to be packed every day by the district nurse. You know what suffering is when you have seen that.'

I nodded and followed Hannes out. We opened the window to feel the air rushing past. The conductor came along the corridor, moving in and out of the compartments, having a bit of banter with the people inside, and getting closer and closer to us. I got the tickets out of my bag, and passed them to him before he could speak to Hannes. His hands were balled into fists in his pockets and pressed against his thighs to stop them trembling. The inspector glanced at our identity cards without opening them, clipped the tickets and said, 'Thanks, hen. Thirty minutes to Glasgow. Your connection will leave at quarter past the hour from Central.'

'Thank you, Sir,' I said, as he squeezed past. Inside, I felt I was betraying the trust of my countrymen. I tried to imagine Hannes in uniform, like the men on the news in the cinema, but I couldn't. I wondered where his uniform was. Perhaps it was hidden out on the Pentlands, pushed into a rabbit hole. He looked ordinary. Strained. I had never deceived anyone in my life and the burden of it slowed me down. I became conscious of every movement of my face as if I was acting in a movie, but I had forgotten the next line, and was making it up. Everything I said sounded false. I was playing a role and I had a sudden memory of Jeff pulling clothes from his mother's wardrobe for me to wear, as if all I had been doing all those days was pretending. Hannes noticed the sadness in my face, and touched my cheek. '*Es tut mir leid, Agnes,*' he whispered. 'I'm sorry.'

I pushed his hand away, and looked out the other window. In my mind's eye, Jeff was sniffing under the arms of his mother's white ball gown after the university reception and complaining that he wouldn't be able to get it dry-cleaned because of the war. He said he should never have let me wear it, as if it had been a crime to sweat, as if his mother had never been damp like a real woman, but a saint carried in the parade of his memory for everyone to worship. I stopped feeling the swaying of the train carrying me along the tracks to Glasgow. I was sliding on a moving platform into a strange world, indebted to a man who might already have killed my countrymen. I leant my head on the cool glass, and then went back into the compartment without him. The old dear was asleep, the needles still clamped under her arms, and I shut my eyes.

There were no lights on at Queen Street Station when we got off. The glass ceiling soared above us, and people with suitcases and gas masks slung over their shoulders moved around us without speaking. They seemed anxious. An ARP warden stood by a bucket of sand, as if he could extinguish the fire of an incendiary bomb on his own, while the crowds fled. We walked without speaking down Buchanan Street to Central Station, under the bridge they called the Hielanman's Umbrella, and caught the train, which rolled out over the Clyde into the light. The sleepers on the bridge rattled. Some of the buildings I remembered had gone. Hannes was staring at the empty spaces. It was another hour to go.

I had forgotten how big the sky was over Ayr, how salty the breeze. The green fields rolled inland from the sea in soft peaks and troughs, crowned with our neighbours' farms, each white house standing at right angles to its byres. The verges of the road were full of brambles and wild flowers, and small birds darted over the hedges between the fields. The black and white cows smelt sweet as we passed, blowing through their noses and watching us as they chewed, grinding the grass, moving their jaws from side to side. Their calves were big now, grazing near their mothers. The bull lay dozing in the last sunny corner of the field, a favourite cow at his side. I breathed in deeply and relaxed. I could see it was the same for Hannes. He walked more lightly here, held his head up higher. *'Unsere Kühe sind braun,'* he said, pointing at them, and I understood. His language didn't seem so foreign, seemed closer to the Scots. We turned onto the farm track at the burn to see my brother Duncan running down the hill towards us, his dogs at his heels. He was tall, deep-chested, with rosy cheeks, and shouting, 'Aggie, Aggie', making the dogs dance and bark with excitement. He birled me round

117

when he reached me. As he put me back on my feet to shake what he thought was Jeff's hand, he stopped smiling. 'Who's this?' he asked.

'A friend of Jeff's,' I said. 'He wants to go back to his family in Ireland.'

It was the first lie I had ever told my brother. 'He can't speak. A bump on the head. He wants to go home to Cork.' A second lie.

I thought Cork might be far enough from Auntie Ina's to stop any questions about shared family and acquaintances. The dogs sniffed round Hannes' feet. He reached down to pat them.

'Well, it's lucky you're such a chatterbox,' said Duncan. 'You can speak for two and no mistake. Come up to the house...' he paused, and looked at me for an introduction, tucking in his chin and raising his eyebrows.

'Hamish,' I said. 'Hamish, this is my brother, Duncan.'

The two men shook hands. Hannes bowed from his shoulders, but Duncan had already turned away, calling the dogs, and didn't notice.

Everyone at dinner was sorry to hear about Jeff, but didn't ask for details, so I knew they thought he had what he deserved for being too feart to fight. Mother had decided puir Hamish should take his dinner in bed and set a fire in the back bedroom for him. 'Well, it may be September,' she said, 'but it can be gey chilly if you are feeling poorly. Why is he wearing Jeff's coat?' she asked when she came back downstairs to hang it up.

'Jeff said he could borrow it,' I replied, as it hung with empty sleeves on the coat stand. It was the third lie I had told my family. Lies standing on end, one in front of the other, and I knew there would have to be more, a long line of dominoes, each ready to bring down its neighbour, and I worried that I might not be able to remember them all, and keep the story standing.

Even so, it was good to be home, but everything was not as it was before. Mother only had one bag of flour in the pantry, although there were still rows and rows of her homemade jam on the shelves, with the empty berry pan shining on the floor below. She had been saving her sugar ration. At tea, Duncan was worried about the price of beasts going South for slaughter. 'They're lighter by the time they arrive, and so is my wallet,' he said, 'At least I am doing better than the slaughtermen here. They have no work now. What was wrong with killing them locally?' He looked round, but no one had an answer.

'Let's eat.' Mother folded her hands and said grace, while Dad scratched and filled his pipe. He knew better than to light it. On the table, there was fresh fish from the boat and Mother had killed a chicken that had stopped laying. After dinner, we played cards and Duncan tickled me for refusing to call him the champ when he won. 'That was the deal,' he shouted, as I begged him to stop. 'If I win, you call me the champ. It was not the best of three.'

As the light faded on the long, late summer evening, the men went out for a smoke and I helped Mother clear the dishes to the kitchen. I saw Hannes had fallen asleep when I collected his plates. He looked like a bairn, undefended, as he had when I first saw him in the flat. I wondered how his family were doing without him. They had waited a long time for news.

'Have you been to see Jeff yet?' Mother asked as we washed up.

'No.' The saucer I was drying clattered as I laid it in the pile. She looked up as she put another plate in the wooden rack.

'I need to apply for a pass each time I want to go,' I said, 'although they booked me in for next week on a first visit. I had a bad cold last time and couldn't go.'

'He'll be missing you,' said Mother.

I didn't reply.

'Are you all right?' She dried her hands and put her arms round me. 'You can't help it that he's a conchy,' she said. 'No one will think any the less of you.'

'Mr Black hates me,' I said. 'So does his wife.'

'Who's Mr Black?'

'The butcher.'

She laughed. 'Well, tell him to go hang himself. You come from a good family and are not to blame for a daft husband with fancy ideas. Jeff will come to his senses soon enough, especially without your good cooking and his home comforts.' She emptied the basin. 'And when he is released, it won't kill him to lift a pen and help out in some office or other.' She lowered her voice. 'Dad doesn't want you to mention this business, if you can avoid it. You understand. We have to keep the neighbours' goodwill.' She held me at arm's length.

I nodded. I wanted to tell her what had happened on the night before Jeff went to prison; that I never knew a husband could take what he wanted from a wife without asking, but I would have had to tell her about Hannes. I wanted to keep his secret, to repay him for saving me. My throat felt tight.

'That's my girl. You are growing up,' she said, and she pulled me close. She smelt of rose water. 'There's a lot we women have to thole.' She patted my back, and turned away to put the kettle on.

I told her I wanted an early night after the journey, and went upstairs. I was anxious to avoid the kind of fireside chat where they would ask for Hannes' story. I didn't feel like I could invent a whole life for the mythical Hamish, complete with military record. I couldn't remember much from the newsreels, just the flattened city I couldn't name, and the marching feet, moving closer; cobble by cobble, heel by heel, and toe by toe.

At the end of the landing, I pushed open my door. My room was exactly the same as before I was married. Time was frozen here. My teddy was still on the pillow and my annuals were in a row on the shelf above the bed. There were rosebuds on the wallpaper, with shiny lines running through the background, like marks on the sand after the tide. My brothers had shared the two rooms next door, but, apart from Duncan, they were married now and living out. They still took the boat out together when the farm could spare them.

I lay under my covers with a hot water pig at my feet as the bed was damp. I could hear Mother and Dad talking downstairs and laughing. Plates and cutlery clattered as she laid the table for breakfast so the men could get something to eat before starting work. I knew she would smoor the fire in the range to keep it going, and tell Dad not to be too long over his last pipe. Then her footsteps would creak on the stairs, she would put on her Pond's face cream in the bathroom, and fall asleep over the first page of her book. Hidden upstairs, I realised that Hannes must have learnt everything about me and Jeff in the silence of holding his breath.

I turned over twice but it was impossible to drop off, and I walked up and down by my bedroom window. The stars danced over the hill and I watched the waning half-moon float up from the ridge to join them. It was like an orange segment, undigested on the black belly of the sky. An owl called.

I picked out one of the annuals and reread my favourite stories, the heroine moving across the pages in black and white line drawings, each scene contained in neat frames, her fate in the hands of the master storyteller. And I remembered being sure, as a bairn, that all would turn out well for her. She would win through and be safe. I had slipped from the page of my own story and I didn't know how it would end. Downstairs, I heard Dad cough and bolt the front door. Duncan's light switch clicked off and within minutes he began to snore. I wrapped myself in my bedspread, and sat on by the window. My room grew chill round the edges and the rosebuds became small, reproachful faces in the gloomy moonlight. I crept out into the hall to get a glass of water from the kitchen. I could feel, rather than hear, the soft breath of my family, drawing in the night air, dropping mumbled words from their dreams into the silence. The crocheted sole of my slipper caught on a nail in a floorboard and, as I bent down to release it, I noticed that Hannes' light was on; a bright line seeping under the door in the darkness. I stopped at the threshold, holding my breath to listen for movement. There was a sharp click of a handle turning and Mother appeared behind me at her door. 'What are you doing up, Agnes?' she asked.

'I just wanted to check Hamish was okay before I turned in,' I said, noticing the joint on her big toe looked swollen.

'Go on, then,' she said. 'We all need to get our sleep.'

'Maybe I shouldn't disturb him,' I said.

'Oh, for heaven's sake, Agnes. Make your mind up.'

I knocked softly on the door and pushed it open an inch or two. A figure lay in the bed, its hips and shoulders muffled by the quilt. I heard Mother yawn behind me, and then saw in the mirror that Hannes was sitting behind the door, a blanket over his knees. His eyes were deep pools in the winter of his face, the shaved skin stretched tight over his skull. He didn't move. My friend was afraid and now I could see only the fugitive. I pushed up the lightswitch and closed the door. 'It looks like he is asleep,' I said, my heart aching for him. I wanted to go to him, to tell him it would be alright and comfort him as he had comforted me.

'Well, off to bed and don't let the bedbugs bite,' said Mother.

'I'll just get a drink of water from the kitchen,' I replied, but her door was already closed. I stood there alone, and then crept downstairs, still seeing his doppelgänger lying on the altar of his fear. The stone floor of the kitchen was cold under my feet and the water gushed out of the tap as I turned it on, splashing onto the floor. I watched my reflection in the window above the sink sip water from a glass, her face pale, and then I turned to go back upstairs, a sleep-walker in a world undreamt of. Hannes was standing two paces away. I hadn't heard him come into the kitchen over the noise of the running water. He pressed his finger to his lips, and then sat down at the table. The bread lay on its board under a cloth.

'Are you hungry?' I asked, wondering why he had come downstairs in spite of his fear.

He shook his head, and standing up walked towards the back door. I ran across the room and put my hand over his as he reached for the key on its nail in the door frame. It was long and silver, the nail head piercing its eye above ragged teeth.

'*Bitte…*Please, Agnes,' he whispered.

I looked down to avoid his eyes. He was standing there in his bare feet. It didn't look like he was running away. I pulled off my slippers and nodded, longing to escape my restlessness. He slid the key into the lock and turned it. The door opened on the night, his breath suddenly visible in a small cloud that heralded the colder days to come. He took my hand and we walked across the grass which was mossy under foot and onto the cinder path between the raised beds of the vegetable patch. The ash stopped at the end of the garden. I could feel the small ends of burnt coals between my toes. Hannes unlatched the gate and we stepped into the field.

I looked back at the house standing against the sea. The moonlight shone on its grey, slate roof and the closed kitchen door. The curtains were all shut except mine and I had a sudden picture of the bed I had left standing silent, its covers tossed back like a gaping mouth. Hannes slipped some black seeds from an escaped allium into his pocket and then took my hand, leading me along the side of the hedge with a smile. The sky was huge and salty, punctured with stars, light shining through the loose weave of old velvet. There was something brighter than us all up there. I sighed and he pulled me close, slipping an arm round my waist as we walked on the land he was about to leave. I could see Orion and the Three Sisters. I remembered Dad naming them for me, pointing up at the sky's unguarded face, and crouching down to hold me in his arms as if I might float away in the vastness. Hannes stopped and looked at me, the names of the same stars on the edge of his lips.

It was still dark when Duncan woke me from my doze in my chair in the early morning. 'Get ready,' he said. 'We're leaving.' He looked as if he hadn't slept much, either.

'I thought we were going on the evening tide,' I said.

'We were, but it appears your Irish friend speaks German in his sleep.' He looked at me. 'I'm not going to ask,' he said. 'You are my sister.'

'He's a farmer, Duncan.'

'Well, he might have been, but he is something else now.'

'He told me they were starving. No one could afford bread. The National Socialists gave them money to live on if they joined the Party.'

'And that makes it all right? Well, he's not staying here. I'll put him ashore and he can find his own way to neutral territory, but I'm doing it for you, not him.'

'He is a good man, Duncan.'

'He didn't come here on holiday, Aggie. We are at war. Don't think because I am not in uniform that I am not fighting.'

I nodded. I couldn't tell him Hannes had helped me. Duncan wouldn't have understood. There was still the sanity of the farm here, man and beast, wheat and barley. Old rhythms, no unpredictable harvests of words. He wouldn't have understood what it was like to live on a dark, spiral stair with taped up windows; to find out that the people who should love you, could also hurt you.

'What is his real name?' he asked.

'Hannes.'

'Hannes. Hamish. Very good,' he laughed, and I saw the man in him who was bigger than the war. I hoped I might find forgiveness. 'Hannes what?'

'I don't know. He's from outside Venice, no, Vienna.'

'And you know that, do you?'

'That's what he said.' I pulled the dictionary out of my bag.

'And books never lie, either,' said Duncan. 'Well, we are not taking that. Tell your man to get his coat. I'll meet you at the harbour.'

Hannes and I crept out of the front door. We could hear Duncan's feet ahead of us on the track. Small stones rattled under his boots and there was the creak of the gate as he climbed over. Hannes now seemed reluctant to leave, and I pulled his arm to make him walk faster. He tried to speak to me, but his voice carried in the early morning air and some of the words were German. I put my finger to my lips. We were almost at the harbour when I thought I saw a man cross the road ahead of us. He had a gun over his forearm, but when we drew level with the trees he had passed, there was no sign of him. Perhaps he had moved further into the wood. Hannes' eyes darted from side to side and he hunched down into his coat. The black handle of one of Professor Schramml's knives stuck out of his pocket. I pulled it out and threw it into a ditch. '*Schon wieder Waffenlos* – defenceless,' he said, and tucked my arm through his. I pulled myself free and walked faster.

Duncan was getting the *Driftwood* ready to cast off when we arrived. Her tyres bumped against the harbour wall as the first swell of the morning tide rushed in at the entrance. Her paint was still sharp in bold green and blue, and her name was freshly painted. I climbed down the ladder, which was slippery with bladderwrack, and Hannes followed. Duncan indicated that he should lie down on the nets at the back of the trawler, and threw folds of it on top of him.

'I hope you're happy with your catch?' he said, taking my arm. 'Don't ever do anything like this again.'

'I'm sorry. I want to come home to the farm.'

'What about Jeff?'

'It's over.'

He nodded as if it wasn't a surprise, but I had thought he liked Jeff. 'Good luck explaining that to Mother. St Anthony's ears will be burning tonight,' he said.

'Well, Dad will support my divorce. He's a Protestant.'

'Divorce? Don't start a war here, Aggie. It's hard enough already.' He waved at the machine gun mounted on the wheelhouse. 'I am supposed to shoot boggles in the night with that.'

He looked over to where Hannes lay in the net, and then turned away and cast off.

I pulled the rope in for him as it trailed in the dark water and he set the boat's course out beyond Ailsa Craig.

It was quiet at sea. The sun was just beginning to rise into a bank of cloud. The waves and sky were grey, and a lone seagull glided in our wake. Duncan smoked his pipe, leaning out of the wheelhouse window. An hour into the trip, I took Hannes a cup of tea from Duncan's flask. It was laced with whisky.

'*Ich möchte aufstehen*,' he said, pointing at his legs.

'Can he stretch his legs, Duncan?' I called.

Duncan looked round the horizon. 'If he keeps low.'

Hannes sat against the side of the boat and rubbed his calves, looking around him. The thin thread of the boat's course was leading him back to his old life; a life larger than the flat where we had known each other. He smiled at me. The skin round his eyes crinkled, but I didn't smile back. I could see the other man he was now. A small furrow appeared between his brows, and I turned away. He sat hugging his knees staring out at the horizon, and I stood in the wheelhouse with Duncan. The sea rolled beneath the boat in the long ridges of an onshore tide.

It was Hannes who spotted the conning tower of the U-boat gliding towards us. The gun was manned and three men in heavy coats stood on the deck, one looking straight at us through his binoculars. 'Take the wheel, Agnes,' Duncan shouted, jumping towards the gun, but Hannes stood up and waved. '*Es lebe Ossian!*' he shouted. '*Es lebe Ossian.*'

His voice carried over the still, cold water. The gull cried.

The gunner on the U-boat lowered his sights and looked towards his captain, who raised a hand. I was close enough to see he was bearded, and then the black wall of the submarine passed in front of us, the propellers churning the water with a low humming sound. Duncan cut the engine and hove to. We were sitting in the water, rising and falling on the swell. The water gurgled in the heads as the huge machine passed in front of us, its black back shining like a whale.

'They let us go,' I said, but Duncan was not happy. He stood looking after the sub, which was submerging, hiding from the sea planes at Lough Erne. 'They are hunting, Aggie. They probably have bigger fish to fry.'

He spat into the water and turned to face Hannes. 'What did he say?' he asked me.

'Ossian,' said Hannes. *Ein Held der Schotten.* A Scottish hero.'

'Never heard of him,' said Duncan. 'What the hell are we doing, Aggie?'

'Wagner,' said Hannes. 'Schubert.'

'Get him back under the nets,' said Duncan, 'before I kill him.'

He went into the wheelhouse and slammed the door, coaxing the engine back into life. I remembered stories of old scores settled at sea. The accidents that weren't questioned, although everyone knew they were the last page of a longer story. As the sun rose higher, Ireland appeared as a thin, grey line on the horizon and grew steadily bigger. The moon still floated behind us, growing paler in the light.

We put Hannes ashore in a small bay. 'Make your way south and go to the authorities,' said Duncan. 'They will find you a place to stay, or lock you up. Either way, it will be an end to this madness.'

'*Herzlichen Dank*, Agnes,' shouted Hannes as he jumped into the shallows to wade up the beach. '*Meine kleine Zauberin.*' He waved and turned away. He looked very small, alone on the shore.

'What did he say?' Duncan asked.

'I don't know. You wouldn't let me bring the dictionary.'

He laughed then. 'You're sixpence short of the full shilling, sis,' he said, and throttled the boat round.

'Maybe Hannes won't fight if he gets back. The vines will need him.'

'Or maybe he will be straight back in a plane.' Duncan sighed. 'He's part of the war machine. It eats all the little people and spits out the bones.'

22

Duncan burnt the dictionary when we eventually got back. Mother looked on but said nothing. I thought I saw some German handwriting on the flyleaf as it curled in the flames, but as I stood up to pull it back out, Mother held it down with the poker. I sat back down. 'Let it go, Agnes,' she said.

I opened my mouth to reply, but from the way she said it, I knew it would never be mentioned again. 'Remember you have a family,' she said, and picked up her pail of scraps for the hens. From the window, I saw her walk down the path and the hens came running to greet her. Duncan stood up and put on the wireless. The RAF had dropped bombs on Düsseldorf or somewhere, and Mussolini had banned people from listening to ghost voices on the wireless. Was that who we were – ghost voices? Hannes was moving back towards that world. Duncan lit his pipe and followed Mother into the garden.

Cocooned in Mother's perfect silence over the guest we had never had, I stayed on the farm through the potato harvest, grubbing in the earth for the tatties, which were hard and round in their bed of soil. I pulled them from the roots of the tumbled, green plants, splitting the thin, white veins that held them. I tried to forget the city and Jeff and Hannes. Douglas seemed like a character in a film, someone who had once loomed above me on the screen. I knew the shape of his lips and the sound of his voice; I knew the way his eyes crinkled when he laughed, but he seemed unreal, as if he lived in another world.

Jeff's letters from the prison grew more and more pitiful, keeping me tied to him. I had sent his ID card to the governor, and Jeff wrote to say that he was disappointed that I had cancelled my visit, but was glad to know I was safe. He was feeling weak with the cold and thought he might be getting arthritis. He said that Douglas' bid to become Rector of Edinburgh University had been defeated despite the best efforts of the student SNP members to have him elected from behind bars. He was running out of paper as Sylvia had flu and was unable to bring more, so it would be his last letter for a while. In my heart I didn't want any more letters from him and I knew I couldn't stay married to him. I didn't want his children, or to live in his gloomy flat, locked in a war over dust with Mrs MacDougall.

Dad had his lawyer draw up the papers to file for my divorce while Mother turned Father Xavier's tea salty with her tears. I could picture them praying for me and I expected to hear all about what a bad Catholic I was when she got home, but all she said was she had found out that a marriage in a registry office had never been a real marriage in the eyes of the Church, so there was nothing to worry about. Father Xavier had been a great comfort, she said.

The land turned over to sleep after the harvest and I took to putting on my wellingtons and walking out along the coastal path with the dogs. The sheep were nibbling at the turnips Mother now made into jam with dye and packets of wooden pips from the Ministry of Food. The fields were muddy when I jumped down from the gates between them, and the dogs flew over behind me, bounding across the bare earth to chase the gulls from their kingdom with gleeful barks. I wished the swing of their tails could wipe my slate clean, and I carried the small, hard stone of my betrayal as a pain in my chest, or rolled it between my fingers in a deep pocket. It never left me and I avoided my old friends, saying I was too sad about Jeff to go to tea, or a ceilidh, even on my birthday.

At the end of October, the usual stream of bairns came guising at the back door on Halloween, and sang in their reedy voices with their arms round each other. I pressed pennies and pieces of tablet made from Mother's sugar ration into the hands of witches, who bristled with brooms to clear the path to hell. Dad drew on his pipe and smiled at their blind turnip lanterns dancing on gales of laughter. I envied them. I was becoming a hollow woman, scooped out, my face a mask. Mother gripped my wrist in the circle between her thumb and forefinger in the morning and said I was getting too thin. 'We'll need to fatten you up before winter, or you'll freeze,' she said, and I nodded, but there was ice on the inside of my window by mid-November, and nothing could warm me.

I applied to visit Jeff in the first week of December to let him know I wanted to divorce him, but when I arrived at the prison the warder told me there was a smallpox outbreak and I should go home. 'I am sorry, Mrs McCaffrey,' he said, 'it would seem you've had a wasted journey.'

I didn't have the heart to leave the divorce papers with him and so I took them with me. Perhaps when the outbreak was over, I could sort it out. I sat on the Morningside tram with my chin pressed down into my scarf.

The flat was dark and cold. When I went down to the back garden to see if I could find a last brussels sprout or stick of rhubarb, there was little sign of my bonfire, just the metal top of one of the coat hangers lying in the grass, dusted with frost. It sparkled, a question mark lying at my feet, but I had no answers. The vegetables had all died back and I ate the pickles and bread Mother had packed, then tried to take Mrs MacDougall a piece of home-cured ham.

'I think it would be better if we weren't seen together,' she said, and shut the door without taking the food. I knew she would be standing just round the corner of her hall, out of sight of the letter box, listening to see what I did next.

'He's gone, Mrs MacDougall. To Ireland,' I shouted through the flap, but I only heard the scuff of her slippers on the linoleum as she scuttled away, and her kitchen door closing.

The next day, I called the switchboard at the prison to ask when I could see Jeff, but the woman said in a very bright voice, 'Please hold the line while I connect you to the infirmary, Mrs McCaffrey.'

A tired-sounding man cleared his throat as he spoke into the receiver and asked me to sit down. 'I understand from the warder who reported your visit yesterday, that you didn't receive our telegram with regard to your husband's health. Are you alone, Mrs McCaffrey? If so, I would advise you to ask someone to come in to sit with you. I have some difficult news.'

'There is no one I can ask,' I said.

'Well, I regret to inform you that your husband has succumbed to the outbreak and has developed bronchopneumonia, which is a not uncommon complication in smallpox. I regret to say that he is very poorly indeed. I was hopeful he might respond to treatment but, in his weakened condition, I'm afraid you might have to prepare yourself for the worst.'

I never heard what he said next. I dropped the receiver and my knees buckled. I lay on the floor crying for a long time and I thought I might choke, the tears came so fast. My head felt too heavy to lift and I heard myself saying, 'My poor Og, my poor Og,' over and over again. Every time I thought of his curly hair on our pillow in the sun all those months ago, I cried harder, and it surprised me because I thought I hated him.

Early the next day, I cycled over to Saughton and a warder led me through the barred gates of the prison and tiled halls to the infirmary, gently, one hand on my elbow, as if I was already a widow. A nurse tied me into a green gown, which smelt of disinfectant, and secured a thick mask over my nose and mouth. When I saw Jeff, I knew it was too late. I was only allowed to look at him from behind a window in the corridor, although they wheeled his bed nearer the glass. He opened his eyes once, but didn't speak. I didn't know if he could see me or not. Small craters had burst on his cheeks and neck, and his chest rose and fell as if he was running. He was trapped in a battlefield. Through the afternoon and overnight, I watched his breathing slow and his face slacken, and then he was gone. His body looked soft, as if he was sleeping on his side, with his hands folded one on top of the other as if in prayer. I couldn't cry, although a howl was growing in my chest, but it seemed wrong to let it out in that moment of stillness, as if it might call him back or disturb him. He looked as if something very big had happened that needed all his attention, and I sat on in a tent of black-out blinds, which shut out the whole world, and the path that had led us here. An orderly entered the sick room, held a mirror in front of Jeff's lips and opened the window to let his soul go. He didn't look at me, as if Jeff's death was shameful and I was part of it. I sat there staring at the floor until a nurse guided me away to a small room, where she gave me a cup of tea. 'I'll need to give you an injection,' she said. 'Please roll up your sleeve… and… all done. Quarantine yourself at home for twelve days. If you feel at all feverish, you must contact your doctor immediately. I am sorry for your loss, dear, but we are unable to release the body, so you must be brave. He's in God's arms now. Our undertaker will deliver the ashes to your house, and I can assure you it will all be carried out with the greatest respect.'

She turned a page of her notebook. 'Now, can you just confirm your address, please?'

She paused with her pen over the sheet of paper. 'Take your time. The doctor will sign the death certificate for you and forward it. Do you have any questions?'

I shook my head.

That night, I cried under my quilt, muffling my screams until I thought I would suffocate, and it was there in the dark as I tried to sleep that I first felt the strangeness in my belly. I lay on my back, my hands exploring the shape of my stomach, which had tightened into a small mound. I didn't know why I hadn't noticed it before. I thought my weight gain was the new regime at home. Mother had been feeding me up with meat from the farm and sago pudding, and I had only ever had to put my rags out on the line once in a blue moon. I thought it was being wartime thin for so long that had stopped Aunt Ruby's visit. I wasn't sure what to do now. I didn't want to be a mother on my own and I began to cry again as if there was an unlimited supply of tears in my body and I hadn't shed a single one. In the morning, I took some castor oil and climbed into a very hot bath, but nothing happened. I didn't know where to find the women I heard helped with these things, and I didn't want to make God angry, so I prayed that I would have the strength to deal with whatever happened. Perhaps it would never come to life.

23

I don't remember that first week after Jeff's death. I think I just sat in the flat, and then Sylvia drove me to Morningside Cemetery on Balcarres Street with Jeff's ashes in a plain urn on my knee. It was too snowy to take the car up the drive. The graves ran in concentric circles round the hillside, locked away from view behind high, sandstone walls and wrought iron gates. It was a place of memory, of sadness. I read the names of the dead as we walked past the gravestones; the lists of family members memorialised with the date of their death; the day they never knew was coming. I pictured them getting up in the morning never knowing it was to be that day when everything stopped, and all the things they meant to say, or do, or put right, became impossible. I hugged the urn of the man I had betrayed, the man who had betrayed me, and tears ran down my cheeks at the confusion of it all. The ground was so cold that the gravediggers had had to warm the earth with braziers to dig a hole that was deep enough. The coals lay smoking to one side. I buried Jeff's ashes in his parents' grave beneath their grey, granite headstone on the seventeenth of December. Their names were picked out in gold, but Jeff's name was scratched in bare letters, and someone had added mine: 'Mourned by his loving wife, Agnes'.

'I thought it was expedient to put yours on now, dear,' said Sylvia. 'Saves them chiselling away at the thing when it's your turn.' At the bottom of the stone, moss filled the legend 'Until a' the shadows flee awa".

I didn't have the heart to tell her that they would never add my dates here. The love that had sewn me to Jeff was unpicked, and only the marks left by the needle in the old cloth of our marriage remained. Sylvia held my arm, and Mrs MacDougall stood a short distance away beside a stone angel, which dripped icicle tears beneath a tree. Although Jeff wasn't Catholic, I said a prayer for him. He couldn't complain now. My words carried over the graves: 'Come blessed of my Father, take possession of the Kingdom prepared for you.'

Sylvia sighed and Mr Lamont stood with his chin lowered into his scarf, watching. He only found his voice again at the wake at the Bruntsfield Hotel, reading out telegrams of condolence as if a great body of people were present. I didn't know many of their names. 'He loves a platform,' said Sylvia, and slipped a sandwich to her dogs under the table.

The animals near my feet comforted me and I lifted the edge of the cloth to see them. 'You should get yourself a dog, Agnes. It would be company for you. You don't want to knock round that rotten, old flat by yourself. Turn into a Mrs MacDougall hiding in graveyards. You are far too young and gorgeous, as I never stop telling you. Take it from an old bluestocking who knows.'

I was too tearful to speak. She squeezed my arm.

'Let's hope Douglas makes it,' she said. 'We could use him in the department now, if the Ancient Greeks in Aberdeen will let him come after this war is over.'

Mr Lamont stopped stirring his tea. 'I believe he will be released in March, all being well, although the Ministry of Labour are putting some pressure on him to clarify what he'll do on his release.'

'They wouldn't lock him up again?' said Sylvia.

'Well, my dear,' said Mr Lamont, 'the issues are still the same. Talking of which…' He turned to me. 'Would you mind most awfully if I came by with the motor to collect Jeff's papers for Douglas? He is a terrible magpie when it comes to the written word. Never throws a scrap out. You'd think everything ever penned was gold. He'll want to take up the reins from where Jeff left off.'

I felt a sense of relief. I didn't want to see if there were any more photos of a life I had never shared, tucked into the papers that had destroyed us, silent in their dark niches. 'You can take his typewriter, too, Mr Lamont. Jeff wanted you to have it, although one of the letters jumps above the line.'

'You are most generous in your grief, my dear. If the SHRA can ever be of any assistance to you whatsoever, you must telephone me. I'll advise the Scottish Mutual Aid Committee of your current predicament as an indigent Edinburgh lady.'

'I'm no Edinburgh lady,' I said. 'I am an Ayrshire lass and I will work for my living.'

He gave Sylvia a look.

'Not on the farm, dear. You can't bury yourself in the country,' said Sylvia. 'I would miss you.'

I squeezed her hand. 'It's all I know, but don't worry, I'm not going all the way down to Ayr. I'll join the Land Army. There's a nursery at Laurelhill. That won't kill me.' But I didn't know what choice I would have. Perhaps they would send me South like the other lassies? I'd seen them in a Ministry film, filling shells with dust in a factory. Their eyes were red-rimmed, and they had looked up and smiled at the camera as a plummy voice talked about their heroic contribution to the war effort.

Mr Lamont and his friend emptied Jeff's study that afternoon. 'Forgive the haste in your time of grief,' he said. 'Are you quite sure you don't want to see if there is anything of sentimental value?'

'Jeff always kept this door shut,' I said. 'It was his ain room.' I sighed.

'He performed invaluable service for the Party, Agnes. His sacrifice will not have been in vain. I know that isn't much comfort to you as his wife,' he said. 'We will all feel his loss keenly in the days to come.'

But I wasn't sure how Jeff drowning in his own lungs had helped any one. I had burned the divorce papers in the range and felt like I was destroying a weapon whose shiny blade reflected my true self.

When they were gone, I rolled up the study rug and beat it in the garden. It made a hollow booming sound, but Mrs MacDougall didn't look out. Upstairs I filled a bucket with disinfectant and wiped down all the surfaces and mopped the floor. I peeled the long, sticky strips of brown paper off the window and washed the glass with vinegar. Then I polished it with handfuls of newspaper, crushing the images of war, and the names of the dead, in my hand. I watched the faces of the politicians grow soggy and peel, and I threw it all in the fire, which sizzled and snapped. I sat on the floor of the empty study until midnight, but it didn't become my room. Memories of Jeff played in my mind: I heard him singing with Douglas, saw him reading to me at the kitchen table about the war. I heard the mumble of his plans for the SNP, the dictionary that didn't move past 'C'. I was eighteen and I was a widow. It was almost 1943 and I was alone at Christmas.

24

On Christmas Eve, I walked across the Meadows to St Patrick's Church. I wasn't feart of the planes any more. I almost wanted to die, to feel an end to the grief that pressed on the back of my head as if its weight would bear me down to the ground, where I would freeze. The sadness was less for Jeff than for the death of my dream. My life with him had been no more than a gilded white lie I told myself. I had been stuck in his teeth, summer fruit picked without thought. Mother had been right about me. I wished Douglas had been the man to take me from my life on the farm, to carry me into a new world in his arms, command it with his voice to 'open sesame'.

The stars shone above the path across the Meadows, sending blue light through the trees' branches that arched overhead. It was a cathedral without a roof, a long nave, the skeleton ribs of a whale that had swallowed me whole, like Jonah. I put one foot in front of the other, trying not to think about the future on my own, letting them carry me forward. I crossed the Cowgate, walked up the cobbled lane to St Patrick's and went in the side door. It was brightly lit, and at the foot of the altar, the Virgin leant over the cradle to gaze at her child. Wooden animals slept at her feet. I put my hand on my stomach.

The Mass began with Christmas carols. I sang the familiar words, but the woman in front of me turned round as if I was out of tune and I stopped singing. An hour later, as midnight approached, a hush fell over us. Above the altar, a silver cloth hung over the carving of Christ on his cross. We were waiting for his birth. There was no crucifixion here, but there were gaps in the congregation, and some women began to cry. Servicemen, home on leave, put their arms round their wives and stroked their bairns' hair. Others, sailors from the port at Leith, stood grim-faced and alone, waiting to take Communion. I imagined Hannes somewhere far away, crossing himself as he received the wafer, genuflecting before the cup. I wondered what the prisoners were doing in Saughton – if Douglas was playing the harmonium at their service. We were all worshipping the birth of a child, who said we should love each other, but it was hard to find that love in this war. I had a cup of tea afterwards, and a piece of Christmas cake, before walking back over the Meadows. The ground was frozen solid, and the snowy ice cracked beneath my wellies.

On Hogmanay, I went to bed. There seemed to be nothing to celebrate, although people crept out to the pubs with taped up torches, and huddled at the Tron at midnight. The seven hills of the city kept watch. We hid in darkness from the coming year, feart that Edinburgh's first foot might be a bomber, but I knew they would be having a ceilidh at the farm with our neighbours. Mother always played the accordion, sweating as she smiled at the dancers flying past, insisting that she only drank tea, but accepting whisky because it was a special occasion. Once in a blue moon, she took what she called a Highland sherry, a wine glass filled to the brim, but then she only drank one. She said she would have to answer to the Lord in the morning for her sins, and winked at Dad, who always looked hopeful.

As the days passed, it was so long since I'd had a blether with anyone, that my lips were sticking together. The postman brought letters of condolence from friends and family and there was one from Douglas. It had a blue sticker, with someone's initials scrawled on it in black ink. I think it had been read before it was sealed in the prison and it made me feel like it hadn't been sent to me. My eyes weren't the first to read the good wishes. It was a burnt-out candle, a prayer for someone else.

Dear Agnes,

I offer my heartfelt condolences over the loss of your dear husband, Jeff. He was a tireless worker in the glorious cause of Scotland's freedom, and he will be sorely missed. It might have made him happy to know that Sorley has been found, although wounded in both ankles. He pitched up at a hospital in Cairo after El Alamein. Perhaps his poem The Cuillin, his hymn to that glorious mountain range on Skye, might comfort you. Jeff helped me with this translation, and I know that you too will 'rise on the other side of sorrow'.

I hope that I will be leaving HM Guesthouse on March 10th, if not before, and that you will visit me at Ardhall. A friend has offered to entertain any sleuths, who might be in attendance, to tea in his pig sty, leaving us free to talk of more significant matters, perhaps of love, and all the things that warm the heart.

Yours aye for Scotland,
Douglas.

I kissed the word 'love'. Of all the words that poured from Jeff's lips, it was the one I heard least, the one whose meaning he never understood. Douglas' letter filled me with new energy. I stopped dithering about and on the sixth of January, 1943, I walked through the snow to the Assembly Rooms on George Street, and volunteered for the Land Army. I didn't tell them I was pregnant. I tried not to think of it.

I was to be sent to Laurelhill Nursery in Stirling at the end of the month. I had little to pack, and I mostly lay in bed in the guest room to keep warm, and listened to the wireless. On my last day in Edinburgh, Sylvia came to collect Jeff's clothes for the Women's Voluntary Service and drove me to the station. 'Chin up,' she said as she took out my bag, and closed the boot on his suitcases. 'Best foot forward.'

She cried as she waved me off, and I closed my eyes on the train, but couldn't sleep. As we drew near Dumyat, I tried not to remember going to the rally with Jeff such a short time ago. It was too painful. My feelings belonged to two different people: the one who had married Jeff, and the one who had wanted to divorce him. I tried to think only of Douglas, imagine him as he stood on the platform at the rally, bold and brave. His name blotted out the small shadow of my husband that still clung to my heart like a wraith, twisting inside me. Stirling was quiet in the cold. A chimney sweep gave me a lift on his cart up to the nursery. 'It's a fine pass we've come to,' he said, 'when the nation is carried on the shoulders of a sweep and an army of lassies. Good luck to you, hen, not that you'll need it here. They'll treat you well. No POWs to mix things up.'

He left me standing in a yard. Greenhouses stretched out to the side of the farmhouse, which stood on a low rise looking at the Ochils. There were houses close by, and the castle crouched on its cliff-top nest.

'Welcome, my dear,' said a woman coming out of the house. 'I'm Mrs Ogilvie. We've been expecting you. I hope Rory wasn't bending your ear on the way up.' She was thin and elegant, even in her wellies. 'Now, don't stare – I used to be a catalogue model,' she said, waving at her boots, 'but Herr Hitler put the kibosh on that, and now I am stuck here. Now, let's get you kitted out. They sent me a stack of the most hideous uniforms you can imagine. Why they want to dress you beautiful, young things as middle-aged men, I can't imagine.'

She threw scratchy shirts, ties and knee breeches on the bed in the spare room and said, 'Take your pick. There is worse to come,' and she held up a pair of brown lace-up shoes. 'Just stuff them with newspaper, if they're too long in the toe. They must have been expecting tattieboggles when they sent me this lot. Put on the dungarees for everyday wear. The other girls live out, and I don't usually bring them in until picking time. You'll meet the nursery man later. I believe they call him "Grumbling Jim" behind his back, but he's not the ogre they make out. You'll see.'

Jim was standing at the door to the first greenhouse after lunch. He had steel-grey, curly hair, and was stocky, with very blue eyes. His shoulders were just beginning to stoop.

'Another townie?' he asked.

'No,' I replied.

'That makes a change, then. Hard to tell in that get-up. Never was a uniformed organisation man myself. Luckily, I am too old for all that conscription palaver.'

'You don't look a day over twenty-one,' I said.

'Oh, a charmer – you'll not get around me like that, young lady.'

His skin was so wrinkled by the sun that he looked a hundred.

'Did you fight in the last war?' I asked.

'Try the one before that,' he replied. 'Put me off for life. Empire is baloney, but I find it doesn't pay to have an opinion, so I grow plants instead. Tomatoes won't bother you with their beliefs. You can always find peace in a greenhouse,' – he handed me a hosepipe – 'but limited rain. The heaters dry everything out. Put that on a fine spray and off you go.'

'Should I water everything?' I asked. The vegetable seed-lings stretched as far as I could see.

'Everything except me,' he replied, 'and don't forget their friends.' He waved at the other greenhouses. 'But if I see any of these boys paddling out the door, there will be hell to pay. I'll be putting the kettle on at four. You'll hear it whistle if you do the west greenhouse last.'

It made me feel calm to water the tiny plants, each one a green thread in its tray. Jim had said they were called Blaby Special after a place in England. The sun broke through and shone on my face, warming the earth.

Mrs Ogilvie put a hot meal on the table at 6.30pm on the dot, ringing an old school bell to tell us it was ready. I was famished and pleased to see she had roasted a chicken, but there was no meat on Jim's plate. It was piled high with root vegetables and tomato jelly.

'He is a vegetarian,' said Mrs Ogilvie, 'insists on it, although I tell him the world won't stop turning if he has a mouthful of flesh.'

'Some people don't understand the meaning of the word vegetarian, although I don't hold with labels, as I said. Pythagoras is my inspiration and he's hundreds of years old,' Jim proclaimed, salting his food without tasting it.

'He's dead, Jim,' said Mrs Ogilvie.

'That's beside the point,' he replied, 'look how clever he was.'

'Well, I don't know what went wrong for you, then. There isn't a whole lot left between your ears,' said Mrs Ogilvie, flicking him with her tea towel. 'You'll scare our guest off with your vegetarian nonsense, and she has only just arrived. You'll have some chicken, Agnes, won't you?'

It tasted as good as Mother's and the heart came back into me. I hadn't eaten much at the flat. Mr Black had closed over Christmas. The woman in the post office hinted that he had had a nervous breakdown, and his wife was running the shop. I doubt Mrs Black would have served me even if I had gone in.

25

As the weeks passed, I began to feel at home. Jim planted out each crop of seedlings with the new moon, and muttered a Gaelic blessing over them. 'It is the price you pay for being raised by a Highland Granny,' he said. 'I didn't do it once and had to get up in the middle of the night and come to the greenhouse. The old ways gnaw inside your head until you do what they say. Darwin got it wrong. There is no survival of the fittest here. It is all to do with planting in the right season. You have to follow the moon for timing. She is the Earth's clock.'

'So you hold with the old ways, Jim?' I said.

'I've told you, I don't hold with anything. It's what you feel inside that makes the difference. The rest is just on the surface,' and he squirted the hose at me. 'Come and prick out these seedlings, madam, and, if you are very good, I might show you my special recipe for the compost, with the exception of my magic ingredient. That will go with me to the grave.'

The tomato plants grew bigger in the early spring sun and Jim kept the heaters on as it was still cold at night. 'The ministry men expect miracles,' he grumbled, adding a little milk to the watering can.

Mr Lamont rang the farm to let me know that Douglas would be released on the tenth of March and that he was starting a campaign to stand in the Kirkcaldy by-election as an SNP candidate. 'He is in much better spirits now,' he reported, 'but come early as they are planning to let their jailbird fly with the dawn.'

Mrs Ogilvie agreed that I could stay overnight at the Edinburgh flat so I could be on time for Douglas' release. I arrived there at five to find Mrs MacDougall going out. She flicked a glance at my Ministry-issue trench coat, and decided to speak, after all. 'This is a big improvement,' she said. 'I have to say, you sometimes looked a bit thrown together in those old clothes of Jeff's mother's. She was always so well turned out, but then that was back in the day. Glad to see you making a contribution to the war effort. It balances the scales.'

I smoothed down my uniform, not trusting myself to speak.

'I am sorry about Jeff,' she said, 'but I think it is better if we return to being nodding acquaintances. Our last... association wasn't the most positive, although the Lord moves in mysterious ways. "Ye cannot serve God and Mammon," Matthew 6:24, although we are but his handmaidens.'

I heard her heels tapping down the street as I unlocked the door to the flat, but it jammed on the post behind it. When I got in, there was a booklet in brown paper, and I was surprised to find a condolence letter from Professor Schramml, postmarked Geneva. He was very upset to learn of Jeff's death and wrote:

Liebe Agnes

Although we have never met, I feel sure you must have brought Jeff great happiness in the short time you were together. He sent me a picture of you on your wedding day and I must say I was struck by your loveliness.

It grieves me that I am too old to take arms against the destructive force which is Hitler, and that the circumstances of war have brought so much tragedy into your young lives. In the not too distant future, I hope to return to my beloved Edinburgh, which was so good to me after the passing of my wife.

Please give my kindest regards to Mrs MacDougall, if you chance to see her, as I am sure you will. I carry the memory of her most excellent soup close to my heart.

Your most faithful servant,
Dieter Schramml.

I tried to imagine the kind-hearted professor in exile from the place he had made his home; all his possessions abandoned upstairs. I wondered if he would mind that I had lost his dictionary, or that an Austrian airman had slept in his bed. Maybe Professor Schramml would hate Hannes for being a Nazi. I wondered if Hannes really did support the Fatherland and Hitler, and had lied to me to escape.

The flat was bitterly cold, and I pulled the mattress through to the kitchen to sleep by the range. There was no kindling so I got it going with torn-up pages from the London Scots for Home Rule booklet that had just come for Jeff. It was strange to see his name on a parcel, as if he was expected home. It seemed to be all about post-war reconstruction. I never knew Jeff had sent Professor Schramml a photo of me, but I wasn't Mrs McCaffrey any more. That person had died with Jeff, and I wasn't Agnes Thorne, either.

Perhaps I was over-tired from travelling, or perhaps the work in the greenhouses had left me more bone-weary than I realised, but I slept in. By the time I cycled over to Saughton, I was just in time to see a piper leading a procession to the end of the drive with the tall figure of Douglas at its head. There was a crowd of supporters and a newshound scribbling in a notebook while a photographer lined up a picture. 'Any complaints, Douglas?' he shouted. He was stooped from his time behind bars, thin and pale, and his beard was longer than ever.

'None against the prison authorities, but the whole criminal system is in need of some reform, as is our whole social and economic condition,' he said.

His voice sounded just as warm and strong as I remembered.

'What did you miss most behind bars? Have you changed your views? Do you have a message for Mr Ghandi on his fast?'

But Douglas was walking on. He disappeared into a car before I could speak to him. A woman next to me said, 'That was quite a moment. They composed a new tune for him on the pipes, Douglas Grant's Welcome. We'll be having the march and the victory yet.'

'Where has he gone?' I asked, trying to see if Mr Lamont was around.

'I think they are heading into town for a supporters' breakfast. I cannae mind where it was to be. Some nice hotel I expect, and then home to Ardhall. Are you a Party member?' She was dressed from head to toe in blue and white.

I wheeled my bicycle away without answering. I had been looking forward to this moment for so long, but he hadn't seemed to be looking for me. Perhaps he had forgotten his letter in all the excitement of getting out.

I tried not to cry on the train on the way back to Stirling. Douglas' release was mentioned in three paragraphs on page three of *The Scotsman*, just above the Imperial Service Medal list of Scottish recipients, and a line about a child's body being found in Leith Docks. No one knew who the poor wee mite was. I put the paper back on the seat where I had found it.

26

Mrs Ogilvie was so concerned at how upset I was when I got back to Laurelhill that she agreed I could go to Ardhall near Leuchars to see Douglas on the fourteenth of March. She even helped me to send a telegram saying when I would arrive.

The bus twisted along narrow country roads, past farm-houses that reminded me of home, and as we drew near Leuchars, I tried to check my make-up in my powder mirror, but the bus was too shoogly. It was hard to look pretty in a shirt, tie and knee breeches. I noticed that the waistband on my trousers was tighter, but it was covered up by my jumper and trench coat, so I wasn't too embarrassed. People seemed to look at me with more respect now I was in uniform, and an old man shook my hand as I got off the bus. Fife was flat compared to Stirling. Large fields stretched out, ploughed and ready for planting, and I could see the sea in the distance. There was a lonely hill and woods near Douglas' house, which I found with a farmhand's directions.

Douglas didn't recognise me at first. It must have been my uniform and I was early, but when he shouted Agnes, and squeezed me in a great bear hug, I was the happiest woman alive. 'I am so sorry about Jeff,' he said. 'But let me look at you. You look so rosy. The country life must suit you. Welcome to my humble abode, although none so humble as my more recent home, as you well know.'

The inside was neat and sparkling. Winter jasmine stood in a pottery jug on the table and seedlings were pricked out in trays on a deep windowsill. 'Still growing your magic beans, Douglas?' I asked.

'They're proving slightly harder to germinate than I anticipated, but I am more hopeful for my gentian, delphinium and daphne for the summer. An army friend sent them from his garden in Bute. I believe he got hold of them in Bombay. One of the more bizarre advantages of war. Cross-pollination.'

He offered to take my coat, but I kept it on.

'So, how are you? You must be missing Jeff?'

My throat tightened and tears sprang into my eyes. Douglas looked dismayed and said, 'They did their best to contain the outbreak, you know, but these things are very difficult when everyone is so run down. Did they let you see him before he died?'

I nodded. 'Let's not talk about sad things. I've come to see you.' I tried to smile.

'Jeff would have wanted you to be happy, Agnes. "Enjoy your youth, dear heart; soon it will be the turn of other men." Theognis. A man who knew what it was to fall from grace, as I do, to my cost. But a cup of tea is the greatest cure of all, at least in the short term. You sit down and I'll make us a pot.'

He wandered into the kitchen, leaving me by a new fire that licked round twigs and pine cones, searching with blue fingers for the small pieces of coal balanced on the wood, and pulling them down. There were brown, glazed pottery mugs on the tray he brought through. It was lined with a hand-crocheted doily, edged with bright glass beads.

'We'll have scones shortly,' he said, 'although they may not be up to your own high standard.'

'You are making me feel like Mrs MacDougall,' I said.

'Ah, the veritable warrior of the stair. How is she? Still sniping at all and sundry?' He sat down opposite me.

'No, the guns have fallen silent.'

'Most unexpected,' he smiled, 'but then I suppose you are hardly there now. Where did you say you were based?'

'Laurelhill in Stirling. You would like it. It's a nursery.'

'Did you contribute to that insane vegetable submarine in the George Street exhibition? HMS Dig? I believe its conning tower was made out of leeks and rhubarb.'

I shook my head. 'Jim mentioned the "Vegetables for Victory" show, but I couldn't go.' I didn't mention I had saved my day off for his release.

He poured the tea. The teapot shook slightly in his hands.

'Help yourself to milk and sugar,' he said.

'Sugar is a real treat. I used to feed my ration to the milkman's horse,' I said.

'The toothless one? The one I was to ride into battle?'

'He was called Flash.' I laughed, pleased he remembered that first visit, and took a sip of tea.

'Are you free for good now, Douglas? They won't send you back to prison, will they?'

'I think they'd like to,' he replied. 'They find my views… difficult. I am trying to get my conviction quashed by appealing to the Scottish Estates.' He sipped his tea. 'However, self-government remains my real focus.'

'Even at the expense of your Greek poet?'

'Never at the cost of culture. Never that. I hope to have finished translating his work in August.'

'And will I be able to read it in Scots?'

'Alas, no. Even my Sorley translation has been downgraded from Lallans, as I originally planned, to English. My publisher wants to put it before a wider audience and I agreed, albeit reluctantly. Money is the real master. More tea?'

I held out my cup.

'Where will they find the paper for it all?' I asked.

'At this rate I will have to ask Sorley to bring some papyrus back from Cairo. And personal projects aside, we can't get hold of enough paper to produce a comprehensive statement of SNP policies to take us forward. I am planning to stand in the Kirkcaldy by-election.'

I tried to look interested but I was thinking how beautiful his eyes were. They sparkled as he spoke, even though he was now blethering on about the new hydroelectric power stations and who would take control of them. 'Can it be right that they suck energy out of the Highlands without directing any of it to the crofters?'

'No,' I said, realising too late that he was asking me a question and not sure if that was the right answer. I stood up, wondering if I might join him on the sofa, when I saw a girl coming up the path to the house.

'That's our scones,' he said, unfolding his long legs to go and open the front door.

'I got the last four, darling,' the girl said, and I heard them kiss. She was holding his arm as they stepped into the room.

'You must be Agnes,' she said. 'Douglas told me so much about your husband. I am sorry for your loss.'

Douglas slipped the coat from her shoulders as if he was unwrapping a present. 'Agnes, this is Isabella. Bella, Agnes.'

'How do you do?' I said, holding out my hand. Her eyes were huge, kind, with a far-seeing, distant quality.

'Bella is an artist,' Douglas said. 'Far better than a bear like me deserves.'

'Have you come far, Agnes?' Isabella asked.

'Stirling.' My throat was dry and I swallowed hard.

'Stirling? Douglas, isn't that where you said Mr Ford chased everyone round, scribbling in his book and scaring people? That must have been awful for you, Agnes, with Jeff in the Party and everything. You have been through so much.'

'Yes,' I said. Such a small word. The roar in my head was deafening. How could I have thought Douglas wouldn't have someone, that it wasn't only politics that filled him? I sat down and added more sugar to my tea. Isabella was staring at me. Douglas had gone into the kitchen to butter the scones, but I wasn't hungry any more. She added a log to the fire.

'So how did you two meet?' I asked, just for something to say, and a little tea slopped onto the table as I set the cup down. Isabella watched the stain spreading on the cloth, but didn't move.

'At Mr Lamont's house in Lochwinnoch. My mother became his housekeeper when we came over from South Africa. I used to visit her there to escape the madness of the art school in Glasgow.'

Douglas came back through with the scones dripping jam and offered me one. I put it on my plate and licked the sticky stuff from my finger. It was sweet and seedless.

'This is delicious,' I said, wondering how I could leave it without offending them.

'My mother's recipe,' said Isabella. 'She strains the jam to make a jelly. Better for the stomach, especially if you have diverticulitis or a sensitive digestion.'

'You and your queer foreign ways,' laughed Douglas.

Isabella laughed. 'He always says that, but he is resisting progress.'

'And you are betraying your good Scottish father,' he replied. 'What is the point in having a name like Auchterlonie if you strain your jam?'

'And what about all the Gossarrees on the other side? Don't they count for anything?' asked Isabella.

I looked puzzled, and he looked at me and said, 'A quarter Basque, a quarter French, a quarter German, from an old Mecklenburg Junker family, and a quarter Dutch.' He said it like a catechism. 'Europa herself sits before you.'

'Bravo,' said Isabella, and kissed him.

I stood up. 'I must be going,' I said.

'But you have only just arrived,' said Isabella. 'You haven't had your scone.'

'I'm sorry – I don't feel very well.'

'Forgive me. We are forgetting you are so recently bereaved,' said Douglas. He moved beside me and stroked my hand. 'You are being so brave,' he added. 'It must be very difficult for you.'

I wanted to blurt out, 'It's not about Jeff. It's you I love,' but Douglas was looking at Isabella. It was impossible to divide the plough from its share. 'There is a bus at twenty past,' I said, looking round at the clock on the mantelpiece.

'Please stay,' said Isabella. 'You could lie down for a while and rest.'

I stood up and straightened my uniform. 'No, must trot on,' I said, in Sylvia's voice, but they didn't laugh. 'I also have some business to attend to.'

They looked concerned. 'We're moving to Glasgow soon,' said Douglas. 'Be sure and look us up if you are through that way. We should be well-established after the wedding in August.'

'Of course,' I said, knowing I never would. I was crying inside. I wanted to remember every detail of his bonny face, the colour of his skin and hair, and the light in his eyes. 'Thank you for the tea.'

I tried not to cry on the bus, but sobs kept escaping and a woman behind me asked if I was all right, and passed me her handkerchief. They were used to seeing grief these days and looked out the window to give me privacy, but I expect they exchanged looks over my head and mouthed the words 'poor, wee soul'.

27

Next day, I watered the tomatoes without even seeing them, pouring can after can over the plants in a transparent hail of water. I thought of the drops clinging to the budding, green fruit as my tears. I would never see Douglas again. I thought of Jeff, his dust buried in a small pot, and the bairn in my womb growing, ripening towards the day it would be born. Strangers would see me as a tragic widow, a woman alone in the world, hand in hand with a child robbed of its father. They would assume he had died a soldier's death, a hero's death, and I would be left to live the lie. I didn't know who I could tell that I was expecting a bairn, so I told no one. The dungarees hid the curve of my belly so well, and I was still very small, although Mrs Ogilvie exchanged looks with Jim at breakfast, as I sat picking at my food. I supposed they had heard me crying in the night and assumed I was disappointed in my trip to Ardhall; disappointed in love. They waited for me to mention it, but I never did. On the fourth day, Mrs Ogilvie announced that she had arranged tickets for a dance at the Miners' Institute and told me that if I moped about for one more minute she would ask the Ministry of Agriculture to repatriate me to the city, as it was unlikely that any tomato could ripen under my baleful stare. I couldn't think of any excuse not to go, so I put on the pink crêpe de Chine dress she lent me. 'Pre-utility, thank God,' she said. It was gathered under the bust, and with a cardigan over the top, my bump wasn't visible. I didn't think she had guessed.

The hall at the Institute was decorated with bunting and a GI swing band had set up with microphones at the far end. The men in their pale-green uniforms softened my memory of Douglas on the same platform. It was a different movie playing in the same cinema. I wondered if Bella had been in that audience at that rally, even as I was longing for him. I had betrayed Jeff with an empty dream, thought to drink from a cup that had already been drained. A spotlight shone on the brass instruments and the trumpeter jumped to his feet to encourage the folk who were filling the room. 'Let's get this room jumping,' he shouted, and the drummer hit his cymbal, which shimmered.

'They're American, dear,' said Mrs Ogilvie. 'Very boisterous.'

'But utterly adorable,' said a voice behind me. I turned to see the blackest man I had ever seen. He bowed and held out his hand. 'Would you do me the honour? Captain Arnold at your service, ma'am.'

'Agnes Thorne,' said Mrs Ogilvie, putting my hand in his. 'She would be delighted, although you might need to remind her how to dance. It has been a quite a while.'

His face lit up. He pulled me into a dance hold and we swung off in a polka. It was like dancing the middle part of a Canadian Barn Dance at a ceilidh. He galloped me round the room, only just avoiding other couples. I was so dizzy I began to laugh, but tears were close behind. He led me off the floor for some lemonade as the music ended.

'So what do you do, Agnes?' he asked, passing me a glass.

'I'm persuading tomatoes to grow at Laurelhill Nursery.'

'Somehow I don't think that is going to stop the Germans,' he replied.

'The wee, green ones are hard enough to stop a man in his tracks,' I said, 'and I have a pretty good aim.'

'David and Goliath?'

155

'Who are you calling David?'

He raised his glass. 'Here's to you, Agnes, and your war.'

'Slainte mhath…' I said, uncertain of his first name.

'Raphael,' he said, filling the pause.

A waltz struck up and he led me back onto the floor. It was good to be held kindly by a man. His chest was warm, and I liked the feeling of his hand on the small of my back. Mrs Ogilvie winked as she span past with Jim, who had gelled down his hair and put on an old dinner jacket from the 1920s. 'You are seeing me at my most debonair,' he had said as we left the farm. 'This tux is my dark secret: there's a trail of broken-hearted lassies from here to Timbuktu.'

I looked up at Raphael. 'You sure look cute,' he smiled.

My face was beginning to relax and my cheeks felt less tense as I sighed, drawing air into my lungs. I had been holding my breath for a long time.

'You okay?' he asked. 'You got a problem with me being negro?'

I shook my head. 'Why would I?'

'You'd be surprised,' he replied. 'I must be the blackest man since Fred Douglass to pitch up in this godforsaken Arctic wilderness you call home. Although I believe he brought more than a little heat to the cheeks of Edinburgh's abolitionist ladies in the nineteenth century.'

'I'm not from Stirling,' I said.

'Oh, how many minutes down the road is the place you're from?'

I punched him on the shoulder. 'Where are your manners?'

'I'm sorry, but Pennsylvania could swallow this whole country in two bites, fence it in and call it a farm.'

'It might be a prickly mouthful.'

'I believe it might, but I am willing to try,' he replied, and pulled me closer. My belly pressed against his flat stomach and he pulled back. 'I'm sorry, Agnes. I didn't realise.' He looked round the room as if he expected to see an angry man approaching.

'It's all right, I'm a widow.'

He looked down at me. 'That is not all right. That is a tough call, and I am sorry for your loss.' He led me back to Mrs Ogilvie and Jim.

'You'd better look after this little lady,' he said, and bowed before walking up to the bar and slapping one of the soldiers standing there on the back.

'Aren't you feeling well?' asked Jim.

Mrs Ogilvie took a long sip of her lemonade, drawing it up through the straw. I knew that when she raised her eyes to me from behind the smokescreen of her blue, powdered lids, that I would see she had guessed, perhaps had always known. But instead she nudged Jim and squeezed past to go to the powder room. It was an invitation to follow her, though I wasn't ready. I told Jim I was going to get some air and walked out into the night. I didn't know how I felt about the child. I had always imagined knitting for my firstborn in a cosy nursery with a loving husband at my side. Not this world, at war.

The night air was unseasonably cold and my breath hung in front of my mouth like a veil. The Ochils were dark, glittering in the frost under a waning moon, which had just tipped past full the night before. The music grew fainter behind me as I walked, my trench coat buttoned up to my chin. I flexed my hands, but the cold was already in my fingers, licking the bones. The Forth slid, inky black, under old Stirling Bridge and my feet echoed on its cobbles. There was no one about. They were all at the dance, or dreaming of husbands, sons and brothers far away. It was a land of women now. The blackout blinds were pulled down on all the big houses, bleak like the empty mansion behind the flat, a pattern of abandoned lives, endlessly repeating. I needed to get off the street, to feel the earth under my feet. Sticks cracked as I began to climb up the path to the Wallace Monument. I wanted to raise myself up above everything; to look out over the small world that was my life in Stirling. An owl called as I reached the foot of the tower, which seemed to grow straight out of the rough rocks.

The jaggy crown on its head loomed above me, as if it might slide down its misshapen body and crash round its feet, crushing me. I tried the handle. The door was unlocked. It creaked as I opened it and the smell of damp stone seeped into my clothes. The stairs spiralled round, past arrow slits. I thought I could hear the faintest sound of the trumpet over the water, carrying on the still air. The stairs grew narrower and the roof got lower, squashing me in and I walked in an ever-decreasing spiral, my hand trailing on the stone spine of the tower, as if I was winding the thread of my life onto a bobbin.

I tried to picture William Wallace, who had stood on this spot before the tower was ever built, looking out at the English camp lying in the Forth's silver loops, and his ghost's cold hands reached round my back and squeezed my belly. I couldn't breathe. My legs were heavy as I reached the top, and pushed open the door onto the narrow walkway outside. The sky flew up above me, filled with stars. Ice cracked under my feet and I held onto the parapet in case I skited on the slippy surface and fell over. I was alone; alone with the bairn swimming in my womb; a featherlight touch as a foot moved, stretching, preparing for life. I looked over the edge. It was a long way down and seemed further with the cliff below. The trees clung to the rock and reached up to me, as if they would catch me if I fell. I imagined dropping into their arms; wondered if they would smile and stroke my hair, coorie me in, sing to me in their twig voices. I held onto the parapet, scared by my thoughts, and with my nail I scratched my name into the frost on the stone wall. 'I can hold on,' I said. 'I am alive.' The letters melted into the sparkling diamond sheet, black furrows on the late winter page, and then I heard the sound of the door at the bottom of the tower click open and feet tapping on the steps. They grew louder and faster as they took the measure of the tower. I looked round for somewhere to hide, but there was nowhere, so I pressed myself against the far wall, out of sight of the door. The hinge creaked as it swung open and a man coughed. 'Agnes? Are you there?'

There was a smell of cigarette smoke. I crept round the corner. Raphael was leaning on the parapet, looking out over the river at the castle. His face was in profile, his shoulders hunched like a great gargoyle.

'Raphael?' I said, wondering if I could squeeze past him, not sure if it was safe to be there with him.

'I don't normally follow ladies home,' he said, 'but since you are obviously a damsel who lives in a tower, I don't think the normal rules apply.' He laughed.

'I wanted to be alone,' I said.

'I don't think you do,' he answered, stubbing out his cigarette, adding a full stop to my name. 'I think you need a friend.'

'I have friends.'

'So why aren't you with them?' He pulled a hip flask from his pocket. 'Lemonade never did it for me.' He passed it to me. I took a sip.

'Bunnahabhain?' I said. 'The river mouth – safe harbour.'

'I'm impressed.'

I stood beside him. He traced the letters of my name with his finger. 'Last will and testament?' he asked.

'No. I don't know.'

'How old are you, Agnes?'

'Eighteen.'

'Eighteen and standing on the edge of a precipice, alone at the top of a tower in a goddamn horror of a fairy tale. Wouldn't you rather come home and get warm?'

'I don't have a home.'

'And why would that be?'

'Jeff is dead.'

'But you aren't. Wake up, Agnes. This war won't last forever. I don't know what happened to your husband, but he wouldn't want you to end your life with his, would he?'

'He didn't love me, and in the end, I didn't love him. Does that fit with your picture-book story?'

'Does it matter?'

'I thought it did.'

159

'God has a plan for you, Agnes, and I don't think it ends with freezing to death on an ice tower on a frosty night.' He put his jacket round my shoulders. 'Now let's go. The people you came with will be missing you.'

'How did you know where to find me?'

'Let's just say that the benefit of having smokes outside is that you get a chance to observe the world and all its passing strangeness. My curiosity was piqued as to why a pregnant lady would toddle off into the middle of nowhere on her own.'

'It is not the middle of nowhere.'

'Well, where is it, then? You tell me.'

I didn't answer him. The stars were tiny pinpricks of blue light behind the mist of his breath.

He held out his arm to lead me down the stairs.

'Thank you, Raphael,' I said. 'I wasn't going to jump, if that's what you were thinking.'

'Do any of us know what we are going to do before we do it?' he asked.

Mrs Ogilvie burst into tears of relief when Raphael dropped me at the farm. He refused a plate of her Eggs Benedict, just said he had to get the boys back to the servicemen's club in Edinburgh. He tooted the jeep's horn and drove off at speed. We sat by the fire, talking until the clock on the mantelpiece struck two, and decided that I should send a telegram to my mother, and go home at the beginning of the week. Mrs Ogilvie had guessed I was expecting, but hadn't wanted to say anything with Jeff so recently dead. 'A bairn isn't the end of the world, Agnes,' she said. 'They bring their own love, and you don't need to worry about the delivery. Mrs Winning at the surgery is a dab hand at hoiking them out, if you want to have it here.' But I wanted my mother.

Jim stopped work on his agricultural census and walked me to the station so I could get the train to Glasgow and on to Ayr. A newspaper seller was shouting, 'Saving stamps for bombs,' and waving a picture of Lord Alness sticking stamps on a bomb, and Jim said the Americans had beaten the Germans in Tunisia. I wasn't sure where that was, but I hoped it was a sign that the war might end soon.

Ayr seemed to be quiet like Stirling and I was glad to arrive. I was looking forward to a warm meal, but Duncan met me at the station grim-faced. I thought he was going to say something about Jeff's death, but he didn't.

'Why so sour, puss?' I said, as he took my suitcase.

'You know,' he said, putting it in the back of the cart, and lifting me up onto the seat. He flicked the reins and Polly trotted on.

'I don't know,' I said.

'The whole Hannes thing is praying on my mind.'

'Why should it? He's gone now.'

He straightened his cap. 'Someone might have seen us.'

'There was no one around.'

'What if someone did? I haven't been able to look the neighbours in the eye since it happened. Whenever anyone mentions the war effort, I feel like I betrayed them. What if he is back on the battlefield now, shooting people we know? What does that make me? I might as well have lifted the gun and shot them myself.'

'Duncan, you're being daft. Believe he was a farmer, like us.'

But as we drove past the ploughed fields, I could hardly remember what had made me take Hannes into my life. He was the figure born from the trees in the rainstorm: Mrs MacDougall's bogeyman, my childish secret against Jeff. He was my humanity and my betrayal. Now I had made my brother unhappy. The child kicked in my womb, and I put my hand over it. Duncan flicked me a look out of the corner of his eye and stared back at the road.

'Is there something you want to tell me?' he said, snapping the reins so the horse trotted on faster.

'Maybe later. Does Mother feel the same as you now?'

'I don't know. She never mentions him. Dad still thinks he was a friend of Jeff's. I don't like lies, Aggie.'

'I am sorry, Duncan,' I said, and touched his sleeve, but he didn't put an arm around my shoulder as he usually did and I knew I wasn't forgiven.

'I feel wrong inside,' he said. 'I can't bear to be with my friends when they are home on leave. Can you imagine how that sits with me? I buy them a drink and I feel like there is so much space between us that I am reaching the glass across the Irish Channel to them, the channel I took a killer across; a man who is fighting for our destruction.'

'Don't exaggerate. You didn't do anything wrong. We didn't ask to go to war. You were helping me.'

'Aye, but the price is too high. I might as well have signed up as a National Socialist.'

'He was a farmer, Duncan.'

'He is a Nazi.'

'Duncan, please.'

He looked at me. 'It is worse than you think, Ag. The Ghillie told me he had an odd story to tell, the story of a hybrid animal he saw early one morning. It had a thick, brown coat, a white head and a strange, guttural cry, and the most curious thing about it was: it was walking along the forest path with a native species, so friendly that they had touched their wee noses together. And later he had seen this animal caught in a net at the harbour, and although it was dangerous, it hadn't been killed. On the contrary, it had been set free. How could I explain a story like that, he asked, because it had left him scratching his head for many a day.'

I remembered the figure with the gun, slipping into the trees.

'You are not safe here, Ag. It was a warning.'

'He wouldn't say anything against you,' I said.

'He's not letting it drop. I buy him a drink when I see him at the bar to keep him sweet, and he raises his glass each time and says, "To the Divine Mystery of God's wonderful creation". He's a big drinker and his tongue gets looser as the evening goes on.'

'Everyone kens he's got mair wind than sense.'

'You shouldn't underestimate him. Don't you remember you turned him down the summer you met Jeff? You are free now. If you refused him again, he might try to hurt you.'

'Duncan, he is twenty years aulder than me. He got the message the first time.'

'All men think they are God's gift to women, Aggie. The face they see in the mirror is not the face you see.'

'And what about you?'

'I am not entirely unkissed. Elaine is keen to get mairrit.'

'I meant, are you safe?'

'Likely no', although he has no grudge against me. It wasn't me he proposed to, but, like I said, he talks when he drinks and he drinks when he's upset. I don't want you here, Aggie.'

'But I want to see Mother.'

'Are you sure she wants to see you?'

'What did you tell her?'

'The truth.'

I didn't know which truth he meant. He stopped the cart. 'Choose, Aggie. You can stay and remind us of your lie every day or you can go back and work in the nursery. Stop the talk before it gets going.'

'Redeem myself?'

'Aye, if you like.'

'A Land Girl growing tomatoes out of season. Do you think that is enough?'

'It will have to be.'

I took the reins from him and turned the cart. I felt like the road no longer connected me to home, but only to Duncan's anger, which smouldered in him, fed by the Ghillie's suspicions, the wireless barking on about the war, his friends' tragedies, the telegrams brought to his neighbours through silent streets. He didn't want me to stay. There was no future here. The past was getting in the way. 'Tell Mother, and Dad, I was asking for them.'

He nodded, but I knew he would just say I hadn't come after all, to spare Dad.

The road back to the station was dreich. Duncan's face was unrelenting. He never looked at me or spoke again. I think he was crying. He kept turning his face away and swallowing hard. He bought me a ticket and left me beside my bag in the waiting room. As I sat there I hated Scotland, the Scotland that had killed Jeff, imprisoned Douglas and left me alone. I'd tried to help someone from another place and she, Scotland, had stolen my family. She seemed less like a great beauty, silver rivers of hair trailing over her misty gown, and more like a hag of petrified rock. I thought of the women they had burned as witches on the dead volcano in Edinburgh, or drowned in the loch at its feet; sacrificing them on the castle rock as if their red blood could run down the cliff face into the heart of the earth and bring it back to life. I thought of the bloody quarters of Wallace's body enshrined in memory at the foot of his tower; the monument hoisting his dream up into the sky, only to smother it in cloud, or throw it up bright against the light as another folly, far above the people who still struggled below. Scotland ate her own children on winter nights as they dreamed, but each new generation still loved her. She was an unkind parent, a deceiver, a monster; she was a lover, an enchantress, a dream.

28

May and my delivery came too soon. The early summer had passed in a slow harvest of picking tomatoes. Jim only allowed me to fill small trugs as I got bigger, and finally he let me sit by the kettle with my feet up. He claimed it was only my tea that kept them all going, and the Ministry inspectors happy on their lengthy visits. I rarely put the wireless on. Hitler was fighting in Russia, and the long reports of Allied troop movements in Africa reminded me of Douglas' injured poet friend who loved the Cuillins. There were pictures in Jim's paper of Douglas, too: in a kilt, haranguing voters on Kirkcaldy High Street. He wanted to give Scotland dominion status like Canada. I folded the page over and didn't read on. I sang to the baby inside me to drown out the sound of the world, but he must have guessed it was not a good place because in the end he joined us only slowly, and it was a long, walking labour.

That first day of my pains, I wandered about the kitchen and sitting room, unable to sit down or get comfortable. It was worse overnight and I lay propped up on pillows, trying to get some sleep, but the contractions came on as a deep ache and kept waking me up. I knelt on my hands and knees, but that didn't help. Mrs Ogilvie came in and rubbed my back with camphorated oil, and Jim came in to say a Gaelic blessing. She bundled him out the door. It was midday before she sent him for Mrs Winning. The contractions were closer together now and the pain had increased. I began to cry and I wished my mother was there. By teatime, they let me hang onto the stone lintel of the mantelpiece to push down, and placed folded towels at my feet. I felt the baby's head turn a corner deep in my belly and then slide downwards. He was born at 6pm and they laid me in bed with him on my chest. He had fuzzy, blond hair and smacked his tiny lips together, casting round for my breast. I could have run up Dumyat and held him up to the stars. Mrs Winning looked at him, swaddled in his shawl, and said, 'What a wee dote. He's been here before.'

Mother never replied to my telegram telling her of little Dougie's birth. If she had winkled the whole story out of Duncan, perhaps she was afraid the Ghillie would use what he knew to press his suit, if I did go home. I no longer had the protection of my marriage. And if I refused him, he might destroy them, too, so I stayed on at Laurelhill through the long years of the war. I was the sick sheep she had isolated to protect the flock, and it made me anxious. Dougie slept in my bed, or in the bottom drawer from my dresser. I tried not to think of it as a tiny coffin when its brass handles rattled as he cried. I would snatch him up to my breast and hold him close, kissing his hair while he fed. We were alone on the raft of my bed in the chaos that tried to pull itself up the country on steel fingers. Death flew in the air and swam in the sea, and I cried for a world Dougie knew only as an illusion; the peace that stretched just as far as the fringes of his shawl, but he brought me joy as he grew.

He took his first steps on the tenth of April, 1944, holding onto my fingers. Jim put him in the wheelbarrow to celebrate and ran round the yard with Mrs O shouting, 'Slow down, before you do yourselves a mischief.' When I rescued him, he kicked his wee legs against me and shouted, 'Again, again,' and I wished there was more for him, that the laughter could be shared with my own family, too. Each inch he grew carried us further from them. We were becoming strangers to each other with every month that passed, and it made me sad, as if we could never go back to what we had. Once, I thought I saw Duncan at the end of the road to the nursery, but I couldn't be sure. He was wearing a coat I didn't recognise, and didn't turn round when I called his name. I arrived back at the farm in tears and, as he did every time I wilted, Jim announced it was time to rally the troops and took us to tea in his favourite café on the High Street, or down the Forth in his boat to Fallin. He always packed a picnic on those summer trips, and we ate fruit from the greenhouses and drank flasks of tea until we were full. We would lie in a solemn row on a blanket, like sardines in a can, and snooze until it was time to go home. 'Always row back with the tide,' Jim would say with a wink, starting the motor on the boat.

As a special treat in May, Jim gave me and Mrs Ogilvie a lift to Perth. He was off to see his supplier about onion sets and a new tomato called Jubilee that had come out the year before. He dropped us by the Tay, which flows through the centre of the town, and we walked along the river's edge to the South Inch park. The wide, green space felt fresh and welcoming with broad paths lined with benches. Mrs O spread out a rug, laid out our spice cake and sponge fingers on a tea towel, and lay back in the weak sun with a sigh. 'You would never guess there was a war on up here,' she said. 'It's like visiting the past. A summer Saturday afternoon like all the others we ever knew, and all the ones we thought we'd see, at least before that madman Hitler and his henchmen started clumping all over the place with their bloody flags.'

I looked at the solid, stone buildings surrounding our little square of blanket, our temporary heaven, and I treasured our friendship. Dougie's wee fist held onto the edge of my blouse. He made little cooing noises, like a dove, as he drank milky tea from his bottle, and his eyes followed a dog chasing a bald tennis ball.

'How are we ever to keep that darling boy safe in this madness?' asked Mrs O, turning on her side to gaze at him. Dougie tried to sit up in the basket of my crossed legs. 'Let me burp him, Agnes,' she said. 'It's the closest I am going to get to having children.'

The beautiful mask of her face smiled, but a traitor tear slid to the corner of her eye. She settled Dougie on the edge of her lap and leant him forward to rub his back in gentle circles. He closed his eyes and burped. 'Better?' she asked him, smiling down into his face and handing him a rusk.

'Mind your dress,' I said, passing her a napkin. 'There could still be handsome men in Perth, roving forestry workers in search of a wife. Sponge finger?'

She shook her head. 'Even if they form an orderly queue, once was enough for me. I have got used to being Stirling's only divorcee and anyway, after the war, if it ever ends, I can reinvent myself as a glamorous war widow. No shame in that.' She wiped Dougie's mouth. 'On the other hand, why bother hiding the truth? Everything is changing.'

'Let's hope it's for the better,' I said, lifting Dougie from her and tucking him into his pram. 'Shall we get you that cloth you fancied?'

She pulled her utility tokens out of her pocket and smiled. 'Lead on, Macduff,' she said, and we wandered over the grass to South Street. Her pleasure in the material at the haberdasher's didn't last long, and with much dark muttering about the low thread count, she selected a length of sky-blue cotton for a new dress. 'I might even get a romper suit for his majesty out of the scraps,' she said, waving a hand at Dougie, who was now fast asleep with a bubble unpopped between his lips.

There was no sign of Jim at the ILP Hall where we had arranged to meet, and after ten minutes fat raindrops began to fall from the sky, which had deepened to a battleship grey. The drops jumped off the river surface in tiny explosions of white, and water began to rush along the gutter and gurgle in the drains. Mrs O dragged me into the hall, saying, 'I am not an SNP supporter, but I certainly didn't sign up for Perth's only monsoon.'

To my horror, their annual conference was in full swing. There was the same Saltire on the table and Douglas, dressed in a kilt, was speaking from the podium, just as he did in my memory. I leant against the back wall to get out of sight, but, after taking sixpence admission and issuing us with tickets, a very kindly, old lady led us to seats in the back row. She waved her hand to get the others already seated to move along, and we sat down. Mrs O pulled the pram alongside her in the aisle. There was no escape. I slid down as far as possible in my seat. My palms were damp. 'Are you all right, Agnes?' she asked.

I sat up. 'Yes, fine.' She followed my gaze to the podium.

'Is that the famous Grant?' she asked.

I nodded.

'How fascinating,' she whispered. 'Tall.' And she raised her painted eyebrows in an arch. 'Positively larger than life.'

'Stop it,' I said, afraid the faithful might start turning round to see who was talking, and draw his attention to us.

Douglas hadn't changed. His voice was as appealing as ever.

'It does not take a genius,' he boomed, 'to realise that the only reason Scots lassies are forced to go south and work in munitions factories in England, is that the Westminster government refuses to invest in Scottish industrial infrastructure. We are not short of land on which to build, but they are short of the will with which to do it.'

The audience cheered. I felt uncannily that Jeff might be sitting next to me, a ghostly supporter rising to his feet, and I kept my eyes straight ahead, afraid to look in case I would see him. Douglas held up his hands for silence. 'And so I say to any young women affected by this, who are isolated from those they love – money, or no money – get on a train and come home. Give the ticket inspector your name and contact the Scottish National Party at our headquarters in Glasgow for assistance as soon as you can. Don't let the fear of fines or imprisonment stop you. This is a matter of principle.'

There was a murmur of approval. Someone at the side of the stage waved a bundle of leaflets. 'Well reminded,' said

Douglas. 'Leaflets on this subject, and others, are available at the back of the hall on your way out.' He took a sip of water. 'Again, dear friends, in order to break the stranglehold Westminster has on Scottish affairs, and in furtherance of our primary aim, which is self-governance, we have written to the Prime Ministers of independent states in the Commonwealth to ask them to support our cause. Has Canada been the poorer since independence from Britain in 1867? No!' he shouted into the silence. 'Ask yourself this. If the Commonwealth is a happy family of self-governing states, but Scotland is the only one without self-governance, then are we not soft in the head? Are we the saftest o' the family to continue as we are?' There was a loud cheer and someone shouted, 'Never.'

I felt the old tiredness wash over me. I thought we were already independent within the union. I wondered if they would drag a Bruce or a Wallace out onto the stage again to wave a broad sword at our neighbour England, while Germany slid across the world in an army of tanks.

'We need to find Jim, Mrs O,' I whispered.

'I'm just beginning to enjoy it,' she said. 'I'm feeling something patriotic stirring in my breast.' She gazed over at Douglas. 'Hasn't that brave man been to prison again? I saw a leaflet about it.'

'Please,' I said, and the spell was broken.

We crept out and stood under a nearby tree that still dripped with water, although the rain had passed. Everything was washed clean. Mrs O shoogled the pram. I looked up from straightening Dougie's covers to see Douglas strolling over to us. His head was bent over his pipe, which he was struggling to light.

'Agnes,' he said, 'I thought it was you. And this is?' He smiled at Mrs O, who almost dropped him a curtsey.

'This is Mrs Ogilvie. She runs Laurelhill Nursery with Jim. Mrs O, Douglas Grant.'

She reached over the pram to shake his hand. 'A pleasure to meet you.'

'What a bonny, wee soul,' Douglas said, looking at the baby, and he reached into his jacket pocket to slip some coins into the foot of the pram. 'Got to handsel the bairn with silver,' he said. 'We don't want him to be poor when he grows up.'

'Thank you, Mr Grant,' said Mrs O, with a dazzling smile.

He drew in deeply on his pipe and let the smoke out through his nose like a lazy dragon. 'Well, my apologies, ladies, but I can't stop. One of the Clydeside apprentices is up next. He has been striking against Bevin's ballot-conscription into the coalmines. It is imperialism run amok,' he said. 'Good afternoon to you, and remember to come and see us in Glasgow, Agnes.'

Mrs O was still gazing after him when Jim pulled up in his van, and tooted his horn. 'Sorry, girls,' he shouted, from the window. 'Got a flat tyre just outside Perth. All ship-shape now, thanks to a passing farmer.' He jumped out to open the door. 'Just move those leaflets over. Some SNP stuff the seedsman forced on me. Wants to know how many Scottish casualties there are in the field. All very hush-hush, according to him. Now, let's get the wee man home.' He lifted Dougie up with a kiss. 'He'll have to grow among the onions for now.'

I wish I had known then that it would only be a year until the end of the war. I danced on VE Day in May 1945 at the Miner's Institute, and remembered Raphael, who claimed he loved me in long letters. When he went missing in action just a month later, I regretted the loss of a friend, but my heart didn't stop as it had when Jeff died, or when Douglas kissed his Bella. Those scars had healed over and, if I didn't think about the past, then the future looked like a land I could inhabit. Mr Lamont told me in a letter that Douglas was looking for a new university job in Classics, but he didn't hold out much hope of success for a man imprisoned as a conscientious objector; the Scots had such long memories. A man called Bruce Watson had become the new Chairman of the SNP, but I didn't care. They belonged to a world I had left.

It was June 1946 before I received Professor Schramml's letter saying he was in Edinburgh and would like to meet the woman who had made Jeff so happy. I had rented out the flat to a man from a London company, which had advertised that it was re-establishing its provincial offices in Edinburgh, and I stayed on at Laurelhill. Anyway, I couldn't have left even if I'd wanted to because of the Standstill Order. The government was worried we would all abandon the farms and rush off to look for better wages, but I was happy where I was. My pay was going to go up to sixty shillings a week, and Jim's to eighty. Falkland Terrace seemed somehow remote, and I assumed that Mrs MacDougall had indeed kept everything in the Professor's flat ship-shape against the day he would return. 'No one should think we keep a dirty house in Scotland,' she'd once said, as she rubbed at the banister on the stair with beeswax and a duster made out of an old pair of flannel bloomers.

Mrs Ogilvie was sitting at the kitchen table cutting the flaps off a bullock's heart, and smiled to herself as I read the Professor's letter out loud. The oatmeal stuck to her fingers as she pushed it into the cavity, and sewed up the hole. The water was already boiling on the stove. She dropped the heart in, and set her timer for an hour, twisting the face on the clock forward. 'How exciting,' she said, wiping her hands on a clean dish towel, 'but I wonder if he has got the wrong end of the stick?'

'Why would you say that?' I asked.

She picked up a knife and began to scrape some potatoes, dipping the blade in cold water to rinse off the skin. 'Only that we have lived together all these years and you have never once mentioned Jeff, unless you were asked.'

'Haven't I?'

'No, Agnes. Never once. I have a good ear for these things. Call me an old romantic. I would know if you missed your husband.'

I rolled some breadcrumbs together on the table. I didn't want to look up. I squashed the doughy bread flat.

'You don't need to tell me, if you don't want to. Are you going through to Edinburgh?'

'Yes,' I sighed. 'I should look in on the tenant and see that the old place is okay.'

'You do that,' she said. 'And if ever that burden, whatever it is, gets too heavy to carry alone, then you know you can share it with me.'

'I know,' I said, and she reached out and touched my cheek with a starchy finger from the potatoes. 'That's cold,' I said, jumping up.

29

Mrs Ogilvie had decided to take wee Dougie to play with her sister's bairns while I got the train to Edinburgh. I was curious to meet the Professor, and see the flat I'd tiptoed round come to life. I took out my darning as we travelled past the still sleeping Ochils, dozing as if they had all the time in the world to stretch out a lazy hand and swat the raindrops, which bit at their necks like midges. They shrank grain by grain and were carried unnoticed into the Forth and out to sea, where they would disappear forever. They didn't care, but time was passing faster for me. I felt older since I had become a mother, strained with worry for Dougie's future without a father, although there was no shame in that as there once was. There were fatherless bairns running about all over the country, happy shadows of their lost parents; fathers blown limb from limb on the battlefield, and if their paternity was ever in doubt, not one of the mothers would admit to those snatched moments with American GIs at the dances. Every child was held up as a testament to his tragic father, no questions asked. Only the men who returned counted the dates off on their fingers over pints in the pub, and in the end they smiled drunkenly at the memory of their own snatched moments, and agreed that it was war, after all, and best not remembered too closely. At least it was life.

The pill box still stood at the West End when I walked up from Haymarket to catch the tram from outside St John's, and when the door opened on the upstairs flat that had so many memories for me, I saw that Professor Schramml had eyes as black as coal and the kindest face I had ever seen. He kissed my hand with old world style and led me into his drawing room, which had been polished until it shone. The neighbours' flats opposite were still obscured by heavy net curtains, but he had pulled his aside and fresh branches of pink blossom stood on a carved table in the window.

'I am glad to meet you, Professor,' I said. 'Jeff was gey fond o' you. He told me how you used to put the world to rights as you walked to work.' I had put away the bitterness. I wasn't that lassie any more.

'I must offer you my most sincere condolences,' he said. 'It was an agony to me to hear of his suffering from Sylvia and be so far away in Geneva. You must have been very upset.'

'Aye, it was a difficult time,' I replied, as honestly as I could.

He patted my hand and poured me a glass of cherry brandy. 'A little schnapps?' he asked.

The glass was like a giant's thimble. He drained it in one with a shout of '*Prosit!*' and waited for me to do the same. I took a sip and then, as he gestured to me to up-end the glass, I drank it down. The clear liquid bit at the back of my throat as if it could burn away the lie of the last days of my marriage to Jeff. He refilled the glasses. 'What would Mrs MacDougall say, Professor?' I said. 'It is only two in the afternoon.'

'That dear lady believes I can do no wrong. Is it any wonder that I am forced to seek refuge from my angelic reputation in a little earthly pleasure?'

I laughed, drained the second glass too fast, and choked. 'Coffee?' he asked.

I nodded. He brought through a little, silver percolator with two wee china cups and a jug of cream. 'It is *wunderschön* to be reunited with my possessions,' he said. 'I missed them, but my time away was a small sacrifice compared to those others made.'

'I have a confession, Professor,' I said. 'I am sorry I borrowed your dictionary and lost it.'

'And why would you have need of a German dictionary in Scotland? Did you think the defences wouldn't hold?'

I didn't know what to say. I hadn't told anyone about Hannes. He had cost me dear. 'I borrowed it to help someone, a friend.'

'A friend?'

'Someone who became a friend to me when I needed one.'

'Indeed.' He smiled and passed me a small plate of biscuits. They were shaped like crescent moons. 'Ein Kipferl?' he asked.

They were sweet and buttery. 'My late wife taught me how to make these when we were courting. I feigned interest in home baking to see her lick the mixture from her fingers, and hoped to wipe the flour from her nose. There is no limit to what a man will do for love, or the price he might have to pay.'

He tapped his waistline and pinged the elastic of his red braces. 'I dare say Mrs MacDougall's stair cleaning rota, which she delights in enforcing, will soon have me trim again.' He put a biscuit in his mouth and chewed. 'I really don't see why we can't pay someone to do it.'

'Hadn't you noticed there was a war on, Professor?'

He laughed. 'If I closed my eyes, I could believe the dear lady was standing before me,' he said. 'You are quite a mimic.'

'I believe she has high hopes of your skill with a duster.'

'I like to make an effort for my neighbours,' he said, and looked at me with his head on one side. 'You are very beautiful, Agnes.'

I blushed.

'I can see why you would be well loved.' He stood up. 'More coffee?'

At that moment, I heard a key in the door. The Professor walked into the hall. '*Grüss Dich*,' he said in his warm voice. '*Schöner Spaziergang? Unser Gast ist schon angekommen.*'

It was strange to hear German in the flat. A picture of Hannes lying injured in bed flashed before my eyes, and then Professor Schramml came back into the room, followed by a man holding a coat over his arm. 'There is someone I would like you to meet,' he said, and stepped aside.

The man behind him was tall and dressed in a navy-blue suit. His brown eyes looked earnestly into mine and he held out his hand. It was Hannes. My hand shook as I took his and he bowed over it. There were tears in his eyes when he straightened up. He took a handkerchief from his pocket and passed it to me. I dabbed my eyes. I felt like I was seeing him for the first time, as if I could look at him and not be letting anyone down. I felt shy.

'Surprise, no?' said the Professor, like a child who had arranged a Christmas present in secret and hidden it behind the tree.

Hannes sat in the seat opposite me and stretched out his long legs. I had never seen him at ease before. He had been taut with fear, trapped as I had been. Now he was himself. I blew my nose again.

'Oh, it is too much of a shock,' said the Professor in dismay. 'If only my wife had been here, she would have known what to do.'

'I wanted to thank you,' said Hannes, in slow English, looking straight at me.

'Yes, he wrote to me. A most expressive letter telling all about the *kleine Schottin* who saved him, like a Flora MacDonald, although he was not a prince. Perhaps you believed him unworthy of your kindness? How could you know the true man? He was a Nazi then, as most were, but you must believe he didn't choose it.'

'Were you a Nazi?' I asked.

'I was a Messerschmitt test pilot.'

'Not a very good one,' I said.

He looked more hopeful, and stopped twisting the watch on his wrist.

'Ah, the *wunderbares* Scottish sense of humour,' said the Professor. 'I have missed it. But all joking aside, this man only just survived the war himself.'

I looked at Hannes. He was very thin.

'I was captured in Russia,' he said, and his hand shook as he reached for the cup Professor Schramml had placed in front of him.

'Yes, he weighed just seven stone when they released him. He was lucky to get out at all.'

'So you didn't get back to your farm from Ireland?'

'I tried, but they came for me and said the land would be confiscated if I didn't fly again. They didn't want to lose one of their pilots. We were only just mastering the machines. They were too fast to control at first.' He put the cup back on the table. 'I am ashamed now, Agnes. Bad things happened that I couldn't stop. Maybe you don't want to speak to me? Can you forgive me?'

'I am happy to see you,' I said.

He looked less uneasy and moved forward on his seat.

'You see,' shouted the Professor. 'I told you not to worry. He wrote to me and apologised for using my flat during my exile. I had to meet the man who was rescued by the good fairy downstairs and, of course, I wanted to meet you, my dear.' He poured another round of schnapps. '*Slainte mhath*,' he said. 'Down the hatch. If only Jeff could be here.'

I exchanged a look with Hannes. He had spared the Professor the story of Jeff's breakdown before going to prison; the day my husband stopped being a friend to me. Hannes' hand twitched, as if he wanted to reach out to me. I wanted to hold his strong fingers and sit in silence with him. Professor Schramml stood up. 'Perhaps I should leave you two alone. After all, I am new to you both and you are old acquaintances. I shall go down and discuss the finer details of stair cleaning with my mentor, Mrs MacDougall, and come back a better man.'

Hannes moved onto the sofa with me and we sat awkwardly together. 'Would you like to walk?' I asked.

He nodded and stood up before following me out. I led him up onto the Blackford Hill and we stood at the top looking out over the Forth estuary. He turned round to look at the Pentlands and rubbed his forehead. I wondered where his plane had come down.

'Do you remember the accident?' I asked. The hills were folded like meringue, tinged brown.

He shook his head. 'I only remember waking up in bed and seeing Mrs MacDougall with a pair of scissors. I thought she was going to kill me, but then she cut off my clothes.'

'She was probably planning to eat you.'

'Then it was lucky for me that you were there.'

He took my hand. 'Schramml told me that Jeff died. Were you friends again after... that night?'

I shook my head and looked out over the hills. A red kite hovered over the golf course.

'*Mein aufrichtiges Beileid*.' He paused. 'My deepest sympathy. Agnes, my English isn't very good. I learned it so I could speak to you one day; to say thank you.'

'There's no need. You saved me, Hannes. I had a debt to pay. Call it fate. I had been thinking of sending you to the hospital, and you would have ended up in a POW camp.'

'Perhaps that might have been better. I could have been near you.'

'You were married.'

'No. I wasn't.'

'But what about Liesl?'

'My niece.' He smiled. 'I thought you might be less scared of me if you thought I was married.'

'You could hardly walk. Why would I be scared of a man armed only with a nightshirt?'

He laughed and pulled me closer. '*Du bist immer noch meine kleine Zauberin*.'

'Please don't talk German.' I looked over my shoulder, but the nearest person was on the way down the hill, calling to their dog, which ran in and out of the yellow gorse.

'I am sorry. You enchant me.'

'There's still a lot of bad feeling,' I said.

'It was a long war. Do you hate me?'

'No. I don't hate you.'

'But you hate Germany? Austria?'

'No. I don't understand them.'

'It was a bad dream,' he said. 'We didn't wake up in time.'

I put my finger over his lips. 'We are at peace now,' I said. I wondered if I would have felt the same if any of my family had been killed at the Front. I couldn't work out when the man became the nation, and the nation became the man. It was chance which side we were born on. What choice did we have?

He held my hand as we walked down the hill, over the springy turf nibbled short by rabbits. The sun turned the Forth turquoise near the Isle of May, and Arthur's Seat rose up above the red cliff face of the Salisbury Crags. He asked me the names of everything as we walked, and I was free to tell him. I let go of his hand as we reached the street. Mrs MacDougall might be watching, or we might be seen by Mrs Black, if she was still alive. I didn't want to upset them. Professor Schramml still wasn't back when we got in. The clock on the mantelpiece chimed five, and I had to go to the station to get the train. 'Where can I find you, Agnes?' he asked. 'I wrote my address in the dictionary. I hoped you might contact me after the war.'

'My mother burnt the dictionary.'

'Was she very angry? Was Duncan?'

'They still won't talk to me.'

'You are alone?'

'No. I have friends in Stirling.'

'Is that far away?'

'No, not far.'

'I have to go back to Vienna tomorrow, to Neustift. I got a short pass. They still don't trust us.'

'Well, you can't blame them.'

'Can I write to you?'

I pulled on my gloves and looked up. We were both reflected in the mirror. 'Yes. Professor Schramml has my address.'

He kissed my hand. '*Auf Wiedersehen*. Until we meet again.'

'Goodbye, Hannes.'

He helped me into my coat in the hall and his fingers brushed my neck, but I opened the front door without turning round. He watched me walk down the spiral stairs. Professor Schramml came out of Mrs MacDougall's flat, straightening his tie. 'She is very strict with me,' he said, and laughed, before kissing me on both cheeks. 'We will meet again very soon,' he said. 'You can talk to me of my dear friend, Jeff.'

I had almost reached the end of Canaan Lane when I heard feet running behind me. I paused and looked back. The shrubs were the same as all those years ago, reaching over the wall with twisted fingers full of flowers. 'Agnes, Agnes,' Hannes was calling. He was running like the wind. 'Mrs MacDougall said you had a child. You never told me.'

He gripped my arms. 'Is it a boy? A *Mädchen*... a girl?'

'Let me go. It is a boy. Called Dougie, after Douglas Grant.'

'Who is Douglas Grant?'

'He was Chairman of the SNP during the war. The Scottish Nationalist Party. Jeff was a member, but don't ask me about that time. I don't want to remember it. I didn't even go to see my tenant today. Goodbye, Hannes. I have to catch my train.' I held out my hand, but he took it in both of his. I pulled it away. 'Don't ask me any more questions.'

'*Bitte*,' he said. 'Please speak to me, Agnes.'

I turned away. I was embarrassed. I walked the last stretch to Morningside Road without looking back. A man was leaning against a bin with a half-bottle of whisky balanced on it. 'I am waiting for friend gull to have a word,' he said, and pointed to the sky.

I nodded and walked faster. I didn't know what I wanted. I liked being on my own with my child. I had work and I had friends. Sylvia had promised to come in her motor and take us to the Fairy Hill near Aberfoyle on Sunday. My life was laid out, under my control. The country was staggering to its feet after the war and one day I thought I could make peace with my

181

family. Douglas was still fighting to get land for returning ex-soldiers, but I saw his face in the newspaper without feeling pain now. He was shaking the country, trying to bend it to his will, without realising that it probably never would. It never did what was expected. It never had. He was the dancing bear of nationalism. Everyone would come out to see him and be entertained, but they would go home with no intention of setting him free.

30

Sylvia drove like the wind, as fast as ever, along the twisting roads from Stirling to Aberfoyle. Wee Dougie was in the back, singing, 'We're going to see the fairies, we're going to see the fairies,' until Sylvia told him it was a secret. She stopped the car on the ridge above the town. The Doune Hill lay like an emerald in the middle of a basin of hills. She picked Dougie up. 'Perhaps we'll see the fairy queen,' she said, and she winked at me. 'You'll like this, Agnes. The story isn't on the scale of the classics, of course, but an interesting study nonetheless.'

She unscrewed the lid of her thermos and poured us all a cup of milky tea. 'They say the local minister, Robert Kirk, was trapped in the tree at the top of the hill by the Gentle Folk, after he failed to return from his daily constitutional. He had abandoned his ministerial studies to write about the fairies, so he was certainly less than conventional – another one swimming against the flow – but whether that contributed to his disappearance is anyone's guess. Politics and folklore, a potent combination, as old as bread and wine.'

Dougie looked at her with wide eyes over the lip of his cup. 'I don't want to go now,' he said.

'But you can make a wish, darling,' said Sylvia. 'They like children.'

She moved the thermos from the roof of the car, and we drove down into the valley. We parked behind the main street of the village and walked towards the hill, which rose straight up from the valley floor. It was covered in trees. A path wound up through the birches. The grass looked softer and greener than in the fields, and patches of sunlight made pools of light on the ground. 'Perfect picnic spots,' said Sylvia, 'just perfect.'

Dougie ran on ahead, jumping over the tree roots that criss-crossed the path, and disappeared up the ladder they made, as if the hill had interlaced its fingers to help his wee feet climb the slope. He ran out of sight. 'Stop at the top,' I shouted. 'There isn't a drop on the other side, is there?' I asked Sylvia.

'Don't worry,' she said, taking my hand. 'He's perfectly safe. Let's enjoy the peace and quiet. I never get you to myself these days. The department is coming back to life. Lots of new faces as the men return, and more students than I can handle. They all seem to think they are classicists just because they sailed past Crete in a warship.'

Dougie was running round and round the tree at the top, not widdershins, thank goodness. It was covered in colourful scraps of cloth torn from people's clothes. Silver sixpences had been pressed into the bark, and scraps of paper were tied on with ribbon or string. Each one was a wish. Some were prayers for the safe return of men abroad.

'Do you think they came back?' I asked Sylvia.

She picked up a tiny doll from the foot of the tree. 'Well, I expect it gave them hope that they might. That is a kind of mercy,' she said. She laid the doll back down and patted its hair into place. 'Curious, isn't it? All this mishmash feels sacred.'

Dougie was jumping up and down, trying to catch a silver ribbon that was twisting in the breeze. 'I want it, Mum,' he shouted.

'You can't peel a fairy hill,' said Sylvia. 'Just leave it or you might get into trouble with the pixies.'

'What would the classicists think of your poor man's superstition?' I said. 'I thought you were a university rationalist, heart and soul?

'University of life, my dear, first and foremost. Don't disallow any possibility until it has been fully examined.'

'So what do you think happened to the good minister?'

'No one knows. He was a most respected Gaelic scholar and the author of a remarkable book for its time, *The Secret Commonwealth of Elves, Fauns and Fairies*. According to him, they were a notable community known to those with second sight. He interviewed enough people locally who believed in it. He had a most questioning mind, but how it sat with the Church, I am not so sure.'

'I'm glad I never had second sight,' I said. 'I might never have married Jeff.'

'I thought you loved him?' She looked at me over her glasses.

'I did. For a while.'

'And then the SNP reared its ugly head.'

'No. It wasn't that.'

'The war, then? That made it difficult for everyone, especially the objectors. If only Jeff hadn't stuck his head above the parapet, stayed safe behind a desk. I never really understood. It wasn't the time for flag-waving and posturing.'

'I think he was fair taken with independence, with Douglas, with his dream, but nationalism isn't glorious. It is a club that pens its members and leaves others to the wolves.'

'Oh, my dear,' she said, holding me close. 'No one could have known it would end so badly. The smallpox was an unforeseen misfortune.'

She smoothed my hair as she had for the doll. 'It must be very difficult for you on your own, but at least you have me and your wee Dougie. Our Douglas is still banging about the country. He never gives up: hydroelectric power, mines, the question of ownership, crofts for servicemen, dead herring. A genuine political animal and… talking of animals…' She looked round. 'Where is that boy of yours?'

The glade was empty. The ribbons fluttered in the breeze and the sun glinted on the silver in the bark of the tree, like teeth.

'Dougie? Dougie?' I called, but there was no answer. I ran towards the path and called again, scrambling down as fast as I could. I only caught sight of him at the second turn. He was holding some grass out to a squirrel.

'You aren't to wander,' I said. The beastie ran off and chattered at us from halfway up a tree.

'This is a braw place, Mum. That squirrel's my friend.'

I sat down beside him and held him close. I could feel his skinny arms and bony chest through my dress. We leant together. I think I was smiling with my eyes closed, and that is when Sylvia took our photo: Dougie, smiling up at her, and stretching out his hand to her Box Brownie. 'To happy reunions,' she said.

We walked back down the hill, retracing our footsteps, the pebbles on the path sliding under our feet. The Reverend Kirk's old church stood on the other side of a marshy field, and we wandered over to the ruin and brushed the moss from his gravestone. They say he doesn't lie here under this impressive memorial to his scholarly work. Never found, as I told you,' said Sylvia. 'Spooky,' and she stretched the word out and waggled her fingers at Dougie, who screamed and ran off. 'Grave robbers were a huge problem, of course. I believe there was a good stock in trade of bodies for curious academics in Edinburgh. The university has a lot to answer for, in its way,' she said. 'Intellectual curiosity running amok.'

Two huge lead weights in the shape of coffins lay by the derelict church door. 'Even those couldn't stop the thefts,' she said, waving a hand at them. I thought of them pressing down on the graves, sealing the dead in the ground.

'I don't like it here, Mum,' said Dougie, coming back and taking my hand. 'I'm hungry.'

We walked back to the village over an arched stone bridge and had a plate of mince and tatties in a wee café on the high street. China models of fairies crowded the windowsills, look-ing out towards the hill.

'Sitting here, it is almost as if the war never happened,' said Sylvia, but I remembered the wishes at the top of the sacred place, the wind carrying the longing on its breath. The fear, the loss and the hope still lived there.

31

The rest of 1946 passed slowly. There were still shortages, but gradually all the men who had survived began to return to their families, and things improved. The prisoners of war were last. Germany was divided and it seemed like the ogre was dead; hung, drawn and quartered; Hitler stuck in his craw like a bitter pill.

Dougie helped in the greenhouses, or thought he did, and Jim read him long stories by the fire on the dark winter evenings. I had my own cottage on the end of a white-painted row. Sylvia's Christmas card came early, as it did every year, and behind the picture of a happy Santa she wrote, 'Expect a visitor. That old rascal Schramml stole my picture of you from my desk to send to a mutual friend of yours. All very mysterious. He swears he will return it, but, if not, at least I have the comfort of knowing you have your own copy. It was a very happy day at Aberfoyle. I wonder if the fairies will grant our wishes. I can't say they are very efficient, but then maybe time isn't as pressing, if you are eternal.'

I looked towards the door, as if I would hear footsteps in that instant, but there was only the sound of the wind. Hannes arrived a fortnight later at the nursery. Mrs Ogilvie had him seated by the fire when I got to the farmhouse, and just as he stood up to greet me, she remembered something that needed urgent attention next door in the kitchen.

'I thought you wanted to leave Scotland,' I said to him, 'but after all the trouble I went to, you keep coming back.'

'I have a good reason to come back, Agnes,' he said, taking my hand, and kissing me on both cheeks.

'I fear you are mistaken,' I said, sounding more like Sylvia than myself.

'There is no mistake.' He pulled a picture of Dougie from his pocket, but there was something wrong. It was an old photo of a boy among vines and there was a white church with a red-tiled roof in the background. 'This is a picture of me as a boy, Agnes.' He handed me Sylvia's photo of me and Dougie at the Doune Hill. 'And this is a picture of my son. Why didn't you tell me?'

'I wasn't sure,' I said.

He raised an eyebrow.

'You can't pretend the war didn't happen. They play Tommies and Jerries at playtime in the school. I thought it would be simpler if he grew up thinking he had a Scottish father. I don't want to lose his love. It is all I have.'

'I am his father,' said Hannes, holding out his arms. 'You can both have me.'

'How could you live here? How could he love you?'

'He could get to know me. I could love him, as you do.'

'It's too difficult.'

'When did you ever let that stop you, Agnes Thorne?'

'Don't laugh, it cost me enough. I am twenty-two now.' I sat down to put some distance between us.

'And it is nearly 1947. Time is moving on. We can make something new for ourselves.'

'What's new?' said Dougie, coming into the room with a biscuit from Mrs Ogilvie.

I looked at Hannes, who had fallen silent and was staring at the wee figure in the doorway.

'Come here and shake hands, Dougie,' I said, but he climbed on my knee and hid his face. 'Do you remember I told you a long time ago that I had a friend who once helped me very much, and that he was an Austrian called Hannes?'

Dougie nodded.

'This is Hannes.'

Dougie picked a raisin out of the biscuit and ate it. 'Is he a Jerry?' he asked.

'Just listen. And do you remember I told you how I helped him to escape on Uncle Duncan's boat. In those days, we were fighting the Germans and Austrians, but I didn't want him to get hurt because he had helped me?'

Dougie nodded again with big eyes.

'Well, the story I told you was not complete. There was silence in it.'

'What do you mean, Mum?'

'The silence is the thing I didn't tell you. The thing I couldn't tell anyone, and I had to keep quiet about it for a long time.'

'About what?'

'About you.' He looked at me with his father's eyes.

'I need to tell you something very important. Do you remember when I told you how angry your uncle Duncan was when he heard Hannes talking in German in his sleep?' I paused, and took his hand.

'Yes,' he said.

'Well, he wasn't talking in his sleep. He was talking to me.'

'I don't understand, Mum.'

'We spent the night together. Dougie, he is your father.'

'Yuk,' he shouted, jumping off my knee. 'I don't like kissing stories.' Then he shouted, 'And I don't want a German dad. I'm Dougie McCaffrey.'

Hannes got to his feet to leave. 'He needs time,' he said.

I reached out for his arm as he passed.

'Just wait.' I walked over to my wee boy and crouched down. 'We don't pick our parents, Dougie,' I said. 'They are who they are. And we don't pick when or where we're born. It just happens. Do you think you could get to know Hannes because he's special to me?'

Dougie took my face in both his hands, then looked at Hannes, who smiled at him with so much love that, for the first time, I had hope. Mrs MacDougall might have said, 'Blessed are the peacemakers,' or, 'There are many mansions in my Father's kingdom,' or just, 'It's past laughing once the heid's aff,' but then she was probably cleaning the stair, or having another word with Professor Schramml.

I put a log on the fire. When I looked up, Hannes had seated himself at the piano and raised the lid. It had been closed for a long time. The first notes of some Mozart sounded, perhaps it was Wiegenlied, which Jeff used to play. Perhaps it was something else. Dougie was leaning on the edge of the piano. When he lifted his hand to move closer to Hannes, his wee fingers left prints in the dust. Hannes looked round over his shoulder, grinned at me and said in Mrs MacDougall's voice, 'Agnes, would you look at this dust? Standards are slipping.'

We both laughed. I knew then that the future lay somewhere in that laughter, not in the past, and if we could find the seed and nurture it, then all might be well. I could teach my son a new song.

32

I lay awake that night in my cottage, knowing that Hannes was sleeping just up the road. Our child made us a family and yet I realised I hardly knew the man who wanted to spend the rest of his life with me. His enthusiasm had swept me off my feet. I got up for breakfast early and walked over to the greenhouses to check that the frost hadn't shattered any of the glass overnight. Hannes was standing in the first one, only just visible through the panes, like a spectre. He turned and trailed his hands over the bare earth, walking the length of the green house and closing the door behind him. He strode up to the farmhouse and, knocking on the door, opened it and disappeared into the light. Perhaps he hadn't been able to sleep, either.

After filling us up with porridge, Mrs Ogilvie waved us off to the castle. 'Keep a calm sough,' she whispered to me as she adjusted the scarf at my neck and stashed three pieces of shortbread, wrapped in greaseproof paper, in my pocket. 'He's lovely,' she said, and I saw her best glasses standing by the sink, and a bottle of single malt with a wheen less whisky in it than it had had the night before. 'He has Jim's seal of approval, too,' she added.

'Is the Hannes man coming with us, Mum?' asked Dougie, and his breath cloaked his wee, red lips. I nodded. He ran off down the path to the main road, and we walked past the King's

Park, then the library and up to the castle. As we came out onto the esplanade, Hannes drew in his breath in admiration. The Carse lay far below us, stretching out to the west, and a toy bridge crossed the river to Causewayside, where the Wallace Monument rose up on its ridge. Hannes lifted Dougie into his arms and, pointing at the tower above its canopy of skeleton trees, asked him what it was. Dougie could have closed it in his wee fist like a stick of rock, and sooked it to a point. 'What's that again, Mum?' he asked.

Hannes raised an eyebrow and smiled.

'The Wallace Monument,' I said. 'Wallace stood there and…"

'Defeated the English,' said Hannes, 'which is more than we did.'

'You fought the Scots, as well,' I said. I didn't know why it suddenly felt like it mattered.

'I forgot,' he answered. 'You seem different.'

'Let's not talk about it,' I replied. 'Anyway, Jim says if the English had crossed the abbey ford at Cambuskenneth over there, and galloped along the far bank, they could have overwhelmed Wallace's army with sheer force of numbers on open land, and taken the ridge. But either they didn't know about the crossing, or they thought Stirling Bridge would be quicker.'

'One wrong turn,' said Hannes, 'and the battle is lost before it has begun. It was lucky for you that Hitler didn't cross the Channel before he turned east for Russia. Maybe I would be wearing the trousers, then.'

'Not up here,' I said.

He looked puzzled.

'We wear kilts.'

He laughed, but it was a poor joke. Without warning, a picture of Douglas in his kilt in the King's Park slipped into my memory, like a piece of paper pulled from a dusty book – a fragment of a different time, old and worn. 'Let's go and see if we can get in. All this ancient history is making me gloomy.'

There was an old man walking his dog just outside the gate. 'Aye, just go in,' he said, as I pointed to it. 'No one is bothered.'

'Don't we have to pay?' asked Hannes.

'You can pay me, if you want,' he said. 'This dog costs enough to keep.' And he turned away, laughing. 'Eats more than the wife. Just ask that soldier over there. He'll show you round. Say old Tam sent you.'

'Agnes, it's still a barracks,' whispered Hannes, taking my arm, but the soldier was walking towards us. Hannes straightened his back.

'We're not at war now,' I whispered to him.

'Who's not at war?' said the soldier. 'Some of the boys are over in Palestine, although I'd wager they are lounging in the sand while we freeze our... while we freeze up here in our eyrie.' He looked at Hannes. 'Where are you folks from?'

'I'm from Laurelhill,' said Dougie, taking the soldier's hand.

'Come with me, then, and I'll show you where you can go and which bits to avoid. Don't want you blowing yourselves to kingdom come on the ammo,' he said. 'Unfortunately, you can only see King James' palace from the outside, but feel free to wander round the garden and the battlements.'

He put Dougie in the front seat of a military car that was painted green. He blew the horn and Hannes jumped. 'Don't scare your pa now, young man,' said the soldier, and he looked at Hannes sympathetically. 'Saw service, did you? I only just made it back from Dunkirk. Took me a bit to get over it, I can tell you, but Goldie over there just strolled out of Stalag 9 in Thuringia in his overalls. Romped in, as grand as you please, after a picnic in Belgium.' He paused.

Hannes looked him straight in the eye. 'I am Austrian,' he said. 'I was a pilot.'

The soldier swallowed. Dougie was wobbling the gear stick from side to side and making engine noises. 'Just a minute, son,' said the soldier, reaching back with a hand to shoosh him. The two men stared at each other. 'Well, we're all Jock Tamson's bairns – noo, anyway,' said the soldier. 'At least that bastard Hitler is dead.' His gaze switched to me. 'Sorry, Miss.'

'Thank you,' said Hannes, and tried to smile. The soldier reached out his hand and touched Hannes' sleeve. 'Come up here one night and we'll talk it over. Wouldn't mind hearing about it from the other side.' There were tears in both men's eyes. The soldier coughed and turned away adjusting his Glengarry. 'Enjoy the view,' he said. 'No rush.'

Hannes walked across the garden and climbed up a narrow flight of stairs cut into the old stone wall to the battlement. I picked Dougie out of the truck and ran after him, sliding on the frozen grass. Hannes was looking out across the King's Knot to the park. The old formal garden lay neglected below the cliff. 'A courtier once jumped off here on home-made wings for a bet,' I said.

'Did he win?' asked Hannes.

'No,' I said.

'You shouldn't have brought me here,' he said. 'There is a whole Highland regiment.'

'I thought you'd like the view. There isn't much else to do round here, especially in winter.'

'It's easier to talk about old battles,' he said. 'We should have gone to the monument.' He took my hand and kissed it. 'Where shall we live, *Schatzi*? Do you have the courage to try Neustift?'

The thought hadn't occurred to me. Me and Dougie were happy here.

'What would I do in Austria?'

'We could run the farm. You should see the vines. I have a bottle of Riesling in my bag for you. My family have been making wine for years. You'd like it.'

'Can you really see me pressing grapes with my cold blue feet?'

'Yes,' he said. 'We could call it a new vintage.'

'And if you stayed here?'

'There is a difference between winning and losing, Agnes. It's how it makes you feel inside.'

'Professor Schramml is happy here.'

'Yes, but he never fought.' Hannes looked down at the courtyard. A truck roared out of the gate. 'There was an order to National Socialism. No one was hungry under Hitler, but I was never a Nazi at heart. That was something different. That had its own power, but I am tarred with its brush. I wasn't brave enough to stand against it. It was easier to say yes. The ones who went to prison didn't come back. So here I am, defeated fighting for something that I stopped believing in, and I feel like a fool. They call me a Jerry here. I am not even German.'

'Blame the Anschluss?'

He looked up. 'Well, we voted for it – but where did you get a word like that?'

'Let's just say I heard it a long time ago, in another world.'

He took my hands and blew on them. '*Ich friere.* It's freezing up here. This wind could blow away all a man's past misdeeds and leave him stripped to the bone.'

'Bare naked?'

He pulled me close. 'Bare naked. Ready to begin again.'

33

The next day, there was no sign of Hannes as I helped Mrs O to wash the breakfast dishes. I kept picturing the Vienna Hannes had described to Jim over tea; the conquerors living the high life in a city filled with flags: Russian, French, American and British. He said the Austrians had painted out the swastikas with red and white paint to make new flags for themselves. They didn't have any new cloth, and everyone scrambled on the black market for food. I dried the last cup so slowly that Mrs Ogilvie whipped the tea towel out of my hand and said in her sternest voice, 'Since when were you a shy and retiring violet, Agnes? You can't hide in here forever. Go and find him.'

I hung my pinny on the back of the kitchen door and walked out into the frozen yard in my wellies, which were warm from drying by the range. It was quiet, and my breath froze in the frosty morning air. I heard laughter from the barn. Hannes was there sawing some old wood into lengths, and Dougie was lining them up by the sawhorse. Hannes' sleeves were rolled up and he smiled when he saw me.

'We're mending the sledge, Mum,' yelled Dougie, running round in a circle. 'Eine Rodel, a sledge,' he shouted. Jim appeared with a roll of old roofing lead for the runners and said he hoped Hannes was going to do a professional job.

'Pass me the nails, please, Agnes,' Hannes said, adding the last piece of wood to the pile at his feet. I handed him the tin. 'Thank you,' he said.

He still sounded a bit like a textbook, but he looked happy to be doing something practical. There was a thin, white line on his temple from the crash all those years ago. I ran my finger along it and he caught my hand and kissed it. 'A memory of you,' he said.

'Well, if love is a thin, white line,' Jim said, laughing at him, 'you have definitely crossed it.'

I blushed.

'I think I am probably superfluous to requirements,' Jim added, wandering off towards the greenhouses to read his seed catalogues.

'I don't understand what he says,' said Hannes.

'It's all hot air,' I said. 'Pay no attention.'

He shrugged. 'It is so good to see you again. To be here with you – and Dougie.'

I squeezed his hand, not sure what to say to this loving stranger, not sure what to say about his suggestion of yesterday.

'Mum.' Dougie pulled at my jacket and passed me a piece of wood. I held the skeleton sides of the sledge up while Hannes nailed on the cross pieces. He pressed the soft lead onto the runners and secured it.

After a bowl of soup and some stewed ox cheek to warm up, we set off for the King's Park. Dougie rode on Hannes' shoulders, singing 'Doctor Carrot' and 'Potato Pete', and I pulled the sledge. When we got there, it had begun to snow, and most people were heading home. Hannes set the sledge at the top of the nearest slope and put Dougie in front of him. He shouted, '*Eins, zwei, drei.* One, two, three,' and pushed off with his feet. They disappeared into the swirling snowflakes, as if they had been swallowed. I could hear them laughing behind the white wall, and I realised that I wanted to be with them. I was tired of being alone. I ran down the slope to join them, and Hannes caught me and spun me round like a child, as if we were rewinding our lives, setting the clock to a new time. Then he set me down on my feet, and kissed me on my forehead in that cold, blank world where the castle sailed on a cloud above us.

'No kissing,' shouted Dougie. 'Sledging.' And he pulled the sledge back up the hill, the snow brushing the top of his wee wellies. 'All do it,' he said as he turned the sledge. We all squeezed on. Hannes' strong arms slid round my waist and we pushed off, but there was so little room for the three of us that he fell backwards into the snow, with a laugh. It was merry like Duncan's. I saw him running to catch up, and throwing himself at full speed onto his belly, he slid past us and beat us to the bottom. I liked this new man, this playmate, and we snowballed and sledged until we could no longer feel our toes. He carried Dougie home, with his arm around me in the dark.

'How was it?' said Mrs O as we tramped into the kitchen. 'You must be frozen.'

'It was good,' said Hannes.

And I realised it was good. It was the kind of day that stood up brighter in my mind than all the others before it, and shielded me from the sad days that had gone before. This man was building walls against my past, a place to shelter and to grow, a place where there was a father for my child. But I was afraid, too. Neither of us mentioned that, on the way home, a boy had shot at us from a hedge with a toy gun, blowing machine gun noises through lips sticky with sweets. Dougie had formed his wee hand into a pistol and shot back from his father's arms. It would be a long time before people forgot, before the names on war memorials became unknown grandfathers, and ceased to be much-loved fathers, brothers and sons, whose touch was remembered. And towering over us was the Wallace Monument, its shadow testament to the Scots' long memory for martyrs. It was all so confusing. Dougie stood here. Whatever love was, it had triumphed in him, created a new generation, overridden history in an instant and taken a place in a new order. It was independent of us all, crossing battle lines on the glance of an eye, the answering twitch of a lip. Love was the traitor who always won, creating her own foot soldiers from stolen moments and filling the silence between the guns.

Glossary

Scots words and phrases

An Cuilithionn: title of a Sorley Maclean poem about the Cuillins mountain range on the Isle of Skye

auld: old

away and boil yer heid: stop talking nonsense (evokes a picture of sheep's head being boiled for broth)

aye: yes

back green: shared communal garden

bairn: child (as in the German verb *gebären*, to give birth)

banter: light-hearted chat, trying to outdo each other's jokes

Barlinnie: a Glasgow prison

(the) belt: a leather strap, used in schools in place of the cane until the 1970s, also called a 'tawse'

bicker: argue

birl round: spin round

blether: chat

boak: be sick, vomit

boggle: frightening apparition, bogeyman

bonny: pretty

brambles: blackberries

braw: good

Bunnahabhain: 'River-mouth' (Safe Harbour), a single malt whisky

burn: stream

cauld: cold

chanty: chamber pot

(to) chap on the door: knock on the door

china knick-knacks: assorted, small china ornaments

conchy: a conscientious objector

coorie up: cuddle up

coo: cow (as in the German *Kuh*)

crabbit: cross, angry

craw: crow (also throat, as in 'stuck in his craw' – stuck in his throat)

dinnae fash yersel': don't upset yourself (as in the French reflexive verb *se facher*)

do: special event/party

doddle: walk slowly

dote: a darling, a baby to dote on

dreich: grey and dull (weather)

drookit: soaking wet

dunderhead/dunderheid: fool

dwam: dream

face like a soor ploom: face like a sour plum, an unhappy expression with sucked-in cheeks as if eating something bitter

fankle: tangled up

fantoosh: fancy

feart: afraid. Also, afeart: afraid of

First Foot: the first visitor of the New Year, usually just after the bells have rung at midnight. It is considered especially lucky if they are tall, dark and handsome. It is traditional to bring a piece of coal to put on the fire for luck

fly cup: an extra cup of tea, not at a recognised time for drinking tea, such as mid-morning or mid-afternoon

folk: people (as in the German *Volk*, although it implies a sense of nationhood in German)

foostie: stale or dusty, usually applied to stale clothes or stale air in a house

gaun: going (as in the German *gehen*)

Gentle Folk: fairies

gey: very

ghillie: servant on an estate/game keeper (usually in

deer-stalking)

glaikit: mentally impaired

Glengarry: soft, usually military, cap

Graham's Dyke: the Antonine wall, renamed for the first man/clan over it

greetin': crying

guising: trick or treating at Halloween

handsel: to make a gift of silver (coin) to a new baby to bring it good fortune, usually by tucking it into the foot of the pram, after pressing it into its palm. Can also apply to the tradition of bringing a gift to a new house for luck

haud yer wheesht: be quiet (in a sharp tone)

haunless: useless, handless

hauns: hands

he has been here before: often said of babies who look wise at birth

hen: term of endearment, as in 'dear' or 'pet'

het up: excited

Hielanman: literally 'Highland man' or 'Highlander'. The railway bridge outside Central Station in Glasgow is still called 'The Hielanman's Umbrella', as it gave shelter from the rain to travellers arriving in the city from the North. There are shops on the street underneath it that became a meeting place for migrants to the city after the Highland clearances

high-falutin': high-handed, snobbish

hoik out: to pull out, usually harvesting potatoes

(the) house: loose term meaning 'where I live'

ILP: Independent Labour Party

it's past laughing once the heid's aff: literally 'it is past laughing once the head is severed'; you can't bolt the stable door after the horse has bolted

Jock Tamson's bairns: a saying meaning 'we are all brothers and sisters under the skin', probably derived from John Thomson's tenements for workers near his Glasgow shipyard (to) keek: to peek

ken: know (as in the German *kennen*)

Lallans: Lowland Scots language

lassie: girl

let that flee stick to the wa': let that fly stick to the wall; don't
stir up trouble

like sna' aff a dyke: to melt like snow off a wall; to disappear
(first)

(the) loodest bummer's no a'ways the best bee: the bee that
hums (bums) the loudest isn't always the hardest worker

MacCaig: Norman MacCaig, the poet (1910–1996)

mair: more

maist: most (as in the German *meist*)

man wi' a ba' heid: a man with a bald, or ball-shaped, head

maukit: dirty

messages: errands/shopping

mind: remember

muckle: great or big; used as emphasis in the same way as
'very'

nae: no

neeps: turnips

nippy sweetie: a sharp-tongued woman or nag who says
things that are hard to swallow.

nous: common sense (also English)

'opened the window to let his soul go': old Scots tradition at
time of death

Ossian: reference to *The Works of Ossian* by poet James
Macpherson, published in 1765. He claimed to have
translated epic poems by the son of Fionn mac Cumhaill
from the original Scottish Gaelic, but there was debate as
to their authenticity

peched out: out of breath, especially after running or exercise

peely-wally: pale

pernickety: fussy or particular about things

pinny: apron

Piskie: Episcopalian

(Edinburgh) press: a built in cupboard with a wooden door

puir: poor

save your breath to cool your porridge: be quiet, wait until there is something important to say

scrieve: write

scunnered: exhausted

shoogling: rocking (a pram), or swaying/swinging (as in the German *schaukeln*)

shoosh: quieten down

SHRA: Scottish Home Rule Association

skinnie-malinkie/skinny-malinky: very thin

skite: slip

skiving: shirking

skivvy: servant/slave

slainte mhath (Gaelic): cheers, literally 'good health'

slater: woodlouse

smoor: to damp down a fire before going to bed, often with peat

sook: suck

Sorley/Somhairlie (Gaelic): Sorley MacLean, the poet (1911–1996)

sough: breath. Also keep a calm sough: keep calm by slow, regular breathing

(the) stair: the common stair to the flats, called a 'close' in Glasgow

stooshie: fuss/commotion.

stour: dust (similar to the German *Staub*)

stramash: conflict/fight

tapadh leat (Gaelic): thank you

tattieboggle: scarecrow

tatties: potatoes

thole: put up with something

thrawn: disapproving

tumshee-heid: idiot, literally 'turnip head'

until a' the shadows flee awa': until all the troubles of the world pass in the light of Christ (grave inscription) wabbit: pale

wee: little or small, also 'young' if applied to a child

(a) wheen: a little less

widdershins: anticlockwise; it is considered unlucky to go
anticlockwise round something

(the) willies: fearful, spooked out or uneasy

yon: that

German words and phrases

Anschluss: German annexation of Austria

auf Wiedersehen: goodbye

beruhigen Sie sich: calm down

bitte: please

das habe ich nicht verstanden: I didn't understand that

Du bist immer noch meine kleine Zauberin: you are still my
little sorceress/enchantress

ein Deutschsprecher wohnte hier, nicht wahr?: a German
speaker lived here?

eine Rodel: a sledge

ein Held der Schotten: a Scottish hero

ein Kipferl?: a Kipferl? (small, crescent-shaped biscuit like
shortbread, but thinner)

eins, zwei, drei: one, two, three

er ist nicht besser als ein Tier: he is little better than an animal

er will Soldat werden?: he's going to become a soldier?

*es ist auch für Dich gefährlich, wenn Ich länger bleibe. Ich soll
doch weggehen, abfliegen:* it is also dangerous for you if
stay any longer. I should go, fly off

es lebe Ossian: Ossian lives. A reference to James
MacPherson's heroic poems, published from 1760
onwards, which inspired German writers and composers,
including some of Schubert's *Lieder*, and a character in
Wagner's opera *Die Hochzeit* (Wikipedia)

es mach nichts. Hände hoch!: it doesn't matter. Put your hands up!

es tut mir leid: I'm so sorry

Gauleiter: area leader

Grüss Dich: hello, literally 'greetings to you' (familiar)

Grüss Gott: formal hello, literally 'Greet God'

Herzlichen Dank, meine kleine Zauberin: heartfelt thanks, my
    little sorceress/enchantress

'Hier auch Lieb und Leben ist': There is life and love here too.
    Auf dem See, 'On the Lake', poem by Goethe (1749–
    1832). *Goethe Selected Verse,* Ed. D Luke, Penguin Books
    Ltd., Middlesex, 1981.

hören Sie auf. Sie hat nein gesagt: stop. She said no

ich bin gegangen: I went

ich bin Österreicher: I am Austrian

ich bin schon verheiratet: I am already married

ich friere: I am freezing

ich meine: I think/believe

ich möchte aufstehen: I would like to stand up

Kino – komme gleich wieder: cinema – back soon

kleine Schottin: little Scots girl

Komm bald wieder: come back soon

Komm der Tag: come the day (literal translation of the phrase
    in English)

Krieg macht Angst: war creates anxiety

Kuh: cow

Liebe: Dear (at the beginning of a letter)

Liesl, Hast Du Kinder?: Liesl. Do you have children?

Mädchen: girl

Mann und Frau: man and wife

mein aufrichtiges Beileid: My sincere sympathy/condolences

meine Frau ist wunderschön, nicht wahr?: my wife is beautiful,
    isn't she?

mein Liebling: my darling

Morgen wird alles anders scheinen: everything will seem
    different tomorrow

noch etwas?: anything else?

Prosit: cheers

Schatzi: (my) dear; literally 'treasure'

schon wieder Waffenlos: defenceless again

schön: beautiful

schöner Spaziergang? Unser Gast ist schon angekommen: good walk? Our guest has already arrived

setzen Sie sich: sit down

Sieg Heil: Nazi salute, literally 'Hail Victory'

Sie können dort oben bleiben. Ab morgen bin ich weg. Sie sind nicht der einzige Gefangener in dieser Stadt: you can stay upstairs. I am going tomorrow. You are not the only prisoner in this town

Universität von Edinburgh? Professor?: University of Edinburgh? Teacher?

unsere Kühe sind braun: our cows are brown (Scots: Oor coos are broon.)

vielleicht gibt's noch Zeit dafür, wenn alles vorbei ist?: perhaps there is time when this is all over?

waffenlos: weaponless, defenceless

Wappen oder Zahl?: Heads or tails?

wer sind Sie?: who are you?

wie geht's (Dir)?: how are you?

wo ist Dein Mann?: where is your husband?

wollen wir uns duzen?: shall we use the familiar form of address? (ie. *Du* as opposed to *Sie*)

wunderbar/wunderschön: wonderful

Author's note

The real events of the 1940s are used as a framework to support the story in this book, but it is a work of fiction. Some of the novel's characters are inspired by real people, but they are fictionalised portrayals and their names have been changed accordingly. One of the main characters, Douglas Grant, was inspired by the real-life Douglas Young, who was leader of the Scottish National Party from 1942 to 1945 – the name has been changed to reflect the fact that the character of Douglas Grant is a construct of the author's imagination.

Historical notes

Some of the real events referred to in this work of fiction occurred at a different time than stated in the text:

Police searches of the homes of SNP members took place in 1941, but it is presented as being 1942 in the case of the fictional Jeff McCaffrey.

Rommel attacked Tobruk in Libya on 20th June 1942 and then invaded Egypt on 1st July 1942. It is implied to be earlier in June in the book to demonstrate the anxiety over Rommel's advance.

The Bethnal Green Tube disaster took place in March 1943, though it occurs in 1942 in the book (*The Scotsman*, 5/3/43, Central Library, Edinburgh).

The body of the Venerable Margaret Sinclair was only moved to St Patrick's Church from Mount Vernon Cemetery, Edinburgh, in 2003.

The Scottish National Dictionary Association was formed in 1929 to compile a dictionary of Scots language. It was edited by William Grant from 1929 to 1946, and then by David Murison from 1946 until its completion in 1976. The researcher Jeff McCaffrey in this book is entirely fictional and the dictionary referred to should not be understood to be the Scottish National Dictionary.

For information about the Dictionary of the Scots Language see http://www.dsl.ac.uk/.

Sources

Manuscripts

Douglas Young Archive, Acc. 6419, Boxes 6, 7, 43, 44, 86, and *The Free-minded Scot* (Douglas Young's Defence, 1958.11), National Library of Scotland (NLS), Edinburgh.

SNP conference Bulletin, June 1944, Acc. 7.110, NLS, Edinburgh.

SNP leaflets and publications, Acc. P.med 3500–3505, NLS, Edinburgh.

Primary works

Finlay, Richard J, 1944, *Independent and Free*, John Donald Publishers Ltd, Edinburgh.

Kirk, Robert, 1815, *The Secret Commonwealth of Elves, Fauns and Fairies*, Longman, and NLS. Ref. PB5. 208.849/4.

MacCormick, John, 2008, *The Flag in the Wind*, Birlinn Ltd, Edinburgh (1955). A special debt to Chapter 16 for the account of the Annual Conference in Edinburgh, 1942.

Mitchell, Mrs JH, undated, *War-Time Cookery*, Thomson and Duncan, Aberdeen.

Robinson, Mairi (Editor), 1987, *The Concise Scots Dictionary*, Aberdeen University Press, (1976).

Young, Clara and Murison, David (Editors), *A Clear Voice*, Douglas Young, Poet and Polymath, MacDonald Publishers, Loanhead, Scotland, (post-1974). Copyright: Douglas Young Memorial Fund.

Publications

Scots Independent, July and August 1942, Central Library, Edinburgh.

The Scotsman Archive, 1942–1947, Central Library, Edinburgh. (See especially: 'Nationalist Chairman, Case of Mr Douglas Young', *The Scotsman*, page 3, 21/7/42.)

Notes

I have quoted or paraphrased text from Douglas Young's correspondence to keep a flavour of his and his correspondents' lively way of communicating. Some information with regard to the legalities of his appeal and the Annual Conference is also quoted from sources.

page 9: Letter from JS Hardy (signature illegible), Manse of Logie, to Douglas Young, 5/3/42, re: 'you are ignorant of how keenly mothers and fathers suffer on their children's behalf' and 'buckle on the armour' and 'puir old Scotland'. Box 6, Acc. 6419, NLS.

page 9: Letter from Douglas Young to John MacDonald, 5/3/42, re: 'MacCaig exam'. Box 6, Acc. 6419, NLS.

page 10 (I could hear Mr Grant saying...): Handwritten notes on 'Report of the Royal Commission on The Court of Session and the Office of Sheriff Principal, 1927: Douglas Young describes Act of Union as an 'Anschluss'. Folder 1, Box 6, Acc. 6419, NLS.

page 11: Letter from Douglas Young, Meikle Cloak, Lochwinnoch, to Helen, 18/5/42, re:'...the shades of Barlinnie are not yet to close about me...but no doubt I shall end up there sooner or later for a space', in response to her letter of 24/3/42, re: Barlinnie as 'Bastille'. Box 6, Acc. 6419, NLS. Same letter: 'the skeleton case knocked together the night before can be fortified.'

page 11: Letter from friend of Douglas Young, 27/5/42, re: citing Dumfries Proclamation in defence. Box 6, Acc. 6419, NLS.

page 12, see also page 140: Letter from Douglas Young, 3/12/42, re: Somhairle MacLean and *An Cuilithionn* translation into Lallans. Box 6, Acc. 6419, NLS.

page 14: 'Internal Differences come to a Head', *Scots Independent*, July 1942, (this report on the SNP annual conference lists the venue as Gartshore Hall, not Shandwick Galleries, as stated in John MacCormick's *The Flag in the Wind*).

pages 14–19: Account of SNP annual conference drawn from John MacCormick, *The Flag in the Wind*, pages 102–107.

page 19: Letter from Douglas Young, 2/6/42, re: 'tired of MacCormick and his caucus', paraphrased by character of Jeff. Box 6, Acc. 6419, NLS.

page 22: Letter from AC, College Bounds, Aberdeen to Douglas Young, July 1942. Box 6, Acc. 6419, NLS.

page 24: Advert for Milton, *The Scotsman*, page 3, 22/6/43 (or 1942?).

page 33: Douglas Young to Mr McNeill, 5/7/42, re: 'Sheriff *ultra vires* in view of the statutes of 1369 and 1371. The 1707 Treaty never gave him more authority than he had before.' Folder 2, Box 6, Acc. 6419, NLS.

page 33: Letter from Douglas Young to Miss Lamont, 7/6/42, re: 'Scots Army under Scots control' (see also SNP Conference resolution, 1937, to refuse conscription by non-Scottish Government). Box 6, Acc. 6419, NLS.

page 38: 'The Two Stirlings', *Scots Independent*, July 1942, re: Councillor Duncan and the baillies.

page 38: Paraphrase of report on SNP special conference, Stirling, *The Scotsman*, page 2, 29/6/42, re: split in party

page 38: Letter from JL Campbell, Isle of Canna, to Douglas Young, 3/6/42, re: 'This exportation of Scottish female labour to England under conscription is a case in point'. Box 6, Acc. 6419, NLS.

page 38: Article by Douglas Young in the *Scots Independent*, August 1942, re: defence of Scotland.

page 39: Letter from Douglas Young to Deorsa, 27/6/42, re: police agents in crowd at Bannockburn rally, '... there were several police men and about five detectives – including the London Chief of the Political Police...' Box 6, Acc. 6419, NLS.

page 48: Letter from David Watson to Thomas Johnston at St Andrews House, 21/7/42, re: his response to Douglas Young's suggestion regarding the 'Scottish War Effort'. 'Scotland is to become an "ally" in the full sense with the "United Nations". Now the sort of peace projected by the "United Nations", or those who manipulate them, would bring no security to Scotland.' Box 6, Acc 6419, NLS.

page 67: Letter from Douglas Young re: prison work as a 'garden party'. Box 6, Acc. 6419, NLS.

pages 67, 69, 75, 149: Theognis: information sourced from Box 86, Acc. 6419, NLS, and quoted from Wikipedia.

page 67: Letter from Douglas Young to David Murison, 7/12/42, re: 'no supplementary diet'. Box 6, Acc. 6419, NLS.

page 67: Letter from Douglas Young to Deorsa, 31/3/43, re: 'HM Guesthouse'. Box 6, Acc. 6419, NLS.

page 68: *Scots Independent*, July 1942, report on SNP annual conference: 'For too long Scotland had faced both ways...'

page 74: Text re: Darwin and Darwin's Rhea, label in Edinburgh Zoo, 2011, and Wikipedia, 2011.

page 74: Letter from HGA, Meikle Cloak, Lochwinnoch to Douglas Young, 14/9/42, re: prison visit/Edinburgh Zoo, 'I gave half your slab of chocolate to a big polar bear and a wee monkey'. Box 6, Acc. 6419, NLS.

page 75: Account of 'Holidays at Home' rally drawn from *The Scotsman*, page 3, 13/8/42. 10,000 children attended!

page 76: 'No species is an island', Darwin quoted on sign, Edinburgh Zoo, 2011.

page 77: 'A Clear Voice', page 76, account of march organised by 'Dr Robert MacIntyre, Secretary of the National Party'. Hugh MacDiarmid was present.

page 77: Salutation at end of all Douglas Young's letters: 'Yours aye for Scotland'. Box 6, Acc. 6419, NLS.

page 84: Argument re: National Services Act of 1939 from *The Free-minded Scot*, NLS.

pages 78, 89: Douglas Young statement to the Scottish People, *Scots Independent*, July 1942, 'Quislings in Scotland/To the Scottish People'.

page 103: Weston biscuits advert, *The Scotsman*, page 6, 25/6/42.

page 110: Public notice re: ration book to replace Main Book, Points Book plus Yellow Supplement Book, *The Scotsman*, 23/6/42.

page 111: 'Augmented Whisky Stocks, Concern in Distillery Towns over Danger of Fire', *The Scotsman*, page 3, 23/6/42.

page 129: 'Ghost-voices' report, *The Scotsman*, 10/3/43.

page 141, 147: 'Mr Douglas Young to be released from Saughton', *The Scotsman*, 10/3/43.

page 141: Paraphrase of letter, 5/2/43, from correspondent (signature illegible), Udny Station, Aberdeenshire, re: 'sleuths… in the pig sty'. Acc. 6419, NLS.

page 147: Paraphrase of Douglas Young's statement on release from Saughton, *The Scotsman*, 10/3/43, 'no complaints against the prison authorities'.

page 150: Letter: Douglas Young and Capt. Stichor re: plants, Douglas Young Archive, Acc. 6419, NLS, Edinburgh.

page 151: 'HMS Dig – a vegetable submarine', *The Scotsman*, page 6, 5/3/43.

page 151: Letter from Arthur Donaldson to Douglas Young, 23/2/43, re: appeal to Scottish Estates. Box 6, Acc. 6419, NLS.

page 151: Douglas Young letter, 28/1/43, re: translation of Somhairle Maclean's work into Lallans/English. Box 6, Acc. 6419, NLS.

page 152: Letter from Douglas Young to Major Hay, 14/8/43, re: hydroelectric power. Box 6, Acc. 6419, NLS.

page 153: Letter from Douglas Young, 11/8/43, re: Helena Auchterlonie's heritage. Box 6, Acc. 6419, NLS.

page 161: 'Savings Weeks', *The Scotsman*, 25/3/43.

page 166: Report on Kirkcaldy by-election, October 1943–February 1944, SNP Interim Organisers' Bulletin, 26th February 1944. Acc. 7498, NLS.

page 171: Letter from Mr Muirhead re: Douglas Young imprisoned again for refusing industrial conscription. Acc. 6419, NLS.

page 171: Douglas refers to campaign to get Scotland dominion status like Canada, *A Clear Voice*, page 79. He also refers to Canada in letter, 11/8/43. Box 6, Acc. 6419, NLS.

page 173: Advert, re: 'provincial offices', *The Scotsman*, 3/1/47.

page 183: Reference to campaign for land for returning ex-servicemen. Acc. 6419, NLS.

page 196: Argyll and Sutherland Highlanders were sent to Palestine after World War 2 (Wikipedia).

page 198: 'A Vienna no Longer Gay', *The Scotsman*, 6/1/47.

Acknowledgements

The author would like to thank Clara Young – Douglas Young's daughter – for her kind permission to base this fictionalised account of Scotland in the 1940s on her father's correspondence and papers held at the National Library of Scotland, Edinburgh, and to partially quote from it.

Thanks to the staff at the National Library of Scotland, and at the Edinburgh and Scottish Collection in Edinburgh Central Library.

The story is indebted to John MacCormick for his account of the SNP AGM in 1942 in Shandwick Place in *The Flag in the Wind* (Chapter 16, Birlinn, 1955, 2008) It is re-imagined here.

Thanks also to the Scottish National Party for permission to use their publicity from 1942, and to Milton Pharmaceutical Ltd for permission to quote their advert.

Finally, thanks to Judy Moir, Dilys Rose, Allyson Stack, Alan Warner, Sara Hunt, Craig Hillsley, Jo Morley and Clare Haworth-Maden.